My darling Remy,

I know some people might think me foolish for writing to you, but who else can I turn to? You've been gone for four years now, yet I still feel you with me every day. Remy, our beloved Hotel Marchand is in serious danger. It's the beginning of Mardi Gras and we are deeply in debt. We suffered after the hurricane, and even before... But there is no point in looking back.

The future should be bright. Because of my little health scare a few months ago, our daughters—Charlotte, Renee, Sylvie and even Melanie—are now at home, working for the hotel, just as we always dreamed. Remy, you would be so proud of them all.

But word of our financial situation must have leaked to the industry because there is an offer to buy us out. Of course I refuse to sell. I may have lost you, Remy, but I will do everything in my power to ensure that Hotel Marchand will be here for our grandchildren. This, my love, I promise you.

Ton amour,

Anne

Dear Reader,

I was thrilled to be invited to write the launch book for the Hotel Marchand continuity series. The opportunity presented an abundance of pleasures: the chance to work with some wonderful editors and eleven dazzlingly talented authors, several of whom are good friends of mine; the chance to tell a fascinating story teeming with family intrigue, danger, love and passion; and the chance to write a book set in sultry, sexy New Orleans, the home of jazz and blues, beignets and po'boys, Mardi Gras and First Night.

Within weeks of my having completed my manuscript for *In the Dark*, however, Hurricane Katrina struck New Orleans. Along with the rest of the world, I watched in horror as televised newscasts showed the swamped streets of the city, the destroyed neighborhoods, the desperate evacuees and the courageous emergency crews who rescued stranded flood victims from balconies and rooftops.

All around me, people mourned that New Orleans would never be the same. Of course they were right; Katrina has altered New Orleans. But as a native New Yorker, I know how cities can rebuild and recover from disaster. I know how, when people love a place, they will nurse and nurture it until it's not just on its feet but dancing. I have faith New Orleans will once again fling a necklace of Mardi Gras beads around her neck and burst into song. No flood could ever wash away the city's magic.

I hope you find that special New Orleans magic within the pages of *In the Dark* and the entire Hotel Marchand series. Happy reading!

Judith Arnold

JUDITH ARNOLD

In the Dark

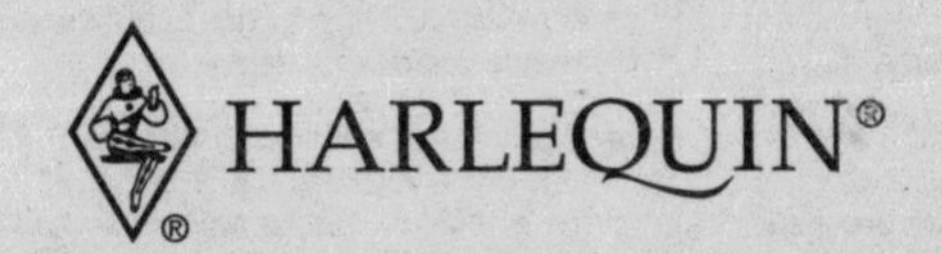

TORONTO • NEW YORK • LONDON
AMSTERDAM • PARIS • SYDNEY • HAMBURG
STOCKHOLM • ATHENS • TOKYO • MILAN • MADRID
PRAGUE • WARSAW • BUDAPEST • AUCKLAND

Recycling programs
for this product may
not exist in your area.

ISBN-13: 978-0-373-38938-4

IN THE DARK

Barbara Keiler is acknowledged as the author of the work.

This edition published by arrangement with Harlequin Books S.A.

www.eHarlequin.com

Printed in U.S.A.

RWA Lifetime Achievement Award nominee **Judith Arnold** has published more than eighty novels, with over ten million copies in print worldwide, and she has received several awards from *Romantic Times BOOKreviews* magazine. Judith can't remember a time she wasn't making up stories. By age six, she was writing them down and sharing them with teachers and friends, and today she's happily sharing her stories with the world. A native New Yorker, Judith currently lives in a small town outside Boston, Massachusetts, with her husband and two sons. Readers can find out more about her by visiting her Web site at www.JudithArnold.com.

PROLOGUE

*J*ULIE *S*ULLIVAN *HAD destroyed him. She deserved to be destroyed herself.*

No one could walk out of a prison after eight years and be the same person he'd been when he'd walked in. Before Julie had opened her mouth and ruined everything, he'd been an amazing man. Successful. Handsome. Generous.

He'd made dreams come true. Pretty girls from around the country would come to New York City and he would turn them into fashion models. If they needed help with hair and makeup, he got it for them. Trouble keeping their weight down? He'd be there. Problems budgeting? He always had good advice. A shoulder to lean on, a mentor they could trust, someone who could get them through the stresses of their daily lives? Glenn Perry was their man.

He'd been kind. He'd truly cared about all his girls—some more than others, but his heart had been open to all of them. Some he'd loved deeply. He'd been a good man, a gentle loving soul.

Until Julie Sullivan had betrayed him.

Now, eight long, difficult years later, he was finally back in New York, his old home, his old haunts. Maybe the world hadn't changed in that time, but he had. His heart was scarred now, his soul shuttered.

Julie would have to pay.

CHAPTER ONE

HE WAS WATCHING HER. Again.

By the time Julie spun her chair toward her office doorway he was gone. She saw only his shadow chasing him down the hall, as silent as the man himself.

Gerard, the former head of security, used to walk in a loud, lumbering gait. Julie and Charlotte would joke that his clomping footsteps were the secret to his success, because troublemakers would hear his approach and flee before they could do any damage. But Gerard had retired right after Thanksgiving last year, and his replacement, Mac Jensen, had a different way of doing things. Julie suspected that he'd prefer catching troublemakers to scaring them away. He moved with the graceful stealth of a panther sneaking up on its prey.

Julie usually sensed his presence without actually seeing or hearing him. She felt his nearness, caught his scent and, if she was quick enough, glimpsed his shadow. On rare occasions she glimpsed *him.* And when she did, more often than not he was watching her.

She rose from her desk, crossed to the open door and peered down the hallway. He was long gone, but his smell lingered faintly, a dark, woodsy, profoundly male scent that probably nobody else would have noticed. Julie was keenly aware of fragrances. And she was keenly aware of Mac Jensen.

Sighing, she returned to her desk and settled in her chair. She didn't have time to waste on the Hotel Marchand's new director of security. Ever since Anne Marchand had handed the hotel's reins to her daughter Charlotte, Julie had more than enough to keep her busy. As Charlotte's second in command, Julie juggled two tasks for every one of Charlotte's—and completing those tasks was more important than wondering whether Mac was paying too much attention to her. If he was, well, it wouldn't be the first time she'd been stared at.

Her computer monitor displayed the menu the restaurant's chef had come up with for the hotel's Twelfth Night party. Robert LeSoeur was a wizard in the kitchen, and Julie would never try to outguess him when it came to hors d'oeuvres or a dessert buffet. She didn't know much about food, except that eating was more fun than starving and that everything Robert prepared was delicious. However, she did need to review his budgets before passing them along to Charlotte. Charlotte's youngest sister Melanie was now working under Robert as Chez Remy's *sous-chef,* but she was more involved with the quality of the food than its cost. And left to his own devices, Robert would offer dishes featuring ingredients that could bankrupt the hotel.

"Julie?" Charlotte called from the adjacent office. Charlotte's office opened onto the hall, just like Julie's, but an inner door connected the two rooms, and Julie kept both her doors open most of the time. She liked being accessible. Even more, she liked allowing the hotel's Old World atmosphere to fill her workspace. Situated on the second floor above the hotel's grand, elegant lobby, her office had the high ceilings, moldings and muted amber walls that defined the building's classic French Quarter architecture, but the decor within her office was strictly utilitarian: industrial strength carpet, L-shaped desk, file cabinets and extensive computer equipment. Because all the high-tech office gear was plugged safely into a multitude of surge protectors in Julie's office, Charlotte could fill her own office with collectables and bowls of fresh flowers, a plush patterned rug and an antique sideboard adorned with photos of Charlotte's loved ones: her three sisters, her niece, her mother, her grandmother and her father Remy, who had died four years ago but whose spirit wafted through the Hotel Marchand like a benevolent breeze.

Thank goodness none of the hotel's treasures—or Charlotte's—had been lost to Hurricane Katrina a year and a half ago. Even Remy's spirit seemed to have returned to bless the hotel and his beloved city.

Julie rose from her chair, this time to cross to the inner door. The sunshine spilling through the tall windows in the adjoining office imbued Charlotte's auburn hair with gold highlights and downplayed the worry lines that accented the corners of her mouth. At five foot ten, Julie towered over her boss, but in every other way Julie looked up to her. Charlotte had hired her when she'd been new to the city, armed with a degree from McGill University in Montreal, Canada, but absolutely no business experience or references. Julie had sent the last person she'd worked for to jail. He hadn't been inclined to write her a letter of recommendation.

"We're still having problems with that guest in 307," Charlotte informed her. "Alvin Grote. His latest complaint—" she held up several pink message slips "—is the shape of the ice cubes. He doesn't like square ones. He wants cylinder-shaped ice cubes, with round holes in their centers. He says he likes his drinks to flow through them."

Julie rolled her eyes and extended her hand to accept the message slips. "The cylindrical ice cubes melt faster and dilute the drinks."

"I'm no expert when it comes to the physics of ice cubes," Charlotte admitted, then sighed. "Mr. Grote is staying with us all this week and through the weekend, unfortunately, so we should brace ourselves for more complaints from him. He's already whined about the temperature of the house Chardonnay in the bar. He thinks it should be three degrees colder."

"Three?"

"He was very precise, according to Leo." Leo was the

hotel's longtime bartender. Just as Julie trusted Robert with the menus, she trusted Leo with the temperatures of his wines.

"Perhaps Mr. Grote should have dropped an ice cube into the wineglass," Julie muttered. "That would have cooled it off. Better yet, he should stay away from liquor altogether. He's so grouchy, maybe he's still hung over from New Year's Eve." The new year had just begun yesterday. Anyone who'd welcomed the new year with robust partying—and that would be just about everyone in New Orleans—would likely still be feeling the aftereffects of that celebration.

Perhaps Alvin Grote wasn't dealing with the aftereffects of too much carousing. He might just be a whiny, grouchy idiot all the time. "Have you met Mr. Grote?" Charlotte asked.

Julie had had that misfortune. "This morning in the lobby. He dragged me over to a window to complain about the weather. 'It's the first week of January,' he said. 'Where's the snow?' I had to remind him he was in New Orleans." A laugh escaped her. "He wears his hair in a ponytail, even though he's bald on top."

"Oh dear." Charlotte chuckled. "Well, his credit card is real and he's paying plenty for his suite. Perhaps we can find some cylindrical ice cubes for him. One of the local convenience stores might carry them. We do like to keep our customers satisfied."

"Even when they're bald men with ponytails?"

"Especially then. Also…" Charlotte crossed to her desk, a beautiful piece of furniture with hand-carved legs and an inlaid surface, the antithesis of Julie's functional steel desk. "Given how hectic this period is—with the Christmas holidays, then New Year's, the Twelfth Night party just four days away and Mardi Gras six weeks after that—I've been investigating the possibility of hiring a party planner." She lifted a folder from her leather-trimmed blotter. "We've always planned our parties ourselves, but I thought I ought to be open-minded about this. At least we should think about it for future events."

"Which planners did you contact?" Julie asked.

Charlotte named a few. Julie had heard of them. The hospitality business community in New Orleans was relatively small and close-knit. "Roxanne Levesque is on retainer with one of the Crewes, isn't she?" When Julie had first arrived in New Orleans, she'd had no idea what a Crewe was. She'd soon learned about the powerful clubs that oversaw the Mardi Gras festival, built the floats, hosted galas and in many ways ruled the city's social scene.

"I believe she's sleeping with one of the Crewes," Charlotte remarked tartly, then laughed. "Her sex life is her own business. All I care is that she stages fabulous parties."

"How much does she charge?"

"Too much," Charlotte admitted. "None of these people come cheap."

"We've hosted wonderful parties without professional help in the past," Julie pointed out. "Our staff is terrific. And Luc can iron out any snafus."

Charlotte's smile relaxed. "He does have charm to spare. The guests adore him."

As far as Julie was concerned, being adored by the guests was a hotel concierge's most important function. Luc Carter sometimes seemed a bit distracted, and he had a habit of straying from his station in the hotel's lobby at inopportune times, but with his boyish good looks and his enticing blue eyes, he was able to smooth every ruffled feather and melt every chilly heart.

That didn't mean Julie would ask for his assistance with any aspect of the party planning. He was a man, after all. Most men she knew—at least the heterosexual ones—thought the perfect party should include potato chips and onion dip, abundant quantities of beer in disposable plastic cups, and a wide-screen high-definition TV set. The hotel's Twelfth Night party was not going to involve poker chips, pretzel bits or any nationally broadcast sports event. Someone like Roxanne Levesque would be far better suited to oversee it, even if she was sleeping with members of every Mardi Gras Crewe in the city.

"I'd love to hand over our future parties to a professional planner," Charlotte said, "but the cost worries me. Would you crunch the numbers so we'll have some idea about whether this would be feasible?"

"Sure." Julie took the folder from Charlotte.

"Don't spend more time on this than you think it deserves," Charlotte added. "Again, we'll be handling all of this season's parties without outside help. I just think we ought to consider the possibility of hiring someone sometime down the road."

Julie nodded. She'd worked for Charlotte long enough to register not just what Charlotte had said but what she hadn't said. Ever since Anne Marchand's heart attack last September had forced her to step down as the hotel's general manager and install Charlotte as her replacement, Charlotte had been overworked and overstressed. Handing off the hotel's party planning responsibilities to a professional would remove one major burden from the many obligations pressing down on her.

But handing off the events planning would mean handing over a generous fee. And despite its prestige, despite its celebrated position among the hotels of New Orleans, despite its ideal location just east of Jackson Square in the heart of the French Quarter, despite its multistar restaurant and its elegant accommodations, the Hotel Marchand was leaking money the way a damaged tanker might leak oil—not enough to pollute the entire Gulf of Mexico, but enough to cause its owner plenty of sleepless nights.

"Anything else?" Julie asked as she backed toward the door to her office.

Charlotte studied her for such a long moment, Julie glanced down to make sure her blouse wasn't gaping open. All the buttons were closed and the tails were tucked neatly into the straight skirt of her suit. Julie loved clothes. Even though she'd gained a good fifteen pounds in the past ten years—fifteen pounds her too-thin frame had welcomed—she was blessed with a body that was flattered by pretty much any garment she put on it. The suit she had on today carried an obscure label—big-name designers didn't impress her—but it was beautifully cut and the fabric was the color of Lake Pontchartrain on a clear day, a mix of green and gray and reflected blue.

She lifted her gaze back to Charlotte. "You had a look on your face when you came in," Charlotte told her. "Is something troubling you?"

"Besides the usual, you mean?" The usual would include the hotel's financial health, her own finances, the fact that her sister lived in New York and they couldn't see each other as often as they liked, and the squeaky noise her brakes kept making. She had other worries, too, specific worries that she wouldn't discuss with anyone, not even Charlotte. She had thought she'd kept those worries well hidden.

"It's the oddest thing," Charlotte observed. "Whenever Mac Jensen is in the vicinity, you get this look."

"What look?" Julie said, wincing inwardly at her defensive tone.

Charlotte quirked an eyebrow. "Just a look."

"Do I have that look now? Is he in the vicinity?"

"He was, a few minutes ago."

"What brought him up to the second floor?" Julie asked.

"He was dropping off his report on that incident last night with the guest who swore she'd heard a ghost pacing on the third floor."

"Oh, God, not the ghost again." One of the several town houses that had been joined to create the hotel had allegedly belonged to the lover of a seaman who had sailed with the famous pirate Jean Lafitte and had drowned in a storm that unexpectedly swept through the Gulf of Mexico. Guests often mentioned that they could hear the pirate's lover pacing the floors, waiting for his return. Julie was too sensible to believe the legend, but if it brought more guests to the hotel, who was she to argue?

"The guest insisted she heard a ghost, so security had to check it out and write a report," Charlotte told her. "And you're avoiding my question. Do you have a problem with Mac?"

"Is my 'look' a problem look?"

Charlotte grinned. "Actually, it's more of a yearning look."

"Yearning?" Julie scowled.

"He's a handsome man, Julie. Those dark eyes of his, and that strong jaw… Surely you've noticed."

"I suppose," Julie said vaguely. No need for Charlotte to know just how much Julie had noticed Mac Jensen's dark eyes and strong jaw, his thick brown hair and his sinewy physique, and the amazing way a man as tall as he was could move so smoothly and soundlessly.

Charlotte was still awaiting an answer. "I think…" Julie inhaled and pushed out the words. "Sometimes I think he's spying on me."

"Spying on you?"

Julie nodded. "I feel his eyes on me sometimes. Like he's watching me and doesn't want me to know it."

Charlotte let out a laugh. "For heaven's sake, Julie—half the men in the city get whiplash from staring at you whenever you walk by."

Julie's cheeks warmed. "That's a bit of an exaggeration."

"Hardly. You're a former fashion model. People can't help noticing you."

"I was a lot younger during my modeling days," Julie argued. "And a lot thinner."

"So now you're older and curvier. It's no surprise that you turn men's heads. I just hope you aren't a distraction to Mac. If you ever see trouble brewing here at the hotel, please run the other way so he can stay focused on his job."

Julie laughed along with her boss's teasing, but as she left the office, she decided Charlotte was wrong. Mac

Jensen didn't ogle Julie. He studied her as if trying to pry loose her secrets.

And he wasn't going to do that, not if she could help it.

Returning to her desk, she hit a key on her computer to kill her screen saver, then entered the URL for Roxanne Levesque's Web page, which was printed on the top of her proposal. The mail icon in the corner of Julie's monitor flashed, alerting her that she'd received e-mail.

Ordinarily, she checked her e-mail only three times a day—as soon as she arrived at her office around eight a.m., at lunchtime and before shutting down her computer and locking up for the night. But she'd been awaiting word from her sister about their father's recent bout with the flu, and Marcie generally e-mailed during working hours. They had learned that they were physically incapable of limiting phone calls to under an hour, so they saved their phone conversations for when they weren't at work.

She clicked on her e-mail icon, hoping for news that her father was on the mend and her mother was no longer running herself ragged taking care of him. The New York area seemed to be in the grip of a minor flu epidemic this winter, and although Julie's parents remained youthful in their early sixties, she couldn't help fretting about them.

The e-mail that had set her icon blinking wasn't from Marcie, however. The return address was "4Julie" and the entire message consisted of a musical staff with a single note on it, tailed by a long, rippling line that scaled from the low end to the high end of the staff: a glissando. And below it the words, "The song is over."

It took all of Julie's considerable willpower to keep from screaming.

IN HIS PROFESSIONAL LIFE, Mac had often been hired to keep an eye on someone. But rarely had he enjoyed that assignment as much as he enjoyed keeping an eye on Julie Sullivan.

He was a professional, and his personal pleasures had no bearing on the way he did his job. But, hell, if an assignment entailed keeping tabs on a woman who could star in a guy's wet-dream fantasies, he might as well enjoy it.

Julie had to know she was a knockout. By her seventeenth birthday, she'd been doing magazine layouts. By nineteen she'd been chosen as the Symphony Perfumes girl, her big violet eyes and pouty lips featured in ads for Arpeggio, Grace Note, Sonata and Glissando perfumes. Mac had a file on her. He'd done the research.

Back when she was modeling, she would never have blipped onto his radar screen—perfume had never held much interest for him. But now... She had him blipping nonstop.

Unfortunately, Julie represented only one of his jobs—the real one. His second job—his cover—was as the Hotel Marchand's new head of security, and it didn't exactly suit him. The security office was a tiny, windowless room down a back hall, right next door to the housekeeping department. He missed having a window. Sitting in that ugly little cubicle made him feel like a mole.

At least he was able to pop his head aboveground at regular intervals throughout the day. There were always reports to deliver to Charlotte—he could easily e-mail them, but he grabbed any excuse to emerge from the dungeon office—and rounds to walk. He liked to circulate through the hotel, checking on things, making sure emergency exits weren't propped open, window screens weren't torn and loiterers weren't hanging around the lobby, behaving suspiciously. He liked to remain visible to the guests; he figured they'd find his presence reassuring. And he liked to keep tabs on Luc Carter, the concierge. Luc seemed helpful and energetic, but something about him rubbed Mac wrong. He wasn't sure what, but he'd been trusting his instincts all his life, and those instincts hadn't let him down yet.

In addition to his rounds, he had to respond to emergency

calls, of which there were several every day. A guest experiencing chest pains. A guest who'd lost her traveler's checks. A guest who'd befriended a sweet young thing on Bourbon Street last night and brought her back to his room, only to awaken the next morning and discover his wallet missing. A guest who'd heard a ghost prowling the upper floors of the hotel. Mac located errant children, arranged tows for rental cars with mechanical problems and discreetly escorted folks who'd consumed one too many in the bar back to their rooms.

Escorting drunks and warning toddlers away from the pool's edge didn't exactly satisfy him, and he was grateful that hotel security wasn't his life's work. At least all those emergencies and quasi-emergencies, all those torn screens and missing wallets, gave him the perfect excuse to keep Julie Sullivan within his sights.

Carlos was manning the office when Mac returned from the second floor. It was barely big enough for two people, and Mac ought to be grateful that he didn't spend as many hours in it as Carlos did. Actually, the kid seemed to enjoy sitting in that cubicle, viewing the large flat-screen monitor that sat on a shelf above the desk and flashed pictures from the many closed-circuit cameras placed around the hotel. A glance at the monitor informed whoever was posted at the desk of what was going on in every corner of the lobby, the back halls, the bar, the courtyard, the event rooms and the elevators.

Judging by Carlos's bland smile, nothing much was going on anywhere. Carlos had been working security at the hotel for more than a year, but Charlotte had considered him too young and inexperienced to take over the head job when Gerard Lomax had retired last fall. Mac would have been grateful to get Carlos's job—anything to place him close to Julie. But Charlotte had hired him for the top slot.

Just as well. Being the director of security gave Mac more freedom to move around the hotel.

Entering the security office, Mac nudged Carlos's shoulder

and said, "Go take a break. You look like you could use some fresh air."

Carlos, thin and boyish, spun in his chair and grinned. "Fresh air, sure," he said, patting the pack of cigarettes in the breast pocket of his beige uniform. Unlike Mac, who dressed in civilian clothes, Carlos and the rest of Mac's staff wore apparel identifying them as security personnel to the hotel guests.

"You ought to quit that habit," Mac said, not for the first time. "You're too young to let nicotine get the better of you."

"My girlfriend gets the better of me all the time," Carlos said with an amiable shrug. "If I can figure out how to quit her, maybe I'll quit smoking, too." Grinning, he hooked his walkie-talkie to his belt, then shambled past Mac and out of the office.

As soon as he was gone, Mac sank into the chair. The computer sat idle; no message lights flashed on the desk phone. A bulletin board running the length of one wall was covered with advisories, notices of public events and recent crimes in the neighborhood, and hotel schedules. File cabinets held folders on every employee at the hotel, complete with the extensive background checks they'd had to undergo to prove they could be trusted entering guest rooms. A wall rack held spare pagers and two-way radios. The monitor above the desk displayed rotations of photos: the lobby, the bar, the elevator empty in one shot and empty again in the next.

Hearing the outer door click shut behind Carlos, Mac propped his feet on the desk, next to the phone console, and pulled his cell phone from an inner pocket of his jacket. He didn't want any record of the calls he made to his own office from the hotel.

Sandy answered on the second ring. "Crescent City Security, can I help you?"

"Hey, sugar," Mac greeted her. "Do you miss me?"

Recognizing his voice, she laughed. "Not for an instant. When the hell are you coming back?"

"When this job is done. Even though every day I'm away from you breaks my heart."

Sandy laughed again. She was the wife of his partner and best friend, and the flirting was just a game between them. When Mac and Frank Romero had started their private security business five years ago, they could barely afford to cover their rent. Hiring a receptionist had been out of the question, so Sandy had volunteered to help out. She wasn't a volunteer anymore, but she was still answering their phones.

"Frank's up to his eyeballs with that nasty insurance case," Sandy reported. "He still hasn't been able to trace the missing money past an account in Costa Rica that's now empty. He could really use your help."

"Sorry," Mac said, though he honestly wasn't. Keeping tabs on a woman as gorgeous as Julie Sullivan was a hell of a lot more fun than tracing embezzled funds through a labyrinth of offshore accounts for an insurance company.

"Doesn't it bother you, double-dipping?" Sandy said. "You're getting paid to watch that woman and you're getting paid to run security at the hotel."

"I earn every penny," Mac said.

"Right." Sandy's sarcastic tone signaled disbelief. "I don't know, Mac. It's been more than a month. It just doesn't feel right to me that the hotel is paying you to do a job and you're doing something else."

Maybe the setup wasn't exactly kosher, but in the private security business, clients cared less about pristine ethics than results. "If I'd known you were going to give me grief, darlin', I wouldn't have called," he said, his gaze drifting to the monitor above the desk. Someone had entered the elevator. A middle-aged couple conferred with Luc in the lobby. The hall outside Julie's office was empty.

"All right. No more lectures. Collect two incomes. See if I care." Sandy's tone was one of fake resignation. "We could use you back, though. Try to tie this one up before Christmas, would you?"

Given that Christmas was nearly a year away, Mac believed

he could manage that. The camera outside Julie's office picked up something new: Julie. There she was on the monitor, stalking down the hall, her arms wrapped around her as if she were hugging herself, trying to stay warm.

He sat straighter and frowned. Her face was naturally expressive, especially her eyes, big and thickly lashed and a color that reminded him of amethysts. Right now her eyes were giving her away. She looked petrified.

"I've got to go," he said abruptly, all playfulness gone. "Tell Frank all's well on this end." Before Sandy could say anything more, he flipped his phone shut and leaned forward, watching the monitor intently.

On the screen Julie moved from one frame to another as she yanked open the doorway to the back stairwell. He didn't like her using the service stairs, which were more isolated than the public staircase down to the lobby, but at least the back stairwell was also monitored by closed-circuit cameras. She wore a suit in a color somewhere between turquoise and gray, and the neatly cropped jacket and skirt looked so good on her, Mac could only wonder how much better she'd look if she took them off. But when she turned at the landing and he saw her face, he forgot about her body, spectacular though it was. Her eyes were glassy with worry, her lips pinched with tension.

He pressed the base of the two-way radio and punched in Carlos's number. "Carlos? How soon can you get your ass back here?" he asked.

"I'm on my way," Carlos said. He must have heard the urgency in Mac's tone.

"I won't be at the desk," Mac said, shoving away from the desk and shrugging to adjust his jacket over his shoulders. "I've got to check something." Not bothering to listen to Carlos's response, he swung out of the office, slamming the door behind him. The fear in Julie's eyes told him not to wait.

CHAPTER TWO

HE FOUND HER in the hotel's central courtyard. A square patio furnished with chairs, tables and planters around a distinctive teardrop-shaped pool and enclosed within the buildings that formed the Hotel Marchand, the courtyard lent a European flavor to the place. Centuries ago, what was now the hotel had been a group of separate town houses, along with a carriage house and some slave quarters. Previous owners had broken down walls and turned the entire block of buildings into a hotel with the courtyard at its center. Mac was no expert when it came to architecture, but he was intrigued by the way different buildings united to create a single entity.

Given the cool, overcast January morning, he wasn't surprised to find the courtyard vacant. Almost vacant. He spotted Julie through one of the French doors that opened from the lobby into the courtyard. She sat beside a table and a planter of geraniums in a corner of the patio, near the restaurant. Her posture was slightly hunched, her arms still wrapped tightly about her, her knees pressed together and her face angled down so her dark hair spilled forward.

He couldn't let her know he'd been watching her on the security monitors. Better to approach her as if he were making his rounds and they just happened to include a stroll through the courtyard. He levered the polished brass door handle and pushed open the French door.

Julie glanced up, then lowered her face again. Even with twenty-twenty vision, Mac couldn't tell from this distance whether she was crying. He strolled closer, and about halfway across the courtyard he could see the rise and fall of her shoulders as she took deep, slow breaths.

"Hey," he said when he was just a few feet from her.

She lifted her face and managed a pathetic little smile. Her eyes were dry, at least. No telltale tracks of moisture on her cheeks. "Hello, Mac," she said.

Wintry clouds drifted across the sky. The gray morning light emphasized the absence of color in the elegant hollows of her cheeks. If she was trying to hide her distress, she wasn't trying hard.

He settled into the chair across the table from her and asked, "Something wrong?"

"No," she said, forcing another feeble smile.

"Anyone ever tell you you were a lousy liar?"

"Anyone ever tell you you were nosy?"

He grinned. "All the time, darlin'."

She relaxed her grip on herself and let her hands come to rest in her lap. Her fingers were long and silky-looking. He wondered how they'd feel on his skin, then shut down that thought before it could take hold.

"I'm not really nosy," he said. "But when the assistant to the hotel's general manager looks like her cat just got hit by a car, I need to know if you want security to mop up the blood."

"I don't have a cat," she said.

The hell with her hands. Her mouth, he thought. What would those full, soft lips feel like? What would they taste like? "I figured you for a cat person," he said, just to keep the conversation going.

"Tropical fish," she told him, then laughed. "If I had enough time and room for a real pet, it would be a dog. One of these days, if I ever own a house with a yard, I'll get one."

A vision of her in old shorts and a baggy T-shirt, racing around a grassy yard with a big, slobbering mutt, sprang up in his mind, taking him by surprise. He'd never seen Julie less than impeccably groomed. But the vision of her with her long, dark hair in an unraveling braid and her feet bare was so vivid, so natural, he needed a moment to bring himself back to the reality of the polished woman seated across the table from him.

"So," he drawled. "No cat. I take it that means no blood for security to mop up."

"No blood. Really, Mac, I'm fine."

Really, she wasn't. Her usual proud bearing was nowhere in evidence, and her lower lip trembled slightly. He found it much more difficult to picture her weeping than romping with a dog, yet she seemed a lot closer to weeping right now.

"Something personal?" he guessed. "Something back in New York?"

She flinched. "How did you know I was from New York?"

"I'm head of security. We've got files on everyone who draws a paycheck here."

"Of course." Her suspicion faded. "Well, it *is* personal. I mean, nothing is wrong, but if something *was* wrong, it would be personal."

He chuckled. She must have realized how much she'd revealed, because she allowed herself a small laugh, too. "If you need help, Julie," he said, earnest despite his smile, "I'm a pro when it comes to helping."

"Thanks, but I'm fine. Honestly." He must have looked skeptical, because she relented. "I got an e-mail that upset me, that's all."

His brain switched gears. No more thoughts about her lovely hands and shimmering violet eyes. This was business. This was why he was here. "An e-mail?" he asked in a deceptively mild voice.

"Spam," she said. "Thank God for the delete key."

He swallowed a curse. "You deleted it?"

"Isn't that what you're supposed to do with spam?"

"Run-of-the-mill spam, sure," he said. "Anything personal you should save. And you should alert someone."

"The police?"

"Or a security professional. Like me." He smiled to keep from alarming her. As if she wasn't already alarmed.

She tried valiantly to pretend she wasn't. "It was nothing, Mac. Not even worth the breath I've wasted talking about it. But thank you for offering to help."

"No thanks necessary." He stood, his brain whirring. He was going to have to hack into her computer and get a look at that e-mail. Who besides her might know her password? Her sister, maybe. "Promise me something, Julie," he said.

She leaned back and raised her eyes. They met his and he was once again stunned by their unusual color, their seductive beauty—and by the fear in them, the emotion she couldn't hide. "What?"

"If you get any more strange e-mails, you'll tell me about them."

"Mac—"

"And don't delete them. Promise me."

She stared up at him for a long, taut minute. "All right," she said. "I promise."

SHE'D PROBABLY OVERREACTED to the e-mail, Julie thought hours later, after she'd compiled all the information Charlotte had asked for concerning the party planners. She'd contacted several of them, typed up their rates and their available services and concluded that, given the hotel's delicate financial health, Charlotte shouldn't farm out any party jobs this year. But that decision was Charlotte's to make, so Julie simply put all the estimates into a folder, along with a sheet outlining her own opinions.

She'd also spent twenty minutes phoning grocery and convenience stores in the area to see if any of them sold bags of cylinder-shaped ice. A deli up on Canal Street claimed to have the right kind, so she'd sent one of the bellhops to pick up a bag, which was delivered to Alvin Grote's room with the hotel's compliments. She'd discussed shrimp prices with Robert LeSoeur and Melanie Marchand in the kitchen and alerted Nadine LeClaire in housekeeping that a guest had noticed a pile of wet towels on the floor near the third-floor elevator vestibule, and she'd gotten an e-mail from Marcie telling her their father was much improved and might even return to work tomorrow. That was an e-mail Julie wouldn't delete.

She rescued the glissando e-mail from her computer's trash bin, too, just in case Mac was right about saving such missives. She wasn't sure what its message was, though she tried to interpret it in the most positive way. "The song is over" could refer to nothing more sinister than the news that Glenn Perry's time in prison had ended. Her testimony had won him a twelve-to-twenty-year sentence, but with time off for good behavior, he'd been released after only eight years.

So his "song," his time behind bars, was over. Fine. Let him get on with his life. Let him pick up the pieces and live on the right side of the law and never exploit young girls again. And, please God, let him stay out of her own life.

By six-forty the top of her desk was clear and she could quit for the day. She slid the handles of her leather tote onto her shoulder and left her office, locking the door behind her. Given her long hours, she hadn't been joking when she'd told Mac she had no time for a dog. She barely had time to sprinkle a few flakes of fish food into her aquarium. Not that she was complaining, but after a long day of work, her feet were sore, her neck was stiff and her mind was wrung out. And her song was over.

Don't think about that e-mail, she scolded herself. *It's nothing.*

She was still assuring herself it was nothing when, on her drive home, she noticed a car following her. It wasn't directly behind her but a few vehicles back—a black BMW sports coupe. She turned left, and three cars later the black sports coupe turned left. She turned right and it turned right. She ran a yellow light and the BMW got stopped by the red, but two blocks later it had caught up to her, drifting in and out of her rearview mirror.

"It's nothing," she said aloud, then turned on her car's radio in time to hear Bonnie Raitt ask her if she was ready for a thing called love. As soon as that song ended, another began. "See?" she spoke to the air around her. "The song isn't over. There's always more music."

She reached her house at the edge of the Garden District, an old, genteelly seedy mansion that still showed water stains on its white stucco surface, just above the foundation, from Hurricane Katrina's floodwaters. She supposed her landlady had more important things to do than get the house's exterior painted. The landlady's apartment and one other were on the first floor of the building, and they'd suffered a fair amount of damage from the storm. Julie's flat was on the second floor, and when she'd returned home after the evacuation and found her possessions all as she'd left them—with the exception of her fish, who'd died from neglect and been mourned and replaced—she'd vowed never to complain about having to tramp up and down the stairs again.

She pulled into the small off-road parking area near the front door and spotted the black BMW easing up to the curb in front of the house. Cursing softly, she grabbed her tote and slammed the car door. Her song was *not* over, and whoever the silhouetted driver of that car was, he was not going to end it for her.

She raced to the front door and jammed her key into the lock, ignoring the tremor in her hand. Once she was inside the foyer, she leaned heavily against the door and let out a shaky breath. Only after her heart stopped pounding did she allow herself to peek out the side-light window framing the door.

The black car remained at the curb. She couldn't tell if the driver had emerged.

At least she was home. She had neighbors. She had a phone. She could dial the police. She could sing. She recalled how, years ago, she and Marcie used to drive their parents crazy when they sang a silly children's jingle that began, "This is the song that never ends..." If she sang that song until the black car left, she would be safe.

She climbed the stairs to her second-floor flat, humming the catchy tune as if it were a mystical chant with which she could ward off evil. Still humming, she unlocked her apartment, entered, shut the door and threw the dead bolt. She stepped out of her shoes, slid off her jacket and started toward the bedroom, singing under her breath.

She had just slipped off her blouse and shimmied out of her skirt when her intercom button sounded. The sharp buzz cut her song off, and the silence that filled her small apartment sent a chill through her.

One e-mail and she was turning into a wreck. One e-mail, sent just weeks after Glenn Perry had been paroled, and now a mysterious black car had followed her home. The intercom sliced through the peace of her apartment again, turning Julie into a basket case.

She threw her robe on over her slip, double-knotted the sash and padded in her stocking feet to the kitchen, where her intercom phone was. "Hello?"

"Julie? It's Mac Jensen."

Mac Jensen? What was he doing here?

He offered some sort of answer to her unspoken question. "You forgot to lock your car."

She'd forgotten to pick up her mail, too. She'd been too anxious to reach the safety of her apartment to waste time on her car door or her mailbox.

Then it hit her: Mac had been driving the black BMW. Mac had followed her home. The bastard, scaring the hell out of her!

What was she supposed to do now? Invite him up for a cup

of coffee? Go downstairs and lock her car? Slap him silly for having frightened her?

She didn't want to invite him up, that was for sure. She didn't trust any man who would follow her home, even if he'd had a good reason for doing so. Mac struck her as the sort of person who never did anything unless he had a good reason.

More important, she didn't trust a man who could extract a promise from her as easily as Mac had in the hotel's courtyard just hours ago. Why had she promised to tell him if she received any more weird e-mails? Why would she promise him anything at all? She didn't need some big, strong, protective man looking out for her. The last time she'd placed her fate in a man's hands had been with Glenn Perry, and he'd done things that had ultimately landed him in prison. She'd learned how to take care of herself then, and she wasn't about to unlearn that lesson now.

"I'll be down in a few minutes," she finally said. She hung up the intercom phone, stalked back to her bedroom and replaced her bathrobe and slip with a pair of jeans and a tunic-style sweater of textured white cotton. A few quick strokes with her brush settled the frizz the evening's dampness had teased out of her hair, and she slid her feet into a pair of clogs and grabbed her keys. She'd lock her car, get her mail and tell the overprotective guy to go home.

Downstairs, she peeked through the leaded-glass side light once more. Mac stood on the brick front porch, clad in the same gray suit and black polo shirt he'd been wearing all day. Maybe he'd look a little less dashing if he were dressed in the security uniform his underlings wore. Tomorrow Julie would suggest that Charlotte put Mac in uniform.

She bet he'd look damn good in that uniform, though. He looked better than damn good dressed in gray and black, with a day-old shadow of beard darkening his jaw.

Sighing, she eased open the door. "Did you follow me home?" she asked.

"Yeah."

No explanation. No apology. If confession was good for the soul, Julie thought his soul could use a little improvement. "Why?" she asked when he volunteered nothing.

"First lock up your car," he said. "It's not safe to leave it unlocked when you can't garage it. Anyone could walk up the driveway and tamper with it."

She scowled and pushed past him, down the porch steps and onto the front walk. "If anyone wants to steal the thing, they're welcome to it. They could save me the cost of a brake job."

"Are your brakes going?" He sounded like her father, stern and patronizing.

"They squeak," she said, hating how defensive she sounded. "The warning light hasn't turned on yet, so I'm sure they're safe. Just noisy." She locked the door, then marched back to the house, trying to ignore how closely he walked behind her.

On the porch, she halted and folded her arms. "Now tell me why you followed me home."

He opened his mouth, then shut it, reconsidering his answer. "I could come up with all kinds of explanations, darlin'," he said, then gave her a sheepish smile. "But mostly it's because I'm worried about you."

"There's no need for you to worry. I'm okay, as you can see." She uncrossed her arms and spread them wide, displaying how okay she was.

He scrutinized her with just a bit too much interest, and she folded her arms over her chest again. "This morning…" he began.

"I had a down moment, that's all. Have you ever heard of moods, Mac? They afflict women sometimes."

He chuckled. "Oh, yeah, I know about women and moods. Would you like to see my scars?"

His grin was knowing and a touch self-deprecating—and wickedly sexy. The thought of his stripping down to show her his scars sent a flush of heat through her. If there had been any question of her inviting him upstairs, it vanished now. Her apartment was too small; she wouldn't feel comfortable with him inside it. As it was, the Garden District seemed too small for the two of them. Even in the open air she detected his scent. It made her think of a forest at night, lit only by the moon.

The sound of a car cruising up the driveway dragged her attention away from Mac. Recognizing the bright red Miata, she felt her shoulders sag with relief. Creighton Bowman lived across the hall from her. He was in his sixties, flamboyantly gay and utterly delightful. He parked his car beside hers, climbed out and greeted her with a booming, *"Bon soir, ma chère!"* Then he loped up the walk to the porch, his silver hair flying and a colorful silk scarf fluttering around his neck. "Who is this adorable man you're refusing to introduce me to?"

"This is Mac Jensen," Julie dutifully told him, even though she didn't want Creighton to think Mac was her friend, or that she considered him particularly adorable. "Mac, my neighbor, Creighton Bowman."

Creighton extended his hand, and Mac shook it. "I like the looks of this one," Creighton confided to her in a stage whisper. "Much better than the last one. Or the one before that. Or…well, let's just say this one looks tall enough to hold his own with you. Most men can't see eye to eye with our Julie," he continued, addressing Mac. "Not her fault, of course. She's such a statuesque beauty—"

"Creighton, I think you've done enough damage for one day," Julie said, although she was smiling. He was so good-natured, she could never get angry with him, even when he was being painfully tactless. "Mac and I work together."

"Ah. A Hotel Marchand veteran."

"Hardly a veteran," Mac said smoothly. "I've been there only since Thanksgiving."

"That place will suck you in," Creighton warned. "It's simply too beautiful for words. French Quarter to the nth degree. The decor… It makes me swoon. And the restaurant… If only I were rich, I'd dine at Chez Remy every night."

"And you'd get fat," Julie pointed out. "You're a fine cook yourself—and your recipes have less butter in them." She patted his arm. "Mr. Jensen and I have business to discuss."

"On the front porch? You Yankees do things so strangely." Creighton turned his shining eyes on Mac. "When she's done demonstrating northern hospitality to you, sweet man, come on upstairs to my apartment and I'll pour you something potent. I adore Julie to pieces, but she doesn't know how to stock a bar."

"Thanks for the heads up," Mac said, shooting a quick look at Julie. He appeared to be struggling against a laugh.

"Well then, I'll leave you two workers to your business," Creighton said, sweeping past them and into the building.

It took several seconds for the air on the porch to settle. "Interesting neighbor," Mac said.

"He's a sweetheart."

"Anyone who knows how to stock a bar is all right with me." Mac grinned. "So, are we going to discuss business on the porch?"

"What business do we have to discuss?"

Instead of answering, he tilted his head back and stared up at the sky, which was dark but for the gray clouds streaking across. Julie realized why he looked up when she felt a cold raindrop hit her forehead.

"Tell you what," Mac drawled. "It's late and I'm hungry. Why don't we go get a bite to eat? We can talk then."

Julie was hungry, too, and tonight wasn't one of the rare occasions she felt like cooking. If they went out, she wouldn't have to invite him into her snug apartment, where his distinctive scent would linger long after he'd left.

"I have to get my purse," she said.

"And a raincoat," he suggested as the sky leaked a few more drops.

Reluctantly she let him into the foyer to wait. She couldn't very well leave him standing on the porch in the rain, and really, he was perfectly safe, even if he made her nerves twitch. She unlocked her mailbox—Mrs. Grollier, the landlady, sorted the mail for her four tenants when the postman dropped it through the slot in the front door—and pulled out the few items inside: a cell phone bill, several circulars for postholiday sales and a fashion magazine her mother had bought her a subscription to, thinking she might still have some interest in the business. She didn't, but she accepted the magazine without a fuss. At least she knew she could leaf through it without seeing any images of herself, looking as sultry as a naive teenager could look while holding a bottle of Glissando or Arpeggio.

Mac was sensitive enough not to follow her up the stairs, and she moved fast once she reached her apartment, tossing the mail onto the dining table that stood in the corner of the living room, then pulling her lined raincoat from a hook of the coat tree and grabbing her purse. She checked her wallet to make sure she had enough cash to cover her dinner if they went to a place that didn't accept plastic. She didn't want Mac paying for her. This wasn't a date.

Since he lacked a raincoat, she dug out an umbrella from her closet before leaving her apartment. He stood where she'd left him, in the entry foyer, tall and powerful, his hands in his trouser pockets and his jacket gaping just enough for her to appreciate the lean contours of his chest.

He looked stylish enough, even with his scruffy five-o'clock shadow—*especially* with his scruffy five-o'clock shadow—to dine anywhere in the city. In her faded jeans and baggy sweater, she wouldn't be admitted to any of the better establishments. Which was fine with her.

"Here," she said, extending the umbrella to him. "You might need this."

He appeared surprised by her generosity. "Thanks," he

said, holding the front door open for her and joining her on the porch. He popped open the umbrella, then leaned toward her so she could stand under it with him.

They hurried down the driveway to the street, where he'd left his car. It looked new, its glossy surface shining in the light of a streetlamp. He opened her door for her, then circled the car and wedged himself into the driver's seat. After shaking the rain off the umbrella, he snapped it shut and tossed it onto the floor behind him.

The car held his smell, along with a whiff of leather from the seats. "Fancy wheels," she observed. He must have earned a lot in his previous job. The Hotel Marchand didn't pay its security director enough to afford a new BMW.

He shrugged and cranked the engine. "It handles well," he said, as if that was the only reason someone would spring for a car like this.

It did handle well, weaving smoothly through what was left of the rush hour traffic, the windshield wipers arcing back and forth in a steady rhythm. Julie distracted herself from his steely profile by trying to make sense of his interest in the stupid e-mail she'd received a few hours ago. She should never have mentioned it to him, but she had—and now he seemed practically obsessed with her safety. Why? He was in charge of the hotel's security, not hers. Maybe he felt responsible for the entire staff, as well.

The hotel had a lot of employees. Mac Jensen was going to wear himself out if he took on all of their personal problems. She'd have to explain that to him—or perhaps Charlotte should be the one to tell him to lighten up. Charlotte was his boss, after all.

"Where are we going?" Julie asked as he steered down a sleepy street of darkened storefronts.

"A little place I know. Great food, cheap prices and no atmosphere. You up for that?"

No atmosphere sounded good. Mac clearly saw nothing remotely romantic in this outing.

The restaurant was located down an alley dark enough that she'd never have ventured there alone. In fact, she'd never have found it. Halfway through the alley, she and Mac descended a short flight of stairs to enter a basement club.

He'd lied about the atmosphere. The place teemed with it: dim lights, scratched wooden floors, paneled walls and a din of cheerful voices competing with the tinny zydeco music emerging from cheap ceiling speakers. Mouthwatering aromas of hot oil and fiery spices wafted through the dining room.

No maître d' hovered near the door, waiting to greet and seat them, but a waitress in blue jeans and white T-shirt swooped down on them as they entered. More specifically, she swooped down on Mac, planted a juicy kiss on his cheek and drawled, "Hello, loverboy! You're lookin' fine tonight. We're pretty full, but I got the perfect table for you. The catfish is so fresh tonight, it might flop around on your plate a little." She flashed Julie a toothy smile, then led them on a meandering path around the tightly arranged tables and chairs to a cramped table for two pushed up against the far wall.

"Loverboy?" Julie murmured once the waitress had departed.

Mac shrugged innocently.

He waited for her to sit before lowering himself onto the ladderback chair across from her. The table was small, and their knees collided underneath. The world, Julie had learned, was not designed for tall people with long legs. Mac apologized, shifted and bumped his knees against hers again. That time he smiled instead of apologizing.

"The food's really good here," he said, leaning forward to be heard above the chattering of voices around them and the lilting rhythm of accordion music pumping through the speakers.

"I like fresh fish, but I prefer that it not be flopping around on my plate," Julie countered. "Do you think they'll kill my dinner for me before they serve it?"

Mac grinned. "Only if you ask nicely."

"Or if Loverboy asks for me. Something tells me that waitress will do anything you ask of her."

"Probably," he said, a playful boast. "Assuming she's not being afflicted by one of those moods women are known to have."

Maybe by "no atmosphere," Mac had meant paper napkins. Maybe he'd meant computer-printed menus and water in plastic tumblers. Maybe he'd meant that more than one waitress seemed to hold him in extraordinarily affectionate esteem. Several stopped by their table to fawn over him.

Finally, one of them took their order. "The crawfish stew is great today," she gushed when Julie ordered it. Then she winked at Mac and said, "I just know you're gonna want that catfish, ain't you, honey?"

"You have a lot of friends here," Julie commented dryly, once the waitress bounced off with a promise to bring Mac's beer and Julie's glass of wine straightaway.

"You'll notice that not one of them has called me by name," Mac shot back.

"No, but they've got plenty of endearments for you, *darling.*"

"You're in N'awlins, Julie. Down here, the word *darlin'* doesn't end in a *g.*"

Their waitress returned with the wine and beer and a plastic basket filled with warm rolls. Another wink for Mac's benefit, and she was gone. "How did you even find this place?"

"I get around," he said casually. He lifted his beer mug, tapped it against her wineglass and took a sip.

"Were you born in New Orleans?"

He shook his head. "I grew up in Cajun country. St. Mary's Parish."

She would not have taken him for a rustic. He was poised, polished and always well dressed. Someone had brought him up to city speed somewhere along the way. "Jensen doesn't sound like a Cajun name," she said.

He grinned. "Even in the bayou, they allow crossbreeding. We didn't all marry our cousins." He pulled a roll from the basket and broke it open. A puff of vapor rose from its steamy center. "I was a jock. Won myself a scholarship to Loyola, left St. Mary's Parish and never looked back."

"How did you wind up in hotel security?" she asked before taking a sip of her wine. Not the sort of vintage Leo would stock at the hotel, but not bad, either.

"I like snooping," he confessed. "I studied psychology, but I couldn't picture myself sitting in an office and charging a hundred bucks an hour to listen to people whine. It's more interesting trying to psyche folks out, catching them at their worst. And keeping beautiful women safe." He took a bite of his roll, his eyes steady on her. "But enough about me, Julie. You're the one I want to keep safe."

"I'm perfectly safe," she insisted.

He appeared far from convinced. "You were whiter than chalk when I saw you this afternoon. Whatever that e-mail said, it had you spooked."

"Sure," she said calmly. "And when someone tiptoes up behind me and shouts 'boo!' I get spooked, too." *Or when someone in a hot black sports car follows me home,* she wanted to add. "Once the scare wears off, I'm not spooked anymore."

"Have you got any ex-boyfriends?" he asked.

She'd lifted her wineglass, but his question startled her and she put it back down without drinking. "I beg your pardon?"

"Any ex-boyfriends who might send you a nasty e-mail."

"Oh." She picked up her glass again and took a long sip, using the time to consider her answer. She'd had a few boyfriends over the years—as he could have guessed from Creighton's comments on the front porch. She couldn't imagine any of those old flames sending her that cryptic message about the song being over, though. The e-mail alluded to her stint as the face of Symphony Perfumes, and she hadn't dated during her modeling days. She'd been too young and too busy. She hadn't dated much in college, either; she'd been too traumatized by the whole ordeal in New York and the way her career had ended. And frankly, she hadn't felt a lack in her life. She prided herself on her independence. She didn't need a man by her side to make her feel complete.

In New Orleans, she'd gotten to know some men, and she'd stayed with one long enough that the subject of marriage arose during a few conversations. But she and Steven had ultimately decided they weren't destined for till-death-do-us-part, so they'd broken up. Afterward, over a devilish concoction Creighton had prepared for her from the contents of his well-stocked bar, her neighbor informed her that Steven had never been good enough for her. "You have more brain power in your earwax than he has in his entire body," Creighton insisted. Julie had disagreed, but Creighton's support and frequent dinner invitations had helped her get through the loneliness she'd felt in the wake of Steven's departure.

And it had been just loneliness, not heartbreak. Julie had recovered quickly.

"If you're asking me whether I've got an ex-boyfriend who would send me harassing e-mails, the answer is no," she said. "Really, Mac—"

"Anyone from your past who might be looking for trouble?"

She was spared from having to answer by the arrival of the waitress with their food. If the waitress hadn't arrived, would Julie have told the truth? Was she turning whiter than chalk again?

Glenn Perry was out of jail. He'd served his time and won his parole. But he had no reason to seek her out, no motivation to look for trouble with her now. She was a thousand miles away, and, God willing, their paths would never cross again. Surely he wanted to put the past behind him as much as she did.

"I ought to warn you, Mac," she said, with as sweet a smile as she could manage, "I don't like overprotective men."

"I'm not overprotective," he argued quietly. "Just protective."

As she recalled, Glenn had said something along those lines when she'd signed with the Glenn Perry Agency. She'd been seventeen, and her parents had said she could work only on weekends and in the summer—and even at that, they'd been worried about their precious young daughter commuting from their suburban home. But Glenn had said he'd take good care of her. He took good care of all his teenage models, he'd assured them. He protected his girls from the creeps and the sharks in the business.

Too bad he hadn't protected them from himself.

Julie might have been young, but she'd never been stupid. Unlike some of the other girls, she'd never trusted him. She'd learned how to defend herself and she'd known her own mind. Some people might have considered Julie beautiful, and others might have considered her freakish, so tall and thin and gawky for much of her childhood, but she'd always taken care of herself. And she'd taken care of Glenn, too, once she'd figured out what he was doing.

She didn't need Mac Jensen to look out for her. Let him protect the Hotel Marchand and its guests. That was what Charlotte paid him to do.

Julie was fine, thank you. One stupid e-mail wasn't going to get to her.

CHAPTER THREE

MARCIE SULLIVAN HAD INSISTED that Mac conceal the truth from Julie, and since Marcie was writing the checks, he bowed to her wishes. "If Julie knew I'd hired someone to keep an eye on her, she'd blow a gasket," Marcie had told him. "She hates anyone fussing over her or worrying about her. And I'm her sister, so I really don't want her hating me. You can't let her know what you're doing."

Not a problem. Mac had engaged in undercover work before, and this particular job was one of his easier assignments. Luck had created an opening at the hotel for him, and he'd stepped into it so he could remain near Julie without anyone realizing he was being paid to keep her safe. If Julie thought he was probing too much about her social life, he could rationalize his concern as simply part of his job as the hotel's head of security. She'd never have to know her sister was involved.

Curious though he was about her ex-boyfriends—and while he was at it any current ones—he steered the conversation in a different direction. "How long have you been Charlotte's assistant, Julie? Four years?"

"Five years this July," she answered. "Why?"

"I'm just trying to figure why a woman would leave a glamorous career as a high-fashion model to push papers in a hotel office."

She chewed, swallowed and speared another chunk of crawfish with her fork. "I was hungry," she said.

He gestured toward her plate. "Dinner ought to cure that."

She smiled. "This is delicious, but that's not what I meant. When I was modeling, I had to keep my weight down. I got tired of starving myself all the time."

"You quit so you could eat?" He laughed, even though he knew she was exaggerating.

"I also wanted to use my brain," she continued, then leaned back and sipped some wine. "Modeling is boring. The perfume ads were *really* boring. Try posing hour after hour with a bottle of Symphony Perfume." She shuddered at the memory.

"You did ads for Symphony Perfumes?" Mac asked, hoping he sounded as if this was all new to him. "Is that a big company? I'm not really up on perfume. Never wear the stuff," he added with a grin.

"Kiss a woman who's wearing it and you'll wind up wearing it, too," Julie returned, her smile teasing.

Staring at her across the small table, he was tempted to ask if she'd splash on some perfume and let him kiss her, just to see if what she'd said would happen. "So Symphony Perfumes…is it a big company?"

"Perfumes are made by drug and cosmetics companies," she told him. "A dozen different labels might come out of one huge company. Symphony was just one brand. Then, within the brand, there were different scents. All the Symphony Perfumes had musical names—Glissando, Arpeggio, Sonata, Grace Note. It's all marketing, Mac. Stick a label on a pretty bottle, take a photo of a bored model holding the bottle and people will buy the stuff."

However bored she'd been, she'd looked damn sexy in those photo ads. He had a bunch of them in a file back at his office.

He'd known his share of beautiful women—and his share of bored women, too. Julie looked beautiful tonight, her hair mussed, her slender body hidden beneath a baggy sweater and old jeans and her eyes dancing with pleasure as she devoured the food in front of her. With her makeup worn off, her professional polish missing and a decade's worth of experience adding character to her face, she looked a lot sexier than she had in the perfume ads.

He convinced her to order dessert and coffee, simply so he could spend a little more time watching her eat. When she hesitated, he ordered a bowl of bread pudding for himself. That seemed to appease her, and she resigned herself to a slice of bourbon pecan pie and a cup of decaf. He asked for real coffee; he'd need the caffeine to keep him alert when he got back to work tonight.

"Tell me about the Hotel Marchand," he said once the waitress had delivered their desserts and coffee. "Charlotte recently took over managing the place from her mother, Anne, right?"

"Last September, " Julie answered with a nod. "The hotel was Anne's dream—hers and Remy's. He built the restaurant into what it is today, and she managed the hotel. The hotel was their home. Their daughters grew up there, in the living quarters above the bar."

"Remy was pretty well-known in the city," Mac commented. "Being a famous chef, spreading the word about New Orleans cuisine. He died in a car crash, didn't he?"

Another nod. "It was horrible. A drunk driver hit his car during a storm on the causeway over Lake Pontchartrain." She sighed. "It was so sad. I'd barely gotten to know him—I'd been working at the hotel a couple of months before he died. But he and Anne were soul mates."

"Was that why Anne turned over the hotel to Charlotte? Because she'd lost her soul mate?"

This time Julie shook her head. "Anne was still pretty much running the show until just before you arrived. Charlotte was taking over more and more of the management, but Anne remained in charge until last September, when she had a minor heart attack and the doctor ordered her to cut back and take it easy."

Although he had access to the personnel records, he wasn't privy to those of Anne Marchand or her daughters. Family—and hotel ownership—had its privileges. That Anne had had a heart attack surprised him. "She looks pretty healthy."

"You've met her, then?"

"In passing. She's not around that much. Charlotte was the one who hired me."

"I remember," Julie said, then busied herself with her pie. He wondered if, as Charlotte's assistant, she'd had any say in his hiring. Wouldn't it be ironic if she'd helped him to weasel his way into the hotel so he could keep tabs on her?

He took a long sip of his coffee. Black and strong, it rinsed the heavy sweetness of the bread pudding from his mouth. "I've gotten to know the other Marchand sisters, too. Sylvie, who runs the art gallery in the hotel—she's got a daughter, right?"

"Daisy Rose," Julie confirmed. "She's three years old and absolutely adorable. Also a handful," she added with a grin.

"Any other third-generation Marchands?" he asked.

"Not yet. I guess it's lucky none of the sisters had other family ties, since they've all been able to help out with the hotel since Anne's heart attack. Melanie was a chef in Boston, but she came home and fit right into the Chez Remy kitchen. Renee was doing PR work out in Hollywood before she moved back, so now she's doing PR for the hotel." Julie scooped up a dab of whipped cream and licked it off her fork.

"Anne knew what skills to develop in her daughters so they could take over the business," he said with a grin. "That took some foresight."

"Growing up with Anne as their mother, maybe they couldn't help catching the hotel-business bug. Anne loves the hotel almost as much as she loves her daughters. She pretty much designed the place herself, picked out the furnishings—all those gorgeous antiques in the lobby, the furniture and the fabrics, the room furnishings, even the teardrop shape of the swimming pool. She's an amazing woman, very strong—

except for her heart problem. I don't think she wanted to give up the day-to-day management of the place, but it was for the best that she handed that responsibility over to Charlotte. Running a hotel is so demanding. Plus the financial pressures…"

"Is the hotel having money problems?" he asked. He wasn't going to worry about his paycheck—as Sandy had pointed out, he was already getting paid plenty by Julie's sister—but the Marchands were nice people, and their hotel was a four-star establishment. The rooms seemed to be booked, the restaurant crowded, the bar lively.

"There are some debt issues," Julie said vaguely. "Nothing insurmountable, but Anne worries about it. Charlotte does, too."

"And you don't?"

This time she didn't bother lying. "Anything Charlotte worries about, I worry about. But the hotel is kind of like Anne herself. It would take more than a heart problem to knock her flat. She's tough. So's the Hotel Marchand." Julie glanced down and seemed startled to discover an empty plate where her pie had been. "That was so good," she said, then smiled bashfully. "I can't believe I pigged out like that."

"You were hungry, darlin'." Most women loved sweets but refused to eat them in front of a man. That Julie had ordered the pie and savored every bite of it… In Mac's book, few things were as erotic as watching a woman suck the sweetness off the tines of a fork.

Too bad he worked with her. Too bad he worked for her sister. Another time, another circumstance, and this evening might have ended back at his apartment. He might have figured out a way to seduce her out of that baggy sweater, out of those soft, worn jeans and into his arms. He might have wound up smelling like her perfume, if she was wearing any.

Julie put up an argument when he reached for the check.

He ignored her protests as he handed the waitress his credit card. Once the waitress was gone, Julie slumped in her chair, sulking. “Why won’t you let me pay for my meal?”

“I brought you here,” he said, wondering whether her annoyance qualified as one of those prickly moods women were so susceptible to. “I’ll pay.”

“Just so long as we’re both clear this isn’t a date,” she muttered.

“Yes, ma’am.” He smiled at her stubbornness. “Clear as the air between us.” Which, he had to admit, wasn’t all that clear, given the dim lighting and the fact that they both were nursing secrets. If he was going to do his job, he’d have to uncover her secrets. She’d probably resent him for that, even more than she resented him for paying for dinner.

Her annoyance had faded by the time they left the restaurant. They huddled together under her umbrella as they walked down the alley to his car, then shared a quiet drive along the wet city streets back to the huge, slightly decaying house where she lived. He walked her up to the brick front porch, and her fingertips brushed lightly over his as he handed her the umbrella. Her fingers were long and slender, as cool and gentle as he’d imagined.

The security expert in him didn’t approve of the uneven lighting on the front porch. The man in him only saw the shadows playing across her face, and the way her large violet eyes glowed, and the curve of her lips.

“Do you want to take the umbrella back to the car?” she offered. “You can return it to me tomorrow.”

“It’s hardly drizzling,” he said, trying not to stare at her mouth. “Be careful, Julie. You get any more scares, no matter how trivial—tell me. Okay?”

She rolled her eyes, then smiled. “Don’t worry about me. I’m perfectly fine.”

Perfect, maybe, he thought as he broke from her and strode down the walk to his car. The rain fell cold against his face and neck, but he refused to run or hunch up the collar of his jacket. *Perfect, but not perfectly fine.*

He drove back to the hotel, left his car in a lot the hotel maintained a few blocks away and pulled his BlackBerry from the console between the front seats. He turned it on and checked his e-mail.

There it was, a note from Marcie: "Our mother's maiden name was Farris. Our grandmothers' maiden names were McConnell and Pasker. Only family pet was Julie's dog, Bella. Why do you need to know this?"

Because it might help me do some breaking and entering, he silently answered Marcie's question. He tucked the Black-Berry into an inner pocket of his jacket, climbed out of the car and strolled down the street toward the hotel's service entrance. The rain had thinned into a chilly mist. His brisk pace kept him from getting too wet.

He entered the hall to the security office. No one expected him to be at the hotel at 10:30 p.m., but if someone spotted him and he hadn't checked in with the night security staff, there would be questions. Mac had learned long ago that one of the best ways to avoid those kinds of questions was to do whatever you were doing right out in the open.

Tyrell was seated at the security desk when Mac swung through the door. "Hey, boss. You come to spell me?" Tyrell asked. He was young and had a sly sense of humor.

"No such luck," Mac told him. "I'm not really here. Julie Sullivan told me she had some weird static on her computer. She's worried about a virus or a hacker. I told her I'd check it for her."

"You a techie?" Tyrell asked.

Mac shrugged. "I can fiddle around a little. I'm betting it's a problem with her power strip. I'll unplug something, plug it back in, and she'll think I'm a hero."

"I wouldn't mind a lady like her thinking I was a hero," Tyrell said appreciatively.

Mac wouldn't mind, either. "What kind of night are we having?"

"A boring one." Tyrell peered up at the monitor above the desk. "Some dude kicked up a fuss at the front desk on his way out to dinner. A Mr.—" he located a slip of paper on the desk and read from it "—Alvin Grote, Room 307. He said someone swapped pillows on him."

"Swapped pillows?"

Tyrell glanced at the slip of paper. "He said his pillows were much softer when he checked in. Now they're hard. The desk clerk assured him no one had changed the pillows in the room, but he got himself pretty worked up. So the desk clerk contacted me."

"Did you have to calm the guy down?"

Tyrell's immediate answer was a snort. Then he elaborated. "He was worked up, but it wasn't like he was swinging or making threats. He's from Chicago. Dressed all in black, bald on top and the rest of his hair in a ponytail.... You know the type. He demands the best, even though he hasn't got a clue what the best is."

"But you were able to keep the situation under control?"

"The desk clerk offered to put him in a different room, but he didn't want that. So I suggested we have the hotel treat him to a drink at the bar. That satisfied him." Tyrell shook his head. "Sometimes I think folks just throw a fit because they're hoping to get something free out of it."

Mac had to agree. He was thankful hotel work wasn't his life's vocation. He hated giving people undeserved gifts just to shut them up. It seemed like extortion to him.

He studied the monitor for a minute. "Other than Mr. Grote, have there been any problems?"

"Nah. The night's young, though," Tyrell added hopefully.

"I like your optimism." Mac patted him on the shoulder, then left the office and headed toward the stairs. Hearing footsteps down the hall, he turned to see Luc Carter emerge from the housekeeping supply room, shutting the door behind him.

Luc bounded along the hall until he noticed Mac. Then he slowed to a halt and smiled. "Hi."

"Hi, yourself. What are you doing here?"

Luc glanced over his shoulder, then spun back to Mac. His tie loose and his hands plunged into his trouser pockets, he had the pleasantly rumpled look of someone who'd put in too many hours at work but didn't really mind. His job as the hotel's concierge shouldn't have required a trip to the housekeeping supply room, though. "I've, uh, I've got a friend who works in there."

Oh. Okay. Mac smiled. "You can't find a better place for your rendezvous than the supply room?"

"Well, she was closing up for the night, and I came downstairs to help her."

"You're all heart, Luc," Mac teased him. Luc's smile transformed from sheepish to wolfish. Mac considered reminding Luc that affairs with coworkers rarely ended happily—a truth he ought to remember the next time he got to pondering Julie Sullivan's magnificent mouth—but dispensing romantic warnings to colleagues wasn't his style. Let Luc learn his own lessons.

"Well…I guess I should be on my way," Luc said, sparing Mac a parting grin. "Catch you later."

"Yeah." He watched Luc leave the building, then lapsed into thought. Where was the young lady Luc had been fooling around with in the supply room? She must have left ahead of Luc—but the supply room was her bailiwick, not Luc's. Odd that she'd leave him to lock up the place.

Frowning, Mac abandoned the stairs for the hall, stealing past the security office and testing the doorknob to the supply room. As he'd expected, it was locked, but he had a master key. He inserted it, twisted and pushed the door open. Reaching around the jamb, he groped for the light switch and turned it on before he entered the room.

Floor-to-ceiling shelves divided the room into narrow

aisles. The shelves were packed with supplies—bed linens, bath towels, boxes of complimentary shampoos, soaps and skin lotions, rows of irons that guests could borrow, spare coffeepots and packets of ground coffee, glasses capped in pleated paper. No sign of Luc's sweetheart—not that Mac had expected to find her lurking in the storeroom.

Where could a young couple fool around in here? he wondered. The room lacked upholstered horizontal surfaces, and the floor was cold, hard linoleum. Of course, a lot could be accomplished standing up, but the aisles were narrow and the shelves were so crowded that a couple getting physical would likely knock things onto the floor.

The floors were clear and the shelves were neat, though. Maybe Luc and his girlfriend had just stolen a few kisses. Maybe they were saving the main event for another venue.

Or else…maybe they'd spread some towels on the floor. Mac noticed that the stack of plush white bath towels on one of the shelves looked slightly uneven. Most people wouldn't have caught that, but Mac had been at this game a long time. He knew how to spot things that weren't quite right.

He strode down the aisle to the crooked stack. If Luc had used these towels, they shouldn't be sitting on a shelf with all the clean ones, awaiting delivery to some unsuspecting guest's room. He pulled the top towel from the stack and shook it out, searching for signs of dirt.

What he saw were tiny glitters imbedded in the plush nap. Squinting, he angled the towel toward the overhead fluorescent light. Each glitter belonged to a splinter of broken glass.

Something must have shattered in here, and Luc and his girlfriend had used the towel to clean it up. And then they'd put the towel back onto the shelf, where it could have been picked up and sent off to a guest's bathroom. The unsuspecting guest would have stepped out of the tub and dried himself off, and wound up with glass splinters in his back.

"Son of a bitch," Mac muttered.

He pulled the next towel out and studied it in the bluish light. More splinters of glass. He unfolded a third towel, a fourth, a fifth. All of the towels in the stack were flecked with tiny shards of glass.

"Son of a freaking bitch." Why would Luc have done something so careless, so downright stupid?

Maybe he hadn't. Maybe the girl had, or someone else on the housekeeping staff. The housekeepers were the lowest paid employees at the hotel. Someone pissed off at the boss or simply at the world might have left the booby-trapped towels on the shelf.

Didn't the hotel ship the bulk of its linens out to a professional laundry? Maybe someone at the laundry was responsible for this.

He cursed one final time, then turned and left the supply room, locking up behind him. He'd have to contact Nadine LeClaire, the head of housekeeping. She'd be gone for the night, but this was worth phoning her at home about. Charlotte would have to hear about it, too, but he could write her a report in the morning.

He returned to the security office, swung inside and reached for the phone. "What's up?" Tyrell asked, shifting his gaze from the monitor and frowning at Mac.

"Glass," he muttered as he punched in Nadine's phone number. The home telephone numbers of all the senior staff were posted on the wall next to the desk. Fortunately, the hour wasn't so late, and he didn't awaken her. As soon as she answered, he told her about the towels.

She was appropriately outraged. "Broken glass in the guest towels? Who would've done that?"

Mac pictured Luc Carter, then shook his head. Too many other possibilities existed for Mac to name a suspect. "I don't know, Nadine. But I think you'd better send that batch of towels back to the laundry service. We don't want to risk having a guest get hurt."

"I'll come down and oversee the job," she said. "God almighty. Thanks for discovering this mess."

"Just doing my job," Mac insisted before hanging up.

Tyrell looked worried. "I missed something?"

"You couldn't have missed it. We have no camera in the supply room—and those towels could have been put there hours ago. When Nadine gets here, give her whatever help she needs. I'll get a report to Charlotte tomorrow." With that he left the office, determined to accomplish what he'd come to the hotel to do.

He took the back stairs two at a time. On the second floor he moved swiftly and quietly down the hall to Julie's office. The master key worked on her door as effectively as it had on the supply room door.

Not bothering to turn on the light, he crossed directly to her desk and hit her computer switch. While the machine warmed up, he pulled his BlackBerry from the jacket pocket where he'd stashed it. Her sister's e-mail glowed on the tiny screen. Farris, McConnell, Pasker…and the family dog, Bella.

Julie had told him she was a dog person. Now he'd find out just how much of a dog lover she was. Lots of folks used the maiden names of relatives as passwords, but some used the names of their pets. Mac had a feeling Julie was one of the pet people.

As soon as the computer was online, he clicked her e-mail icon. The cursor flashed at the "password" box and he typed in *B-E-L-L-A*.

"Yeah," he whispered as her e-mail inbox filled the screen. A dozen unopened e-mails awaited her, and he skimmed the return addresses. They featured recognizable names or companies. He hoped that meant she wouldn't have any ugly surprises awaiting her tomorrow.

Issuing a silent prayer that she hadn't deleted the e-mail that had upset her, he scrolled down to her already opened e-mails. One return address stood out: "4Julie." He clicked it.

The e-mail showed a musical notation of some sort—a

staff with a wriggly line sloping up it, and underneath it the message: "The song is over."

What the hell did that mean? Obviously, Julie had some idea. This had to be the message that had shaken her to her bones.

He pulled out his flash stick, plugged it into her computer and downloaded her entire e-mail folder. He had no interest in all those e-mails from vendors and banks and the hotel's reservations department, but only by collecting all the data would he have half a prayer of tracking down the sender of the musical e-mail. Not a full prayer, but half was better than nothing.

Once the download was complete, he removed the flash stick and shut off her computer.

The song is over, he thought. What song? Whose song? Over in what way?

He left Julie's office, locked up and took the back stairs down to the security office again. "Did Nadine get here yet?" he asked Tyrell.

"No."

"Phone me if she needs to talk to me. I'll keep my cell turned on."

"Okay. Broken glass in the towels?" Tyrell snorted in disbelief. "Pretty crazy."

"It's a crazy world," Mac agreed as he pivoted and stalked out of the office.

A crazy world, indeed, he thought as he exited the building into the damp, raw night. Someone sabotaging the guest towels with glass, and someone sabotaging Julie Sullivan's equilibrium with a cryptic e-mail. A crazy world full of crazy people—no wonder the services of Crescent City Security were in high demand.

He patted the pocket that held his flash stick. He'd gotten lucky at guessing how Julie would choose a password for her e-mail software. If his luck held, he'd be able to track down who'd sent her the e-mail that had freaked her out.

Even with luck, however, he had a long night ahead of him.

SHE'D MADE GLENN SUFFER, so she should suffer, too. Fair was fair.

Not that what she'd done to Glenn was fair.

Tracking her down had been easy enough. Anyone could be Googled these days. The name Julie Sullivan had summoned thousands of hits, but patience paid off. You had to be patient to survive an eight-year sentence, being cut off from the world, your job, your lover. That same patience made it possible to click Web site after Web site until the right one appeared.

The New Orleans Times-Picayune *had provided the goods: a photograph of some antiques on display in a hotel lobby, with a few of the hotel's executives standing around. One was identified as Julie Sullivan, and the photo offered proof. All these years later, Julie was still tall and poised and gorgeous. And she was in New Orleans, working at the Hotel Marchand. A phone call to the hotel's switchboard was all it took to get Julie's e-mail address.*

Bingo. Or as they said in New Orleans, voilà.

Thank God for computer cafés and libraries—the twenty-first century's version of pay phones. Send a nasty e-mail from a public computer and no one could ever trace it back to you.

Not that the e-mails needed to be openly hostile. That would be too obvious. Julie was the kind of woman who'd get huffy and indignant if you confronted her directly. Better to undermine her subtly. Give her a quiet scare. Soften her up bit by bit, so when the time came, her stiff resolve and her smug self-righteousness would be worn down and she wouldn't have the will to fight back.

She'd deprived Glenn of his business, his freedom and his ability to love. Let her suffer and squirm for a while. Make her miserable.

She'd be put out of her misery soon enough.

CHAPTER FOUR

MAC HAD BEEN in her office. Julie noticed his scent, faint though it was, as soon as she entered the room the next morning.

Nothing appeared to have been moved or even touched. Her desk looked exactly the way she'd left it last night. Her chair was pushed in, her computer turned off, her file cabinets closed. Her pen angled out of its brass stand and her day calendar still showed yesterday's date. She tore off the page and gazed around the room. Mac had left no evidence behind, other than his woodsy, sexy scent.

What had he been doing in here? When had he done it? *Why was he watching her?*

She had to admit his scrutiny bothered her less now than it had before she'd spent an evening in his company, stuffing her face with delicious food at that unpretentious back-alley eatery. If he unnerved her now, it wasn't because she felt he was spying on her. It was because he was so damn…*male.*

Maybe she'd eaten all that food last night to sublimate another hunger. She hadn't been with a man since she and Steven broke up a year ago—and Mac wasn't just some guy. He had those dark eyes and that chiseled chin, as Charlotte had pointed out yesterday, and he had a heart-melting smile, a wicked laugh, height to match Julie's and a soft, seductively drawling voice that could make the word *darlin'* sound X-rated. He was smart and confident, just this side of arrogant. And he had that scent, warm and tangy and obviously loaded with pheromones, considering Julie's reaction to it.

Her reaction to it this morning wasn't as simple as a rush of girlish giddiness, however. The man was head of hotel security, so perhaps he'd had a legitimate reason to have invaded her office in her absence. He possessed a master key which enabled him to enter any room in the hotel. Charlotte had vetted him and she trusted him. Julie ought to trust him, too.

Even so, as soon as her computer warmed up, she clicked into the hotel's personnel records. Mac had access to all the employee files. Her access was limited to basic information, but if he could check her out, she could sure as hell check him out, too.

The portion of his record she was able to open informed her that he was thirty-five years old and single, that he lived in the Carrollton neighborhood, that his previous position had been as an associate with Crescent City Security Services and that he'd declined the hotel's health insurance plan. That last item tweaked her curiosity. Why would he have chosen not to be covered? Usually, when an employee opted out of the health plan, it was because he or she was covered under a spouse's insurance. But Mac didn't have a spouse.

Well, he certainly seemed healthy, anyway.

She would have loved to take a peek at his total employment history, his referral letters and any observations Charlotte or the head of personnel might have included in his file, but those pages were off-limits for her. She considered it unfair that Mac could read her entire file if he wanted, and she couldn't read his. But that, she supposed, was the difference between being the assistant to the hotel's general manager and being the security boss.

Sighing, she opened her e-mail software, typed in her password and checked her in-box. Most of the messages were standard fare: daily reports for Charlotte from the business office, the Reservations Department, the restaurant and bar; solicitations from assorted vendors, two more responses from professional party planners and an announcement of a store-wide sale at the pet supply shop where Julie bought her fish food. She ignored all those and instead clicked on the one new e-mail that caused her stomach to twist into a pretzel-shaped knot. Like yesterday's troubling e-mail, this one had as its return address "4Julie."

Today's communication featured the musical symbol for a grace note and the words, "Say goodnight, Julie."

That message seemed more menacing than "the song is over." It didn't actually threaten anything, but... Someone was definitely trying to scare the spit out of her.

Whoever had sent her the "4Julie" e-mails knew of her past as the Symphony Perfumes model—but that hardly narrowed down her list of suspects. Models often attracted groupies and weird fans, as Julie had learned during the years she'd been in the business. People used to send her marriage proposals and tawdry propositions through the agency, but Glenn Perry's secretary would discard the most offensive fan mail so Julie wouldn't have to see it. Back then, of course, she'd believed that Glenn was truly acting in the best interests of his girls, protecting them from all the creeps who liked to fantasize about fashion models.

Julie had changed her e-mail address half a dozen times since ending her modeling career, however. She simply couldn't imagine who, from that period of her life, would have tracked down her current address.

Maybe the "4Julie" sender wasn't someone from her past. Maybe he was one of the business people she corresponded with in the course of her work at the Hotel Marchand. Someone might have figured out Julie was the onetime Symphony Perfumes girl and decided to taunt her about it anonymously. Why? Jealousy or fanatic devotion or...who knew? As her father always said, trying to figure out why idiots did idiotic things was a waste of time.

She slid her mouse to delete the grace note message, then hesitated. Mac had told her not to erase any creepy e-mails she received, and she'd rescued the glissando one from her computer's trash bin yesterday. She supposed she ought to save today's e-mail, too, just in case.

At the sound of voices in the adjacent office, she took several deep breaths to settle her nerves and then went to open the inner door to Charlotte's office. One of the voices belonged to Charlotte and the other to her mother, Anne Marchand.

Seeing Anne was enough to put all thoughts of weird e-mails out of Julie's mind. Ever since her health scare last fall, Anne had kept a low profile at the hotel, partly because her doctor had ordered her to take it easy and partly, Julie suspected, because Anne wanted to give Charlotte a chance to establish her own style as she took over the hotel's management. These were both good reasons, but Julie missed Anne. She was such a classy woman, poised yet passionate about the Hotel Marchand and loyal to all the people who worked there.

Before Julie could say hello, Anne swept across the room, her arms open for a hug. "Julie! How are you?"

Julie bent so Anne could reach her cheek with a kiss. "You're looking great, Anne. How are you feeling?"

Anne rolled her eyes. "If you must know, I'm sick—sick of people asking me how I'm feeling. I'm sick of being babied and fussed over. My mother, bless her heart, is going to give me a heart attack with all her nagging." Anne had moved in with her mother for her recuperation. Julie had never met Celeste Robichaux, but she'd heard the family matriarch was temperamental and domineering, and not particularly enthusiastic about the family's hotel business.

However oppressive Celeste's nursing was, Anne seemed to be flourishing. She twirled about the office radiating energy and confidence. She'd let her hair grow long, and today she wore it pulled back from her face in a ponytail held by a tortoise-shell barrette. She also had on comfortable-looking khaki slacks. Julie couldn't recall a single instance when Anne had come to work in anything other than an impeccably tasteful dress or suit, back before her heart attack had put her out of commission. Slacks suited her, though. She looked slim and fit and energized.

"Charlotte told me the menu for the Twelfth Night party still hasn't been finalized," she said. "If there's going to be a discussion about food, you all know I want to be involved."

Julie laughed, and Charlotte shook her head. "We won't be making the final decisions until the last minute, Mama. Robert and Melanie will want to see what's available, what's fresh—"

"I'm so glad Melanie is here to help us with the menus," Anne said. "All those years she was working as a chef up in Boston when she could have been putting her culinary skills to use here at the hotel. If my little health scare last fall was enough to bring her home, it was worth it. And flowers, Charlotte," Anne continued. "Have you ordered the flowers for the party? I always ordered them at least a week in advance."

"I know, Mama," Charlotte said, her tone an interesting mix of impatience and indulgence. "The flowers have been ordered."

"Of course they have." Anne smiled wistfully at Charlotte. "You have everything under control. You all don't need me here, fussing over this and that."

Charlotte exchanged a look with Julie, then reached for her mother's hand and gave it a squeeze. "If you want to oversee the decorations in the event rooms, that would be great."

"You're humoring me, I know," Anne said, sounding not at all sorry. "But since you offered, I will most certainly oversee the decorations."

A light rap on the door to the hallway stole their attention, and they turned to find Mac filling the doorway. He wore a dark blue suit, beautifully tailored. Julie thought back to the equally stylish gray suit he'd had on yesterday, and his black BMW, and his refusal to accept the hotel's health insurance. Was the man independently wealthy?

That question disintegrated in her mind as Charlotte greeted him and he entered the room. He'd shaved since Julie last saw him, but even without a shadow of beard, he looked slightly weary, slightly dangerous. His eyes were perhaps a bit too dark, his angular features a bit too harsh. Or maybe the only danger he posed was that Julie found him intolerably attractive.

"Charlotte, I'm sorry to interrupt," he said, tapping his fingertips against the folder he was carrying. "There's something I need to discuss with you." He smiled at Anne. "Mrs. Marchand. Good to see you."

"Mama, you remember Mac Jensen, don't you?"

"Gerard Lomax's replacement in security," Anne said, returning his smile and extending her hand. "We've met."

Mac shook her hand, then glanced at Julie. One corner of his mouth skewed up in a tentative half smile. She hoped her own smile was noncommittal. What had happened yesterday was…nothing. They'd eaten dinner together, that was all. And shared an umbrella. And exchanged a few searching looks, although Julie had no idea what Mac had been searching for when he'd gazed at her that way—the way he was gazing at her right now.

"Well, I'd love to stay and chat," Anne said, "but I want to visit the event rooms and wait for inspiration to strike."

Charlotte nodded. "Sylvie had some thoughts about the party decor, so you might want to talk to her."

"Sylvie has a marvelous eye," Anne conceded, her smile growing mischievous as she headed toward the door. "But I'm her mother, so I get more votes than she does." With that, she waltzed out of the room.

"She's looking well," Julie said as she backed toward the door to her office, where a full day's work—and that damned e-mail—awaited her. "If you don't need me, Charlotte—"

"Stay," Charlotte requested. "Something tells me Mac's got bad news. You might as well hear it, too."

"Not bad news," he corrected her, then grinned. "Well, yeah, it's bad. Maybe we ought to sit down."

They each found a chair, Charlotte behind her desk, Julie

and Mac in deep, upholstered armchairs facing her. Mac placed the folder he'd been holding on Charlotte's desk and said, "Last night, I found chips of glass embedded in some of the towels in the housekeeping supply room. These were clean, folded towels in a stack, ready to be left in guest rooms."

"Glass?" Charlotte's cheeks paled.

"I notified Nadine LeClaire immediately, and she sent the entire batch back to the laundry service. She blamed the glass on the service and demanded that they launder the batch for free. They agreed. So it's not all bad news. We incurred no extra laundry expense."

Julie listened not merely to his words but to his tone. She heard more in it than just what he'd said. "You don't agree with Nadine, do you," she guessed. "You think the laundry service wasn't to blame for the glass, right?"

"I'm not sure what I think. Yet," he added. "Just before I found the glass in the towels, I saw Luc Carter leaving the supply room."

"Luc?" Julie and Charlotte exclaimed in unison. "What on earth would he be doing there?" Charlotte added.

"He said he was helping a friend on the housekeeping staff."

Charlotte appeared bemused. "A friend?"

"A *friend,* Charlotte," Julie clarified, once again able to interpret the nuances in Mac's tone. She turned to Mac. "Is Luc getting biblical with one of the maids?"

Mac laughed at Julie's euphemism. "He didn't go into detail about the extent of their relationship, and I didn't ask."

"So it's possible Luc was in the supply room fraternizing with one of the maids," Charlotte said tactfully, "and that has nothing to do with the glass in the towels."

"Yeah."

Again Julie heard more in Mac's voice than just the single word. "You can't very well confront Luc with accusations if you have no evidence he's done anything wrong," she said.

"I know." Mac turned to Charlotte. "With your permission,

I'd like to investigate Luc a little, see what I can dig up. He'd never have to know—unless I found something incriminating."

Charlotte tapped her manicured fingers together as she considered his suggestion. "I hate the idea of spying on hotel employees."

I hate it, too, Julie thought, sending Mac a scowl that he didn't notice, since he was focused on Charlotte.

"Chances are, what I find will exonerate him. And again, he'd never even know. I'm good at doing that kind of thing."

I bet you are, Julie thought churlishly.

"Well…all right," Charlotte conceded. "But please be careful. Luc has done a good job behind the concierge desk. I'd hate to lose him. And if he finds out he's being investigated—"

"He won't find out," Mac promised, then pushed himself to his feet. "I can be very discreet."

Can you really? Julie recalled the way he stared at her, the way he grinned at her, the way he'd stood so close to her under her umbrella last night. Then she remembered the way he moved around the hotel, so silently he could come and go without being detected. She supposed that proved he could be discreet, even if his stares and grins and closeness were anything but.

Charlotte nodded, flipped open the folder, shut it unread and sighed. "Thank you for noticing that broken glass before it wound up in a guest's bathroom. Imagine what a disaster that would have been."

Mac nodded at Charlotte, then shot Julie a pointed look. She might have been able to interpret the undertone in his voice, but she couldn't begin to guess what this particular look meant. Lacking a better response, she turned away.

Charlotte flipped open the folder, skimmed Mac's report and muttered, "Dear God." Julie glanced toward the door to see him vanishing down the hall, his footsteps as silent as ever. "I shudder to think what could have happened if he hadn't discovered that glass. You don't really think Luc could have planted it there, do you?"

"Why would he?" Julie asked. "He's got a good job here. He seems satisfied with it. The guests adore him."

Charlotte sighed again. "Let's assume Nadine was right and the laundry service screwed up and sent us a batch of dirty towels. Though heaven knows how towels would end up with glass in them."

"Someone might have used them to wipe the floor after breaking a mirror," Julie suggested.

Charlotte eyed the folder and grimaced. "If so, someone's got seven years of bad luck heading their way. Fortunately, Mac spared us a similar fate. Do me a favor, Julie, and in a half hour or so, go downstairs and see what my mother is up to."

"You don't want her overseeing the decorations?"

"I'd love to have her working on the decorations. She has such a flair for that sort of thing. I just don't want her tiring herself out. And if she catches me checking up on her, she'll hand me my head on a silver platter. Better you than me. You're not her daughter."

"Thanks," Julie grumbled, although she was smiling. "I think I can handle her." She stood and walked across the room to the door leading into her office.

Two steps across the threshold, she halted. There, leaning casually against the file cabinet nearest the hall door, stood Mac, his hands in his pockets and his head slightly cocked, as if nothing could be more natural than for him to be in her office, waiting for her.

She tried not to notice his lopsided smile, which produced a dimple in one corner of his mouth. She tried not to notice the smooth drape of his shirt across his chest or the length of his legs or his thick, dark hair. She couldn't help but notice his scent, though. It stirred something deep inside her, making her feel vulnerable.

She crossed the room to him so she could speak softly. If she closed the door between her office and Charlotte's, Charlotte would become suspicious, so she left it open. But she'd rather Charlotte didn't overhear anything she and Mac might say to each other.

"What are you doing here?" she asked.

"Did you get any more badass e-mails?"

She hoped he didn't detect her slight hesitation before she answered. "No. And what were you doing in my office last night?"

"I wasn't in your office," he drawled.

"You're a liar."

His smile grew. "Takes one to know one, *chère.*"

Was that his way of admitting he *had* been in her office? Or his way of demanding she tell him about the second e-mail? Or both?

"If there's something you want from me, Mac," she said, "ask me. Don't go sneaking around in my office behind my back."

He surprised her by sliding his index finger under her chin and tipping her face up until their gazes locked. He used his thumb to trace the edge of her chin. "If there's something I want from you, Julie, I will surely ask," he murmured, his voice so thick with meaning she didn't dare try to make sense of it. She was relieved when he let his hand drop, pushed away from the file cabinet and glided out the door.

Relieved and also inexplicably disappointed.

HE'D CROSSED A LINE.

He knew it the moment he'd touched her, the moment he'd felt her cool, smooth skin, as silky as he'd imagined it, as tantalizingly soft. It had taken all his willpower not to slide his hand down to her throat, around to the nape of her neck, and pull her to him for a kiss.

Sure, he could justify getting close to her. He could tell himself he was just doing his job: watching out for her, serving as her secret bodyguard. He couldn't very well protect her long-distance, could he?

Still…touching her that way, even if only for a few seconds, made him far too aware of her. To do his job properly, he had to remain detached and objective. One look into Julie Sullivan's shimmering eyes and his objectivity jumped into the river and swam away.

Meanwhile… She'd lied to him. She'd gotten another bad e-mail. Her *no* was irrelevant. He'd seen the truth flash across her face, as bright as lightning.

He'd lied to her, too, of course—but he'd had a good reason for sneaking into her office last night. Her sister was paying him to keep her safe, and if he had to hack into her e-mail software to do that, he would do it and never apologize.

He wondered how she'd guessed that he'd been in there, though. Short of dusting her keyboard for fingerprints, how could she tell? He hadn't touched anything besides her computer. He hadn't even turned on the light. His hair wasn't falling out, so she couldn't have detected short, dark strands on her desk, and her carpet had a shallow nap, so his shoes left no obvious imprints in it.

Maybe, like him, she had instincts. Maybe sensing a man's former presence in a room was one of those women's intuition things. Or maybe she'd just tossed out the question to see how he would react.

Hell. He'd reacted by touching her. Not good.

And for all that, he hadn't been able to trace the e-mail to its source. After spending several hours searching through her e-mails and finding little of interest—if the woman had a private life, she sure didn't discuss it via e-mail—he'd isolated the one e-mail from "4Julie" and rooted through various Internet systems, hoping to find out which one the sender had used. By one in the morning, he'd given in to exhaustion and headed for home, leaving his flash stick on Louise's desk. Louise was Crescent City Security's tech genius. He hoped she'd track down the sender.

He descended the stairs to the service entrance and turned

down the hall to the security office. Carlos had just arrived; he was removing his jacket as Mac swung into the tiny room. "Carlos, my man," he greeted the kid robustly. "Do me a favor and find Nadine—see if everything's okay with housekeeping."

Carlos gave him a curious look. "Nadine LeClaire? What's up?"

"It's a long story," Mac told him. "We had a little trouble last night. I'll fill you in later."

"Okay." Carlos hung his jacket on the chrome coat tree in the corner, then left the office.

As soon as he was gone, Mac settled in at the desk and called up Luc Carter's file on the computer. The screen filled with Luc's personnel data. Mac had pored over it already, but he needed to jot down a few specifics. He had the file closed by the time Carlos returned to report that Nadine had encountered no problems that morning.

Mac ceded the desk to Carlos. "I've got some people to talk to," he said, hooking a two-way radio to his belt on his way out the door. "Hold down the fort, okay?"

"Any chance you could bring me back a coffee?" Carlos called after him. "I didn't have a chance to pick one up on my way in today."

"Cream, two sugars," Mac shouted back before heading toward the lobby. At Charlotte's behest, the hotel's restaurant kept Mac's department supplied with free coffee throughout the day. Charlotte believed that one good way to keep the security staff alert was to pump them full of caffeine.

The lobby was bustling, as it usually was at this hour of the morning. Hotel guests streamed up and down the grand curved stairway, gathered along the antique credenza that served as the check-in desk, sat on the sofas and settees, which were arranged in cozy conversation groupings, or milled near the doors, clutching tourist maps and cameras. A short line of people waited to confer with Luc at the concierge desk. Luc was so busy recommending tours and marking routes on maps that Mac could scrutinize him without being noticed.

Luc seemed friendly and helpful. He genuinely appeared to be enjoying his work. Why would he put glass in the hotel towels?

After observing him for a few minutes, Mac continued through the lobby to one of the French doors that opened onto the courtyard. Yesterday's clouds had drifted away, leaving a cool, crisp morning beneath a pale blue sky. The water in the pool glistened as if someone had painted its surface with sunshine.

Mac moved across the courtyard to a shadowed corner, pulled out his cell phone and speed-dialed his office. "Crescent City Security Services," Sandy recited.

"Hi, sugar," Mac said quickly, urgently. "Got a pencil?"

"Sure, Mac. What's up?"

"I want you to find out what you can about this guy. Luc Carter. *L-U-C.*" He pulled from his pocket the slip of paper on which he'd made notes in the security office, and read off Luc's Social Security number, his birth date, his birth place—Reno, Nevada, according to his personnel file—and his previous job at a hotel in Lafayette.

"Is this for the Sullivan case?" Sandy asked.

"As a matter of fact, no. It's for the hotel."

"And I'm supposed to bill this how?"

"I don't care how, Sandy. You're in charge of the bureaucracy. I trust you to figure it out."

She laughed. "Anyone ever tell you you're a pain in the ass?"

"Nope. You're the first," he joked before hanging up.

He reentered the building near the two event rooms, across the courtyard from the lobby. According to the plans he'd reviewed, one of the two rooms would be cleared for dancing on Saturday, and the other would contain a portable bar and small tables for partygoers to rest their feet. Right now, neither room was set up, but Charlotte's mother, Anne, stood in one, hands on hips as she surveyed her surroundings. He'd overheard enough of Charlotte's discussion with her mother to know that Anne would be in charge of decorating the rooms. No doubt she was mapping the entire scene in her mind right now.

Mac abandoned the event rooms and headed upstairs, hoping to find someone from the housekeeping staff. He needed to question everyone who had access to the supply room, not only to see if any of them could explain the towels but also to shake loose any information about Luc's alleged romance with one of the maids. He might indeed be "getting biblical" with someone—Mac grinned at the memory of Julie's sweet voice wrapping around that phrase—but if he wasn't, then his story last night had been bogus. If he was covering something up, Mac needed to know.

Reaching the second floor, he should have turned right to search for a housekeeper's cart. At—he checked his watch—nine-thirty, the maids would be starting their rounds.

But his feet carried him in the opposite direction, toward Julie's office. He'd just take a quick peek, just one tempting glimpse of her black hair, the slope of her spine as she sat at her desk, the grace of her fingers dancing across her keyboard or the gentle murmur of her voice as she talked on the phone. He remembered she was wearing a burgundy outfit, a top and matching slacks that denied him the glorious sight of her legs. The color had enhanced the natural rosy hue of her cheeks.

But if he saw her cheeks now, that would mean she could see him. Not a good idea. She figured he was a liar, and she was right. God knew what she'd thought when he'd caressed the underside of her chin.

Luck was with him. Her back was to the open door. She was at her desk, staring at her computer monitor. Her shoulders were hunched; he could see the tension in them. Her hands weren't dancing. They were clenched in fists on either side of her keyboard.

He hovered in the open doorway, squinting to make out what was on her monitor. He couldn't read the words, but he could discern shapes and the flow of the text.

It was an e-mail she was staring at.

Another badass e-mail.

CHAPTER FIVE

"HI, DARLIN'." Mac's voice, smooth and warm, reached her like a caress. "Can you spare me a few minutes?"

Actually, she couldn't. She was standing in one of the event rooms, having just performed the daunting task of urging Anne Marchand to take a break. "Go get a cup of tea," Julia had suggested. "Or a glass of iced tea, if you'd rather. You've been fussing over these rooms for hours."

"I haven't been fussing," Anne had retorted. "I've been imagining. I know we're on a tight budget, but we could do some wonderful things. Not just with the flowers and centerpieces, but…I was thinking about draping some panels of fabric on the walls. It would give the rooms a mysterious feel…"

Julie adored Anne, but she didn't want to babysit her. She could use a snack herself. Her lunch today had been a cup of low-fat yogurt consumed at her desk while she worked. She had too much to do and too little time to do it and eat. Lunch breaks were an indulgence she couldn't afford.

Worst of all, no matter how intently she'd focused on her various responsibilities, a part of her brain clung tenaciously to the two creepy e-mails she'd received yesterday and today. And a part of her soul clung to a memory of Mac standing too close to her that morning, stroking her chin and gazing so deeply into her eyes she'd felt as if he'd seen all the way to the center of her being.

She shifted her gaze from Anne, who was bustling about

the event room, muttering to herself about how she'd like the tables positioned, and turned to look at Mac. "A few minutes?"

He smiled crookedly. "Okay, if you insist—a half hour."

She checked her watch. Three-thirty…and plenty of work still awaiting her upstairs in her office. "No, I can't spare a half hour."

"Sure you can," he said, tucking her hand through the crook of his elbow and escorting her out of the room before she could inform Anne she was leaving. Not that Anne would have cared. She was too busy visualizing the party decorations and jotting notes on a sheet of hotel stationery to notice Julie's departure.

Sighing, she let Mac lead her down the hall to the lobby. "Where are we going?"

"Out for a little walk. You look like you could use some Vitamin D."

"Vitamin D?"

"The sunshine vitamin." He swept her through the lobby and outside before she could object.

Five years after moving to New Orleans, she still wasn't quite used to the city's springlike January temperatures. In New York at this time of year, the ground would be caked in soot-gray snow and the air would be raw. Up in Montreal, where she'd gone to college, the wind would have felt like needles of ice against her skin. And here she was, strolling down Chartres Street with Mac, and even without a coat she wasn't cold. No wonder Alvin Grote, the guest in Room 307, kept grumbling about the lack of winter.

He'd phoned guest services that morning and been transferred to her line. She'd thought maybe he would have thanked her for finding him the cylindrical ice cubes, but no. He'd been calling to register his displeasure with the courtesy bottles of conditioning shampoo the maid left in his bathroom. "Everyone knows it's better to have a separate shampoo and conditioner," he'd complained. "This two-in-one stuff isn't good for your hair."

Julie considered conditioning shampoo one of the great wonders of the world. Anything that saved her five minutes was a blessing. And having seen Grote's scruffy little ponytail, she hardly considered him an expert when it came to hair grooming. "It's a high-quality product," she'd assured him over the phone. "We supply our guests with top-end toiletries. If you don't care for it, however, there are plenty of stores selling shampoo within walking distance of the hotel."

Alvin Grote wasn't her problem now. Mac was—although he didn't seem to be posing a problem at the moment. He simply strolled beside her, leaving her hand tucked into the bend of his arm as he steered her around pedestrians and smiled at a saxophone player occupying a corner across the street, his instrument case open and filled with dollar bills from passersby.

They walked another block and Mac ushered her through the gate into Jackson Square. The small urban park was quiet, its lawns green but its shrubs and bulbs not yet in bloom. Directly ahead of them loomed a towering statue of Andrew Jackson astride his horse. Beyond the statue, the three sharp spires of St. Louis Cathedral poked the sky. It was a lovely park, even in the heart of winter, and the city had done a wonderful job of repairing and replanting it after Hurricane Katrina.

Lovely as it was, though, Julie had no idea why Mac had brought her here. "What's going on?" she asked.

He led her to an unoccupied bench and motioned for her to sit. "You looked like you needed some outdoor air."

"There's outdoor air in the hotel's courtyard," she argued.

"Non-Marchand air. Do you ever get out of that building, Julie?"

She sighed. "It's a busy time of year," she said, rather than coming right out and admitting that she didn't leave the hotel very often. "We just finished our New Year's festivities, we've got the Twelfth Night party this weekend, and Mardi Gras's coming up…"

"It's always a busy time of year," he said. The afternoon

sun imbued his skin with a golden sheen. "As my mama used to say, the right time never comes."

What a depressing thought. "Your mother must have been very sad."

Mac chuckled. "She's pretty happy, to tell the truth. Her point was, if you wait for the right time to do something, you'll wait forever. May as well just go ahead and do it."

"I see."

"So it's probably not the right time for me to ask you this question," Mac continued, "but I'm going to ask anyway. Is the Hotel Marchand for sale?"

"What?" Julie's eyes widened in shock. "Of course not. It's a family business, and I'm betting it'll remain in the family as long as there's a Marchand alive to run it."

Mac absorbed her statement with a nod. He looked skeptical, though.

"Why in the world would you think it's for sale?"

"I've been doing some digging." He leaned forward, rested his forearms on his knees and tilted his head to look at her. Two pedestrians strolled past them, casting their shadows across her and Mac, but her attention remained riveted to him. "The financials aren't good," he said. "Bookings are down from a couple of years ago."

"Hurricane Katrina threw everything out of whack," she reminded him. "It's a miracle the city—and the hotels—have recovered as much as they have."

"Anne Marchand took out a second mortgage on the place a few years ago, *before* the storm," Mac said. "That's a lot of debt to carry."

"It's a four-star hotel. Business has been picking up. And with all the Marchand daughters here in New Orleans, working for the hotel… I just don't see the family ever giving up its hold on this place."

"Even if that hold's tenuous?" Mac asked. "The place is ripe for a takeover."

She let out a slow breath, as if she could exhale the uneasiness his questions had roused within her. "Would-be buyers have sniffed around the hotel before, but Anne has no interest in selling. It's a family business."

"So you've said, several times."

She eyed him dubiously. "Have you heard something I don't know? Is Charlotte talking about selling the place?"

"No. I haven't heard anything." He laced his fingers together, studied his thumbs, then turned back to her. "I don't know a lot about finance, Julie, but my—this guy I used to work with before I took the hotel job does. He's told me that when you've got a venerable business like the Hotel Marchand, where the name and reputation are more valuable than the business itself, and its financial health is shaky, it becomes a prime target for a takeover."

"You've been discussing the hotel's financial health with some guy you used to work with?" Julie's eyes widened again, this time with outrage.

"I haven't talked about this with anyone, until now. With you. All I'm saying is that he used to explain this stuff to me. And I'm looking at the hotel and thinking, this seems like a good example of what he used to describe." He straightened up, ran a hand through his hair and then leaned back, stretching his arms out along the back of the bench. If Julie shifted slightly, he could arch his arm around her. She held her posture rigid so that wouldn't happen. "You may think this is none of my business," he conceded. "You may be wondering why I give a rat's ass about whether the hotel is at risk. But it *is* at risk when stuff like that glass in the towels happens. If those towels had wound up in a guest room, and a guest cut himself while drying off with one of the hotel towels, word would get out and the hotel would become even weaker and more vulnerable to a takeover bid. You'd wind up with horrible press. Maybe a lawsuit. It could be a disaster."

"Which is why we're very lucky you found the glass before the towel wound up in a guest room."

"Play let's-pretend with me for a minute, *chère.* Let's pretend someone deliberately put the broken glass in those towels because they wanted to weaken the hotel and make it vulnerable."

Julie swallowed. Mac was making her nervous. Everything he said made sense. "I can't imagine who would be trying to undermine the hotel. The laundry service certainly wouldn't. They've got a lucrative contract with us. We pay them a fortune to do our towels and sheets."

"The service ate the cost of relaundering that one batch of towels. This could mean either they wanted to protect the hotel, or they were guilty and knew their reputation was on the line."

"Do you believe they're responsible for the glass?"

Mac thought for a minute, then said, "No."

"Do you think it's Luc? Or someone from housekeeping?"

"I don't know." He gazed steadily at her, as if hoping she could help him puzzle it out. "I'm wondering if it could be someone on the outside, someone with his eye on the hotel, causing problems that'll hurt the hotel just enough that he can sweep in and buy the place at a bargain-basement price."

"Who would do that?" Julie considered Mac's theory and shook her head. "I've heard nothing about any outsiders interested in buying the hotel. And if they were outsiders, how would they have gained access to the towels?"

"An ally on the inside."

She didn't want to play let's-pretend, not in the context of the Hotel Marchand's future. "You've got a good imagination, Mac, but I don't know why anyone would want to buy the hotel. Everyone knows it's a family business. That's part of its appeal."

"Its appeal, sweetheart, is that it's in a prime location in the French Quarter and it's cash poor, which makes it a cheap takeover target. Some bad press, more falling revenue, that second mortgage pressing down on the budget like a two-ton weight, and someone could pluck this baby right out from under Charlotte's nose."

Julie was surprised by his knowledge of business economics. He was a security officer, after all, not an MBA. "It's not a publicly held company," she argued. "It can't be bought if it's not for sale."

"If Charlotte can't bring in enough income to keep up with her payments, she'll have to sell it. Either that or she'll lose the place to the bank holding her mortgage."

Julie wished he didn't sound so convincing. "The cash-flow situation isn't that dire," she assured him. "The hotel has had its ups and downs, but that's normal in this industry."

"The hotel needs another up," he argued. "It's had more downs than ups lately."

She wondered how much she could trust him. He'd been thoroughly vetted before Charlotte had hired him, and he was soliciting her advice out of concern for the hotel…and most important, he'd been the one to find the broken glass in time to remove those dangerous towels before they caused serious harm. Surely that marked him as trustworthy.

On the other hand, she was pretty sure he'd been in her office sometime between last night and this morning, and he'd lied about it. As a security professional, of course, he had access to every office. He hadn't stolen anything, hadn't sabotaged anything—hadn't even touched anything, as far as she could tell.

She supposed she could trust him, at least a little. "A huge chunk of money mysteriously disappeared from the budget a few years ago," she told him. "As I understand it, this happened right around when Remy Marchand died. That money still hasn't been tracked down."

"A huge chunk? How huge?"

"One million dollars."

He digested that bit of information with a nod. "There are ways of tracking down missing money," he pointed out. "Security firms can trace it."

"I'll suggest that to Charlotte." That was actually an excellent idea. Her respect for Mac jumped another notch. "It was a staggering loss at a time when the Marchand family was reeling from the tragedy of Remy's death. If the hotel's finances are shaky, it probably dates back to that period. But we still have bookings. The restaurant still requires reservations on weekends. Ever since we reopened after Katrina, money has been coming in."

"I hope it's enough money to keep the hotel afloat," Mac said, squinting as he gazed into the sun. "And I hope to God we don't have any more episodes with broken glass." He shoved himself to his feet and extended his hand to Julie. "I'd appreciate your keeping your eyes and ears open, and letting me know if there are any big changes in the financials. I can monitor the security situation, but you're in Charlotte's office. You can monitor what happens there."

"Why didn't you discuss this directly with Charlotte?" Julie asked as they started down the walk toward Decatur Street. He released her hand, and she flexed her fingers, as if that would remove the lingering warmth of his clasp.

"It's her family," he said. "She may not be ready to face the facts, or she may already know the facts and be ten steps ahead of me." He shrugged. "Or maybe she wants to sell and isn't ready to let the staff know. I just thought it would be better to talk to you about it."

Julie sighed. She wished Mac had confided in someone else, if only so she wouldn't be burdened by this new worry. But he'd chosen her because… He trusted her.

The sidewalks were beginning to fill with people leaving work early and tourists swarming the French Quarter in search of food and entertainment. The saxophonist one block down was still playing his heart out, a sweet bluesy wail emerging from the bell of his instrument. At the corner Mac patted Julie's shoulder and signaled her to wait, then darted across the street. She expected him to toss some money into the man's case, but he didn't. Instead he waited until the sax player ended his song, then clapped him on the back. The musician grinned wide enough to split his face in two and the two men embraced.

Who is Mac Jensen? Julie wondered, watching as he and the other man chatted for a minute. Mac was a glorified rent-a-cop working for the hotel, but he had a sophisticated understanding of business. He knew something about tracking missing money. He was a street jazzman's pal.

And standing near him, sitting next to him, feeling his fingers close around her hand or brush against her chin did dangerous things to her equilibrium.

After a brief exchange, Mac and the saxophonist bumped fists and Mac crossed the street to her side once more. "A buddy of mine," he said unnecessarily. "I would have introduced you, but he can be kind of crabby sometimes if you interrupt him while he's playing."

"He didn't seem crabby today," Julie observed, wondering how Mac would have introduced her. As a friend? A coworker?

"I didn't know that until I was already over there. Next time, I'll drag you along."

What did he mean by *next time?* Did he plan to take regular walks to Jackson Square with her?

Her brain was full to bursting. She had enough worries on her plate with her weird e-mails, the financial straits the hotel was in and Mac's suspicions about a possible buyout. Thinking about what was going on between her and Mac—assuming something *was* going on—pushed her into overload. She could practically hear alarms clanging inside her skull, warning her of an imminent short-circuit.

Fortunately, he didn't run into any more old friends as they walked the rest of the way back to the hotel. A bellhop held the door open for them, and they stepped into the lobby. Julie usually arrived and left using the service door out back. Entering the Hotel Marchand's lobby from the street was an entirely different experience. The gold-hued walls, the dark hardwood floors, the plush rugs, the sofas and chairs upholstered in cream and ruby fabrics and accessorized with tapestry pillows, the majestic curved staircase to the second floor and the mirrors, artwork and antiques combined to give the airy room the atmosphere of an eighteenth-century plantation house.

Behind the credenza that served as a check-in desk lurked computers and telephones, and a short walk down one hall led to vending machines, but the lobby allowed as little of the modern world as possible to taint the atmosphere. Anne had handpicked most of the furnishings herself years ago, rummaging through antique shops and estate sales, mixing genuinely valuable pieces with inexpensive, comfortable furnishings to create the hotel's warmth and welcome.

The wooden shutters framing the windows had in fact come from a plantation house on the Mississippi River, miles north of the city. Julie still remembered helping the maintenance workers to bolt those shutters before Hurricane Katrina. They'd protected that old plantation house through nearly two centuries of storms, and they'd protected the Hotel Marchand, too.

That someone might attempt to snatch this precious hotel out from under the Marchands was simply unacceptable. Julie hated that Mac had planted the notion in her head, even though he'd done so with the intention of preventing such a thing from happening. He wanted the hotel to remain in Marchand hands, where it belonged.

He was one of the good guys.

She peered at him. His gaze had zeroed in on Luc, who was at his post behind the concierge desk, cheerfully describing something to a middle-aged couple, shaping the air with his hands. Mac's attention veered from there to the French doors leading out to the courtyard, and from there to a bellhop arranging luggage on a cart, and from there to a check-in clerk wearing a telephone headset and typing on her computer. At last he'd completed his inspection of the lobby and turned to Julie.

"Thank you," she said.

He favored her with his devastatingly sexy grin, and she wondered just how good a guy he was. "For what?"

"For caring what happens to this place," she said. She touched his arm, smiled and then pivoted and headed for the stairs, refusing herself a backward look. If he was still grinning, if his dark eyes were still luminous and his skin still gave off that seductive scent, she didn't want to know.

"GOOD GOD, JULIE, you look like an extra from *Night of the Living Dead*," Creighton exclaimed as Julie climbed out of her car. He'd driven into the parking area just ahead of her and waited by his car to greet her.

"Really?" She attempted a smile. "Not even one of the stars?"

"Come with me," Creighton said, hustling her up the front walk to the porch, his silver hair rippling in the evening breeze and his open duster coat flapping with each step. "I'm going to fix you a drink."

"Thanks, Creighton, but I don't think—"

"It wasn't a question," he said, silencing her. She waited patiently while he unlocked the front door and they entered the ramshackle old mansion together. "Is it that handsome man you introduced me to yesterday?" he asked as they collected their mail.

"Is *what* that handsome man?"

"Is he the reason you look so dreadful?"

Creighton was such a sweetheart, Julie couldn't take offense at his criticisms. Instead she laughed. "I don't think I look dreadful. I look like someone who's put in a long day. Which I have."

"I put in a long day, too, and I look magnificent," Creighton said grandly. He tucked his mail under his arm and gestured toward the stairs. She preceded him up them, pausing only to riffle through the envelopes she'd pulled from her mailbox. Nothing important—bills, solicitations, the usual.

At the top of the stairs she crossed to her door. Creighton followed her, as if he feared she might slip inside and refuse him the opportunity to fix her a drink. She wouldn't do that. As exhausted as she was, and as dreadful as she looked, she wouldn't mind spending a few minutes in the company of someone whose agenda was obvious.

"I promise," she said as she shoved her door open, "I'll come over as soon as I change my clothes."

"Five minutes, love, and then I'll be banging down your door with a battering ram."

"You're a very bossy man," she scolded before stepping inside. It took her less than five minutes to change out of her suit, hang everything up and slip into her old jeans and a soft gray sweatshirt with McGill, her alma mater, printed across the front in bright red. No messages awaited her on her answering machine, so she pocketed her key and crossed the hallway to Creighton's door, which he'd left unlocked for her.

Creighton was the art director of a regional magazine, and his apartment was filled with framed photos and artifacts. Although his place was slightly larger than hers, Julie always felt a little claustrophobic when she settled onto the love seat in his living room and found herself surrounded by painted ceramic animals, hand-thrown pottery, wooden carvings and walls covered with landscapes and art photos. Creighton owned a house on the north shore of Lake Pontchartrain, but he spent most of his time in his cramped Garden District pied-à-terre.

"So, tell me," he called to her from the kitchen, where he was no doubt concocting some complicated beverage. "What's the story with that luscious man?"

"There's no story," she called back, kicking off her clogs and tucking her feet under her on the love seat. "He's just someone I work with."

"Why don't I believe you?"

Because I'm lying, Julie muttered under her breath. *Because I know damn well Mac is more than just someone I work with—only I don't know how much more, or exactly what.* "I think you have a crush on him," she teased, figuring her best defense was a good offense.

"Well, who wouldn't? Straight men and dykes, I suppose." He swept into the living room, carrying two tall tumblers containing something brown and frothy. He handed one glass to her, then settled into the wing chair that faced the love seat across a coffee table adorned with a jade sculpture of a crane, a brightly colored set of Russian *matrioshka* dolls and a pair of scallop shells polished to a pearly white. "I think you should ask him to escort you to the hotel's Twelfth Night party."

Julie took a sip of her drink. It was cold, sweet and wonderful. "He works at the hotel all day. Why would he want to attend the party at night?"

"Why would you? You will, though, won't you? It's always a marvelous time. I've reserved two tickets. I'll be taking Stanley. You remember him, don't you?"

"You broke up with him," Julie recalled.

"Amicably. He always enjoys a good party, too."

"Well, if I go..." Julie leaned back into the cushions and sighed. Sinking into the spongy upholstery, she felt every ache, every twinge, the accumulated fatigue of an overlong day. "I probably won't decide until the last minute."

"Nonsense. You'll go. You'll dress like a fashion diva and everyone there will fall at your feet. Including that adorable man you 'just work' with. If he's giving you a hard time, Julie, I want to know."

"He's not." Another lie, perhaps, but as much as she trusted Creighton, she wasn't ready to discuss Mac with him. Even if she was, she wouldn't know what to say.

"*Someone* is giving you a hard time, love. You look wrung out. Gray is not your color, by the way," he added helpfully, gesturing toward her sweatshirt.

"There's a lot going on at work," she admitted. That, at least, was the truth. She had to help Charlotte and now Anne put together the party, the hotel's finances had Mac worried about a possible takeover attempt, someone had seeded guest towels with broken glass, she'd received two ominous e-mails from somebody who wanted to remind her of her days as the face of Symphony Perfumes, and Mac... Whenever he was close to her, her entire nervous system flew into a frenzy. And he was spending too much time close to her. She couldn't tell Creighton all that, but she had to tell him something. "Anne Marchand has decided she wants to help with the party."

"Good for her." Creighton clapped his hands, nearly spilling his drink. "Her health is up to it?"

"She thinks so, and since I haven't talked with her doctors, I only have her word for it."

"You don't want her help?" he guessed.

Julie took another sip. What was in this amazing drink, anyway? Crème de cacao? Rum? Milk and crushed ice? She hoped it wasn't so potent that she'd have trouble finding her way back to her own apartment once she'd finished it—and she intended to consume every last drop. "Of course I welcome her help," Julie said. "She's got such good instincts. She's changed, though. She let her hair grow, and she wasn't wearing her usual perfect makeup. It's like she's cut loose a little."

"Maybe she needed that. I can't wait to see her at the party. She'll be there, won't she?"

"Before today, I wasn't sure. But now...well, she certainly looks ready to party."

"I wonder if she'll bring her mother," Creighton said, then cackled. "The Dragon Lady."

Julie had heard a few things from the Marchand daughters about their grandmother, but she'd never met the woman. "Do you know Celeste Robichaux?"

"Darlin', anyone who's lived in this city long enough knows

the players. Celeste is very old wealth. Rich as sin and tough as nails. You know the type. A steel magnolia and then some."

"That would explain where all the Marchand women inherited their strength," Julie said.

"Ah, but they're sweet. Celeste is ferocious. You'd get a kick out of her, if she didn't scare you to death."

Julie laughed and took another sip of her drink. She'd rather listen to Creighton gossip about New Orleans society than think about all the worries weighing down on her. "How is Stanley doing?" she asked.

It was just the right question. For the next half hour, Creighton regaled her with stories about his ex-boyfriend, his colleagues at the magazine and his ninety-two-year-old mother, who still plaintively asked him when he was going to get married, even though he'd told her about his sexual orientation many times. He mentioned a new technique he'd learned for frying okra that didn't spatter so much and left the vegetable remarkably tender, and he described a vacation trip he was planning to Alaska that summer. "Twenty-three hours of daylight," he rhapsodized. "I'll be able to take photos in natural light at three in the morning."

Imagining Creighton photographing glaciers and fishing villages at three in the morning was preferable to fretting over towels embedded with glass splinters. Imagining him sailing along the arms of the ocean that reached between mountains and riding on the back of a dogsled was preferable to trying to puzzle out who "4Julie" was and what her mystery correspondent was trying to tell her. Imagining Creighton winning over all of Alaska with his high-octane energy and abundant cheer sure beat contemplating the Hotel Marchand's precarious finances.

And anything was better than thinking about Mac, about the way his piercingly dark eyes seemed able to cut right through her, the way his fingers felt against her skin, the way his honey-smooth voice wrapped around her. It was better than thinking about the way he treated her with a strange kind of intimacy, even though she hardly knew him.

Anything was better than wondering whether he would lead her someplace dangerous, someplace she shouldn't want to visit. Someplace she was dying to see.

CHAPTER SIX

MAC WAS SURPRISED to discover Frank at the Crescent City Security office when he arrived there around seven-thirty, armed with a roast-beef po'boy, a jumbo coffee and a download of Julie's most recent e-mails—including a new one from "4Julie"—on his flash stick. "What are you doing here?" he asked his partner. "If I knew Sandy was sitting all by her lonesome tonight, I'd be at your place instead of here."

Frank took Mac's taunting in stride. "Be my guest," he said with a snort. "Go spend your evening with her. She's driving me crazy." He ran a hand through his curly brown hair and trailed Mac down the semilit hall to his office. "She wants a baby."

"So make a baby with her." Mac shoved his door open, then turned to stare at Frank. "You don't want *me* to make a baby with her, do you?"

"What I want is a little sympathy," Frank retorted, following Mac into the office and flopping down in a chair. "I love her, okay? I'd like to have a baby with her. Just not yet."

"What are you waiting for?" Mac asked as he settled into the swivel chair behind his desk.

"I married her, didn't I? Is it a crime for me to want a few more years of fun before I take on more responsibility? If anyone should understand, it's you, Mac. You're still a free man. You haven't even figured out commitment yet."

"I've figured it out," Mac said. "I just haven't found the right woman to commit to." A vision of Julie Sullivan spread across his mind, and he let it linger for a moment. She wasn't the right woman. She was a damn Yankee, and she kept herself locked up emotionally…but man, she could get under his skin if he let her.

If only he could figure out how to win her trust—which wouldn't be easy, since his presence at the hotel was part of a huge deception. If she knew the truth—that her sister had hired him to protect her—she'd flay him and her sister both. He hadn't even dared to bring Julie across the street that afternoon when he'd spotted his friend Reuben blowing his sax for spare change on the corner of St. Louis Street. Reuben might have asked why weeks had passed since Mac had last stopped by the club where Reuben usually played, and Mac would have had to answer that he couldn't hang out at clubs listening to good jazz because he was spending his nights holed up at his office, trying to catch up on his real job—an answer he didn't want Julie to hear. Or Reuben might have made some comment about Crescent City Security and Mac would have had to respond that he was now working for the Hotel Marchand, and Reuben would have demanded to know why Mac had walked away from the business he'd founded to work security at a hotel, and Julie would have smelled something fishier than the gulf at low tide.

When it came to her, honesty was not the best policy right now.

"Well," Mac said, unwrapping his po'boy, "some of us have to work. And some of us haven't eaten dinner yet."

"Work. Eat. Who's stopping you?"

Frank's intense scrutiny from just a few feet away was almost enough to steal Mac's appetite, but one bite of the thick sandwich, dripping with gravy and Cajun mustard, got his digestive juices flowing. He swiveled toward his desk and noticed a memo from Louise lying on his blotter. "Louise tracked down the creepy e-mail Julie got yesterday," he said after skimming Louise's note. "If I was going to fall in love, it would be with her."

Frank knew Mac was joking. Louise was a tiny woman. If she stood on tiptoe, her gaze would be level with Mac's navel—which could make for an interesting juxtaposition, except that Louise was also shy and solemn and in a serious romance with a medical student from Tulane. Even so, Mac loved her for her technical wizardry, much the same way he loved Sandy for her organizational skills.

"Louise couldn't track it all the way to the user," Frank pointed out. Evidently he'd already read the memo.

Mac took another bite of his sandwich while he read Louise's note more carefully. "The main branch of the New York Public Library, on Fifth Avenue. What does that tell us?"

"Sandy talked to Glenn Perry's parole officer today. According to the P.O., Mr. Perry is being a very good boy. He hasn't left the jurisdiction since his release."

"In other words, he's in Manhattan. On the same skinny little island as the New York Public Library." Mac swiveled back to Frank. "He could have sent that e-mail."

"He could have," Frank agreed.

"Except you'd think he'd have his own computer. Why would he trek all the way to the public library if he could send the e-mail from the comfort of his home?"

"So someone like Louise wouldn't be able to trace it back to him."

Mac wasn't convinced, but then, skepticism was an asset in his line of work. "How easy is it for a person to send an untraceable e-mail from his own computer? Louise might trace it back to Yahoo or Comcast, but could she trace it back to his specific computer?"

"This is Louise you're talking about," Frank pointed out.

"True." Louise could probably trace it as far back as she wanted to. Mac didn't pretend to understand how she performed her high-tech magic. He simply accepted her genius and paid her a hefty salary. "Conceivably she could tell us which computer in the library that e-mail was sent from. Maybe a librarian in the reference area saw who used it on the day in question. I've brought Louise another e-mail from Julie's in-box," he added. "Ten dollars says it was sent from a different computer."

"The guy is sending the e-mails from a public computer for a reason," Frank concurred. "He doesn't want to be identified." He leaned back in his chair and jiggled one sneakered foot. "Do you think Sullivan is really in danger, or is her sister just paranoid?"

"I've talked to her sister. She sounds pretty levelheaded to me," Mac said. "She's an investment banker in New York."

"So she got the brains and her sister got the beauty?"

"Julie's got brains," Mac argued. "And for all I know, her sister is gorgeous." He lowered his sandwich and pried open the lid of his cup. The heavy, slightly burnt aroma of coffee laced with chicory filled his small, square office. The smell alone was enough to jolt his nervous system. "Anyway, Marcie—Julie's sister—said Perry made lots of threats when Julie reported him to the police. He made more threats when Julie testified against him in court. He vowed that once he was out of jail he was gonna get her. I don't think her sister is being paranoid to worry that now the son of a bitch is out, he might make good on that promise."

"Except his P.O. says he's a model citizen," Frank reminded him. "He's taking a real estate course, staying away from models and teenage girls, avoiding his old drug connections. He's turned into a regular Boy Scout."

"Yeah." Mac's cynicism was as strong and bitter as his coffee. "I've dealt with guys fresh out of prison. So have you. Their haloes could blind a person—because they're neon, Frank. They aren't real." He abandoned the coffee and returned to his sandwich. "And now she's getting these scary e-mails from someone who wants to remind her of when she was working for Perry. I think the potential for danger is there."

Frank shrugged. "You're the expert."

"Speaking of which, you're the money expert," Mac said, catching a drip of gravy with his thumb before it fell from his sandwich onto his lap, which was protected only by a cheap paper napkin. "Four years ago, a large amount of money disappeared from the Hotel Marchand's accounts."

"How large?"

"One million dollars."

Frank sat straighter and stopped jiggling his foot. "Tell me more."

"I don't know much. Apparently Remy Marchand died right around the same time this money disappeared."

"I remember that accident. Got lots of press because he was Remy Marchand of Chez Remy. Celebrity chef, co-owner of Hotel Marchand, and his car plunged off the causeway and into Lake Pontchartrain. It was the stuff of tabloids."

"And also a tragedy for his family," Mac said pointedly.

"That, too."

"So, Remy's wife, Anne, ran the hotel end of things while Remy was working his magic in the restaurant. He died four years ago, and now Anne's daughter Charlotte is running the hotel. Another daughter works in the restaurant, and two other daughters are on staff at the hotel. Which is neither here nor there." He devoured the last of his sandwich with some regret. It was delicious. He should have bought two. "Anyway, I've done some probing, and the hotel's finances are pretty tenuous. I'm wondering if this vanished money triggered something nasty."

"You think Remy Marchand was embezzling?"

"I don't know." Mac winced. "I *do* know that if anyone ever suggested such a thing, they'd be hogtied and hung upside down in the courtyard pool. The memory of Remy Marchand is sacrosanct at that hotel."

"But a million dollars disappeared and he died."

"In a car 'accident.'" He shaped quotation marks in the air

with his fingers when he spoke the word *accident.* "What are the odds that it wasn't an accident?"

Frank held up his hands. "Let's not slip into the *Twilight Zone* here. What does this have to do with Julie Sullivan's safety?"

"Nothing. But I'm also the head of security at the Hotel Marchand. And the hotel's budget problems may have something to do with security."

"You're the head of hotel security only so you can keep an eye on Julie."

"Yeah, but while I'm keeping an eye on Julie, I've also got to do the job the hotel hired me to do." He gave Frank a beseeching look. "Surely you could spare an hour or two and see if you can dig up anything about this missing money."

"I can't just make a million dollars miraculously reappear, Mac. You've got to give me something to work with."

"I'll find out where the Hotel Marchand did its banking four years ago. Then you can go through the transactions and see what's there. Okay?"

"I've still got my hands full with the Garrick Insurance fraud case," Frank muttered.

"So, the next time you're mucking around in the records of some off-shore bank, maybe you'll stumble over a million U.S. dollars with Remy Marchand's fingerprints on it. That's all I'm asking."

"That's *all* you're asking." Frank shook his head. "If I'd known you were going to dump this in my lap, I would've gone home and knocked Sandy up."

"Go home and knock her up now," Mac urged him. "Tell her I expect to be named the godfather."

"Right," Frank said as he rose from the chair. "Listen, pal, don't work too late. I don't want you falling asleep at your desk."

"With this coffee?" Mac gestured toward the jumbo cup beside his computer keyboard. "After drinking that, I won't be able to sleep for a week."

Once Frank had left the office, Mac rotated his chair to face his desk. He turned on his computer, then wiped his fingers on a spare paper napkin and pulled the Sullivan folder from the walnut tray that occupied one corner of the desk. He opened the folder, flipped past pages of neatly typed notes and halted when he got to the first photograph.

He had more than a dozen photos, collected as part of his background research into Julie's modeling career. The top of the stack was one of her first jobs, a photo of her and two other girls in bikinis standing in front of the most bogus-looking beach scenery he'd ever seen. Julie's hair was longer than she wore it now, and it was pulled into pigtails. The body on display in the skimpy blue swimsuit did nothing for him. She'd been just a child when that picture was taken, skinny and gangly. But her face…even then, even when she was smiling, her eyes were filled with mystery, with knowledge and longing. And her mouth looked—well, no, not kissable. The thought of kissing a girl as young as Julie had been in that ad gave Mac the willies. But he could see in her soft, full lips the potential, a hint of what she would become once she grew up.

He flipped through the photos, some from old magazines, the paper starting to wrinkle, and others hard copies of images he'd downloaded from Internet archives. Incredible cheekbones, he thought as he studied another photo of her. Her face was a little fuller now, that emaciated look blessedly gone. What had she said last night about having to starve herself during her modeling days? Thank God she wasn't doing that anymore.

At last he reached her Symphony Perfumes pictures. She looked older in them, older even than she looked today. He ascribed part of that to the makeup slathered onto her face, her eyes circled in black, her lashes artificially thick, her skin pale and smooth and her mouth coated with a coral-hued lipstick. But part of what aged her in the photos was the way she stared directly into the camera, her jaw taut and her gaze almost accusing. Her expression was chilly, haughty. *I want this perfume,* she seemed to be saying. *I want this perfume and I don't want you.*

In the Glissando ad, she was framed against a nondescript cream-colored background, just her face and her bare, elegant shoulders and an enlarged bottle of perfume. Her lips were neither smiling nor pouting, her eyes were cold, her attitude inaccessible. In the Grace Note ad, her surroundings were midnight blue, which made her eyes look even darker and more inscrutable. In the Arpeggio ad, the backdrop was wine red and she looked…damn. She looked sexy as hell.

But still aloof. Still chilly. Still communicating the message: *You want me and you can't have me.*

Unlike the photos of her as a scrawny, playful teenager, these photos mocked him. Yeah, he wanted her. And he couldn't have her…although when she looked at him now, in real life, she didn't appear quite so cold. Scrape off the cosmetics, add a few pounds, give her a sweet, rich dessert or a walk in the sunshine and she became a genuine human being, talking, laughing, knocking herself out for her job, plagued by worries but too proud to admit to them.

Yeah, he thought as he studied the photo of Julie surrounded in seductive red. *You guessed. I want you.*

THROWING FITS was not Mac's style, but the next morning, when Carlos showed him the reservation list for the Twelfth Night party, he felt sorely tempted to kick and break things. "What the hell is this?" he roared as he scanned the list of more than a hundred names.

"Those folks all reserved tickets to the party," Carlos explained calmly. He clearly didn't share Mac's irritation.

"These are just last names. *Smith?* That's supposed to identify someone? *Mr. and Mrs. Smith?*"

"I guess the hotel should have gotten first names," Carlos said, struggling to appear concerned.

"That and credit card numbers. When someone reserves a room, the reservation clerk gets a credit card number. Why didn't they get one for these people?"

"Oh, they'll pay," Carlos assured him. "If that's what you're worried about. The hotel never gets stiffed for events like this. Folks show up, they pay and then they go in. If they don't pay, they aren't allowed in. Simple."

"Not simple." Since Carlos was seated at the desk, Mac leaned against the door jamb and flipped through the computer printouts. "We have no way of identifying these people. No way of checking to see if any of them represent a security risk."

"Like their credit card numbers would do that."

Mac gave him a withering look. "Credit card numbers, Social Security numbers, phone numbers—first names, for crying out loud. Who are these people?"

Carlos hesitated, as if unsure whether Mac wanted an answer. Hesitantly, he provided one: "They're Mr. and Mrs. Smith."

Mac cursed and slammed the printout onto the desk. His gaze veered to the monitor. The security cameras revealed a couple chatting in the elevator; a woman who'd draped her legs in a hotel blanket as she sat in the sunlight of the courtyard, reading a book; the lobby teeming with activity, as usual; the bar empty at this early hour; a housekeeping employee pushing a cleaning cart down a third-floor hallway. Julie hadn't been caught by any of the cameras, which meant she was probably in her office.

He could storm upstairs and confront her, but he was too ticked off to inflict himself on her. Besides, if he saw her, he might blurt out his greatest concern: "Mr. and Mrs. Smith" or one of the other anonymous folks on this list might be the person behind her nasty e-mails. She was already unnerved enough about those messages; no need for him to add to her stress. Besides, she wasn't ready to confide in him about what really had her scared. He had his own theories, based on what her sister had told him, but so far Julie hadn't even admitted to him the existence of the second "4Julie" e-mail.

He needed to know—not just for her sake but for the safety of all the partygoers—who the intended guests were.

He lifted the phone and punched in her office number.

"Julie Sullivan speaking," she recited.

"Julie, it's Mac," he said, refusing to close his eyes and picture her and think about her elegant beauty. "I've just seen the reservation list for the Twelfth Night party. It's a disaster."

"A disaster? Why?"

"It's completely lacking in ID. Just a list of names. Does the hotel have any sort of identification for these people?"

"Of course we do. Why do you need it?"

Because I'm the freakin' head of security, he wanted to yell. "So I can make sure none of these guests represents a security risk," he said as calmly as his impatience would allow. "This is important. Can I get a more comprehensive list?"

He heard her sigh. "I can put something together for you, but everything would have to be cross-referenced. It could take awhile."

"Six o'clock tonight," he said. "You'll be done with your other work by then, and so will I. I'll come by your office and we'll straighten this out."

She sighed again, but when she spoke she didn't sound upset. She didn't even sound resigned. She sounded almost… expectant. "Six o'clock. All right, Mac."

SHE WASN'T SURE why he was in such a sweat about the party's reservations list—except that everyone was in some sort of sweat or another about the Twelfth Night party. Anne and Sylvie were bickering over the decorations. Charlotte and Renee were worrying about whether Anne was overtaxing herself. Anne was irked at Charlotte and Renee for worrying about her. Leo was feuding with one of his suppliers regarding the liquor order he'd placed for the event. Robert was arguing with Melanie about the buffet menu. Nadine was worried about how big the housekeeping department's overtime budget for the party clean-up would be. Alvin Grote in Room 307 wanted to know whether he could wear jeans to the bash.

"There's no dress code, Mr. Grote," Julie had explained, "but it's a festive event. People pull out all the stops."

"Great," he'd moaned over the phone. "If I'd known, I would have brought my tuxedo. How am I going to rent a tuxedo down here on such short notice?"

"You don't need to wear a tuxedo," she'd assured him. "But I think you might feel more comfortable in a suit and tie than in jeans."

"If you'd ever worn a suit and tie, you wouldn't say that," Grote had retorted.

God knew what he'd show up wearing. Last year, quite a few attendees had arrived sporting Mardi Gras masks and strings of beads. Since Twelfth Night was essentially the opening night of the Mardi Gras season, the masks and bead necklaces had made sense.

If Alvin Grote wore a mask, he'd still be easily identified. His bald pate and ponytail would give him away.

Evidently, Mac Jensen was just one more person stressing out over the fete, which was all of two days away. Fine. Let him stress out. Julie would review the reservation list with him, and then she'd go home and ask Creighton to fix her one of those creamy, chocolaty, heavily spiked alcoholic drinks like the one he'd served her yesterday.

By six, her desk was cleared of clutter. Her lipstick was long faded, and so was her energy—but if Mac felt double-checking the reservations list was that important, she'd get through it with him. And she'd keep her distance, so he wouldn't touch her and scramble her gray matter, or give her that I-know-what-you're-thinking look. And if his scent started to get to her, she'd hold her breath.

He surprised her by tapping on her door, even though it was open. Usually he came and went without making a sound, and she'd assumed he would invade her office in his usual silent manner. But he did her the courtesy of knocking, and when she spun around in her chair she saw him pushing a wheeled cart into the room. "What's that?" she asked, eyeing the lidded silver platter and the neatly rolled linen napkins on the cart.

"Supper," he told her. "I asked Melanie to put a snack together for us."

"Room service?" She laughed. "That wasn't necessary."

"As far as I'm concerned, it was. I'm hungry. And I bet you're starving." He shot her a teasing smile and squatted down to lock the cart's wheels. His tie hung loose around his neck and his jawline was darkened by a day's growth of beard. It occurred to her that he'd probably put in a day just as strenuous as hers had been.

He pulled a chair close to her desk, draped his jacket over the back and rolled up his shirtsleeves. "I'm sorry I'm making you stick around after hours," he said, "but I've got to get this list in order." From a lower shelf on the cart he lifted a clipboard to which a computer printout had been attached. After setting it on her desk, he reached down to the lower shelf again and pulled out a half bottle of wine.

"What's that for?" Julie asked warily.

"To make the chore more bearable." He produced two stemware glasses from the lower shelf, then unwedged the cork, which had already been popped. "It's a Cabernet. You like red wine, right? That's what you ordered the other night."

She was touched that he remembered, but also concerned. "Wine may make the chore more bearable, but what if we get tipsy?"

"On half a bottle? I don't reckon we will," he drawled as he filled the glasses. He passed her a napkin, then lifted the lid off the platter to reveal an array of cheeses, sliced fruits and crusty wedges of French bread. "I tried to con Melanie che...

Mac gr... have a special re... good care of us." He set... and dragged over another chair... or you, but she said I'd ... his feet up on it. "May as well get sta... he lifted the clipboard.

Julie took a delicate sip of her wine and tried ... the ... re at Mac's long legs, his sinewy, lightly haired forearms and thick, strong wrists. She swiveled to face her computer and tapped a few keys to call up the master reservations list. "I'm still not clear why it's so important for you to have the exact identities of all the guests," she said.

"Ever hear of 9/11? This is going to be a big gathering. Lots of strangers pouring into the hotel. Basic security says we ought to make sure these strangers aren't going to cause any trouble."

"We've never had trouble before," Julie told him. When Gerard Lomax had been the head of hotel security, he'd never reviewed the guest list with her before Twelfth Night parties. Maybe he'd been lazy, though. Maybe she ought to be grateful Mac was so diligent.

"Let's make sure you don't have trouble this year," he said, then read a name off the list in his lap. "Adams?"

Julie scanned the list on her monitor. "Joseph and Evelyn Adams. They live in the city and come every year. He works in the mayor's office and she's active in the historical society."

"They sound reputable enough. Anderson?"

Julie skimmed the master list. "Matt Anderson. He's a guest at the hotel. He's a wine critic. Your buddies downstairs in the restaurant were all in a tizzy about his staying here. I'm not sure he'll be attending the party, but he made a reservation, just in case."

...hat he'd
...ard Julie before
...priced vintage."
...ended it. Drinking wine while
...ac might not be the wisest thing she'd
...t he was right—the wine certainly upped the
...ity quotient of the evening's task.

Mac plucked a sprig of grapes from the platter and popped one into his mouth as he studied his list. "Bowman and guest?"

"That's my neighbor, Creighton Bowman. You met him."

"Right." Mac lifted his gaze to her and smiled. "He's the one who said I was an improvement over the guys you've been dating."

Julie felt a blush heat her cheeks. "He was joking."

"You mean I'm *not* an improvement over the guys you've been dating?"

"I'm not dating you, so the question is irrelevant." She realized that might have come out sounding blunt, but she didn't want Mac insinuating that anything romantic existed between them. They were colleagues, and she couldn't allow herself to imagine them as anything more. Affairs in the workplace were always tricky and fraught with peril. And while Mac was attractive, she didn't like his overly protective attitude. Granted, he was in security, so overprotectiveness probably came naturally to him. But she didn't want or need him looking out for her. She knew how to take care of herself—and experience had taught her to be suspicious of men who tried to take care of women.

Besides, much as Mac seemed to want her to trust him, and much as she wanted to, she didn't. Not quite. There was something about him, something about the way he watched her, the way he stole around the hotel, the interest he took in the hotel's precarious finances. Something about him that made her wonder whether he was more than he pretended to be. His expensive car, his expensive suits, his refusal to participate in the employees' health insurance program... He obviously had more money than the typical security guy.

All right, so she didn't trust him. And she wasn't dating him. They could still work together, get through that long list of names on his printout and drink wine together. And munch on cheese and fruit and bread. Her stomach sent her brain a message about how empty it was, and she cut herself a small wedge of Gouda.

"Carlyle," he said.

"That would be Holly Carlyle. She's a singer. She performs here at the hotel a few nights a week."

"Will she be performing at the party?"

"No. We hired a dance band. I guess Charlotte extended an invitation to her. It must be nice for her to come here sometimes just to party, rather than to work."

"Will you be attending?" Mac asked. "Just to party, not to work."

"I don't know." Julie helped herself to a sliver of pear. "It'll depend on how tired I am. It'll also depend on whether I want to put up with Creighton's wrath if I don't go." She reminded herself that Creighton had suggested she ask Mac to be her escort for the night. She was under no obligation to fulfill Creighton's matchmaking fantasies, however. "How about you?" she asked casually. "Will you be at the party?"

"If I'm needed to beef up the security staff, I will." He leaned back and gazed at her, his dark eyes seductive, his mouth quirked in a crooked smile. "Of course, if you'll be there, I won't miss it."

Yet he wasn't asking her to go with him. Which was good, she assured herself. Even better would be if she stayed focused on the job and stopped thinking of Mac in the context of parties and dating. "Who else is on your list?" she asked.

They continued through the names. Many of them Julie could easily identify; they were either current hotel guests or regulars who attended every year. She looked up the others and provided Mac with information that would enable him to clear them. She hadn't known that a hotel security officer could learn about people through their credit card numbers, but he assured her he could. He seemed a lot more technologically savvy than Gerard had ever been.

By seven-thirty, they'd completed reviewing the list, but the platter on the serving cart was still heaped high with cheese, fruit and bread, and they had yet to refill their glasses. Mac divided what was left in the wine bottle between them, and Julie slid off her shoes and perched her feet on an edge of the chair he'd appropriated as a footstool. She carefully smoothed her skirt around her knees so he couldn't see up it. The floral pattern of her skirt and her turquoise sweater brightened the room, which seemed even more blandly utilitarian at night, when Charlotte was gone and the workday bustle subsided.

"That wasn't so bad, was it?" Mac asked as he slid his clipboard back onto the cart's lower shelf, then stood and busied himself filling a plate with grapes, chunks of cheese and a slab of bread. To her surprise, he handed the plate to her instead of keeping it for himself. "If you're as hungry as I am, you need this."

"I'm hungry," she conceded with a smile, balancing the plate on her knees. "Thanks."

He filled another plate for himself, settled back into his chair and raised a piece of bread to her in a mock toast. "So, you really had to starve yourself when you were modeling?"

"Not starve myself," she explained, "but I definitely had to watch my weight."

"You don't look like a woman who has to watch her weight."

She laughed. "I hope that's a compliment." She bit into a cube of cheddar and let the aged cheese flake across her tongue. Once she'd swallowed, she elaborated. "You have to be really thin to succeed as a model. Supposedly the camera adds ten pounds, though I'm not sure I believe that. But the fashionable look these days—and back when I was modeling, and thirty years before then—is a very thin look. That's what the clients want."

"I think most models look too thin," Mac said. "I can't speak for all men, but I bet a lot of them would agree. We like women with a little flesh on them. Curves. Hips and breasts."

"Even skinny models can have curves."

"If they go to the right surgeon, maybe. It's kind of obvious when you've got a woman without a lick of fat on her, and she's got huge boobs. It doesn't look natural."

"Well..." Julie shrugged, amused to be discussing women's bosoms with Mac. "If that's what the clients want, that's what the modeling agents give them."

"Models have agents, then? Like actors?"

"Sort of. Models sign with an agency, and that agency finds jobs for them. It's different from actors because the agents don't hear about jobs and go after them. Instead, the clients come to the agency, and they work with the agent to find a model with the look they want."

"So you were with one of these agencies?"

Julie tried to keep her face neutral. If Mac seemed overprotective now, imagine what he'd be like if she told him about Glenn Perry and the part she'd played in getting him convicted. If Mac knew Glenn had been recently paroled, he would probably connect that info to the e-mails she'd recently received—which, she had to admit, was a connection she herself had made. She'd dismissed it; surely Glenn had better things to do with his new freedom than hound her with silly e-mails. But still, the possibility lurked in the back of her mind. The morning she'd received the first one, the e-mail itself hadn't frightened her so much as the understanding that Glenn was out of jail, that she'd been the one to put him in jail, that he might harbor the world's biggest grudge. That he'd been a mean son of a bitch ten years ago and could be even meaner today, and he might blame her for his fate.

"What?" Mac goaded her gently.

Her troubling thoughts must have shown in her face. She sipped some wine for fortitude, then said in an admirably bland tone, "I was with an agency, but I wasn't happy there."

"Did you move to another agency?"

She shook her head. "I wound up quitting the business, going to college and never looking back." Except for an occasional nervous glance over her shoulder.

"Just because you weren't happy with the agency?"

"I told you, Mac, modeling was boring."

"And you were starving." He helped himself to another piece of bread and some cheese. "So why did you go into modeling in the first place?"

One more sip of wine, and she realized she didn't mind answering that particular question. "You really want to know?" she asked. At his nod, she crossed her legs at the ankle, cradled the bowl of her wineglass in her palms and smiled. "I was a tall, gawky, funny-looking kid. People were always making fun of me."

"No." He scrutinized her thoughtfully, then scowled. "I'll buy tall, but not gawky or funny-looking."

"I really was. I was skinny, too. I was all knees and elbows, and my eyes were too big for the rest of my face, and I had a pointy chin—"

He laughed. "And your ears flapped like Dumbo the Elephant's, and you had zits all over your nose. I'm having trouble picturing you looking bad, darlin'."

"It's the truth. I towered over the other kids in elementary school. They used to call me freakazoid."

"Freakazoid?"

"Freak, for short. I always got picked first for basketball teams, but I wasn't that athletic, so my height did me no good there. Even in high school I towered above most of the boys. No one ever asked me out. My sister advised me to slump my shoulders so I'd look shorter—she's tall, too, but only about five-seven. Nowhere near freakazoid proportions. I didn't like slouching, though. So I held my head high and tried to ignore the idiots shouting up at me, 'How's the weather up there?' and 'You ought to wear a flashing red light so planes won't crash into you.' They all thought they were so original."

"I grew up tall, and no one said those things to me," Mac argued.

Julie snorted. "Because you're a guy. It's okay for guys to be tall. Not girls."

"Unless they go into modeling," he guessed.

"Exactly. I grew up in a suburb north of New York City, and one of our neighbors was an editor at a fashion magazine. She said I had the perfect build for modeling, and she offered to put me in touch with some people in the business. I'd never really thought about modeling, but I figured if I succeeded there, I'd show all those jerks at my school that I wasn't a freak."

"And you did show them," Mac said.

"I did."

"Did they treat you better once you started modeling?"

She lapsed into a memory and grinned. "As a matter of fact, yes. What a bunch of phonies. They decided I must be hot stuff if people were paying me for my looks. They also assumed I must be rich, because models supposedly made lots of money. I wasn't exactly earning millions, though. My parents would allow me to go to shoots only on weekends and during the summer. They weren't going to let the modeling interfere with my education. Some girls drop out of school once they start getting jobs."

"They model full-time? Even when they're that young? What about child labor laws?"

"Once they're sixteen, they can leave high school and work full-time," Julie explained. "There were quite a few girls at my agency who'd left home and come to New York from all over the country to make it as models. They were sixteen, seventeen—no high school diplomas. All they had were their looks and their dreams."

"Was that enough? Did they succeed?"

Julie hesitated. To explain about the girls Glenn had exploited would bring her to the subject she wanted to avoid: her part in sending Glenn to prison and his threats of revenge. "No," she said carefully. "They would have been better off staying home and finishing school."

Mac studied her, as if he knew there was more to her story. But she wouldn't say more. She still remembered how Glenn used to get the girls to open up, to share their problems with him. She remembered how he'd promise to make everything better, then would gradually take over their lives until they were so dependent on him they'd do anything he asked of them: take weight-loss drugs, take other drugs, hand over their earnings to pay for their drugs…and in a few cases even sleep with him, because he told them if they did he'd get them the best jobs. And the best drugs.

Not that she thought Mac was capable of using and abusing people the way Glenn had. But she'd learned that trusting powerful men and relying on them, believing in their promises of protection, could lead to disaster.

She knew Mac was powerful, not just because he seemed independently wealthy or was technologically savvy, not even because he was tall and no one had ever called him a freak. Simply his confidence, the way he navigated through the world, the way he gazed at her, the way he smiled…

The man had charisma to spare. Charisma and power. And she wasn't going to let down her guard with him.

"Thank you for bringing this wonderful food," she said as she drained her glass. "And the wine."

"Thank you for going over the reservations list with me," he countered, lifting her empty glass from her hands and placing it on the tray. "Are you all right to drive home?"

"I'm fine."

"I can follow you, just to make sure—"

"Really, Mac, I'm fine." *Don't fuss over me. Don't try to manage my life.*

He stood, stretched and rubbed the back of his neck. "If you get more reservations before the party, let me know, all right?"

"Sure." Let him fuss over the hotel instead of her.

He watched her as she slid her feet back into her shoes and maneuvered her computer mouse to shut off the machine. "Any more strange e-mails?" he asked casually, as if the subject was of no great interest to him. Given the way he'd reacted to the first one, she suspected he cared more about her answer than she wanted him to.

In fact, she had received three more strange e-mails that day. All three had come from "4Julie" and included musical symbols and brief, menacing messages: "It ain't over till the fat lady sings." "You sing, you suffer." "I will never forgive you."

If she told Mac, he'd do something drastic—hire a bodyguard for her, force her to leave town, refuse to let her check her e-mail. Yet, paradoxically, the more weird the e-mails she received, the less they alarmed her. They struck her as the ravings of a lunatic too impotent to take action. Sending nasty e-mails was cheap and easy. Someone—possibly Glenn himself—was letting off steam, nothing more.

She refused to let the creep get to her. She hadn't been afraid of Glenn ten years ago, and she wasn't going to become a slave to fear now.

In reply to his question, she smiled. "No strange e-mails," she lied smoothly. "You can stop worrying about me."

"I don't worry about you," he murmured, returning her smile. "It's strange e-mails that I worry about." He lifted his jacket from the back of his chair, tossed it over his shoulder and pushed the cart to the door. "And it's my job to worry, so I reckon I'll just keep worrying. If you see me following you home, don't panic, *chère.* It's just me doing my job."

She watched him as he wheeled the cart out of her office and down the hall toward the elevator. She could bolt now, race to her car and be halfway home before he'd even gotten his sporty little coupe's engine started…or she could take her time and give him the chance to follow her. She didn't like being fussed over, but…

But Mac was as stubborn as she was, and that was something she respected, even admired. He worried; he'd follow her home. Then he'd leave her alone.

She could live with that.

TOO MANY MEMORIES in New York City. Too many memories of money, drugs, parties, sex. No—love, it had been love. Now Glenn didn't know how to love anymore.

Of course he didn't know how to love. How could a man who'd spent the past eight years behind bars, sleeping on a cot and watching his back, ever open up to love again? For God's sake, look at him: he was taking a real estate course. He'd once owned and operated a successful modeling agency, and now, if he was lucky, he might someday man the desk in the rental office of a high-rise building.

The time for payback was drawing near. First, Julie had to be frightened a little more. More e-mails, meaner e-mails, e-mails coming at her from all directions. Easy enough to do with a good friend who was a flight attendant and who landed at several different cities in a single day. Julie might not know where the e-mails were coming from, but just in case she was smart enough to track their origin…

She thought she was pretty damn smart. So let her be smart and scared. Let her suffer a little bit more before the end.

CHAPTER SEVEN

CREIGHTON WAS OUT, which was just as well. By the time Julie was inside the Garden District house, peering through the front door's side light as Mac flashed his headlights at her and drove away, her watch read nine-fifteen, too late to start gulping down alcoholic drinks.

Besides, the wine Mac had brought to accompany their fruit and cheese had left Julie mellow enough. The wine, the conversation and the knowledge that Mac at least knew she found his protectiveness annoying and he could joke about it. The headlight-flashing had simply been Mac's way of saying, "I realize you don't want me to follow you home, but what the hell. Humor me."

She gathered her mail and climbed the stairs to the second floor. Even though she hadn't seen Creighton's bright red car in the lot, she rapped on his door. The lack of a response didn't surprise her.

In her own apartment, she dropped the mail on her kitchen table, stepped out of her shoes and then padded into the tiny living room to check on her fish. The filter pump droned in a gentle hum and the water looked clear. As usual, her fish swished back and forth in the rectangular tank, ignoring one another. The Tetra hovered near the rock formation at the bottom of the tank, the Angelfish swam on a higher plane—closer to heaven, Julie thought with a smile—the Koi glinted coppery orange and the Shubunkin rippled flamboyantly to and fro, its fins fluttering like decorative fringes.

She sprinkled some food flakes across the water's surface. The fish jerked, stared and then propelled themselves upward to devour the feast. Closing the tin, Julie fought off her wistfulness at the fact that fish weren't dogs. You couldn't hug them or talk to them. Julie hadn't even bothered to name them.

Carrying her shoes, she left the living room for her bedroom to change out of her work clothes. A dog would be a blessing, she thought, keenly aware of the emptiness of her apartment. A dog snuffling around, its tags jangling and its voice emerging in a canine rumble punctuated by an occasional spirited bark would warm the place much more than the subdued hum and gurgle of the fish tank's pump.

If possible, Julie would choose a dog just like Bella, the sweet, sloppy mutt who'd followed her home from school one afternoon when she was eight years old. Bella had been wearing a tag, and Julie's parents had insisted on returning Bella to her rightful owner, even though Julie had been certain from the moment she'd seen that dog's uneven ears, soulful brown eyes and poignant smile that *she* was the dog's rightful owner, that fate had delivered Bella to her for some cosmic reason. It turned out that Bella's previous, not-so-rightful owner had moved out of town. Neighbors told the police the owner had tried for two months to find another home for the dog, because she was moving to an apartment that banned pets. Unable to find anyone, the woman had simply left the dog behind.

Julie had begged her parents to let her keep Bella. She'd promised to take care of the dog, walk her, feed her, clean up after her…and when her parents had acquiesced, Julie had lived up to her promises. Bella had been her companion for nine sweet years, until old age, arthritis and blindness claimed the poor animal. To this day, Julie missed her.

Bella had never called Julie a freakazoid. She'd never asked Julie how the weather was up there. She'd simply loved Julie, played with her, snuggled up to her while they watched

TV and listened uncritically to Julie's heartfelt confessions. When Marcie acted like a bossy big sister, Julie would complain to Bella, and Bella would issue a sympathetic whine. When classmates made fun of Julie, she would report the incidents to Bella, who would growl. Perhaps it wasn't a coincidence that less than six months after Bella's death, Julie had agreed to meet with Glenn Perry, who ran a modeling agency that specialized in teenage girls. She'd been lonely and sad and feeling insecure. Modeling had seemed like a good way to fill the hours she would otherwise have spent with Bella.

If her beloved dog were here now, she thought as she sank onto her bed and pulled off her nylons, she wouldn't burden Bella with her stress over the upcoming party or her worry about the hotel's financial health. No, she'd probably just cuddle Bella to herself and tell her about Mac. "He has the most amazing forearms," she'd say, remembering the male muscle and sinew beneath the bare skin. By exposing just a small, G-rated bit of his body, an extraordinarily sexy man had made her aware of how drab her nights were, how huge her queen-size bed seemed when the queen was sleeping alone.

Maybe she'd responded to Mac's forearms because she'd gone a year without sex. But she doubted that. She'd endured long stretches without male companionship in the past, and she'd never turned into a mooning fool. Until now.

Could she actually bear to let a man in her life who followed her home to make sure she was safe? In theory, the mere idea repelled her.

But Mac wasn't a theory. He was simply the kind of man who did things like that. And Julie wasn't sure what to think…except for wishing that while he'd sat with her in her office that evening, she'd been brave enough to reach from her chair to his and run her fingers down his arm, through those wiry black hairs, over the bones of his wrist and across his palm. She wished she'd taken the chance.

MAC HAD THE OFFICES of Crescent City Security to himself tonight. Louise was probably off somewhere, contemplating issues of anatomy with her med-school sweetheart, and Frank and Sandy were no doubt at home, either making a baby or arguing about whether they should. Mac hoped they were making a baby, not only because he liked the idea of becoming a godfather but also because somebody ought to be getting laid tonight, and it sure as hell wasn't him.

He slumped in his chair, turned on his computer and rubbed the fatigue out of his eyes. And cursed. He was crossing lines all over the place. Never should have taken food to his meeting with Julie tonight. *Never* should have taken wine. Never should have sat with her after they'd completed their task and talked to her and joked with her and polished off that Cabernet Sauvignon with her. And wanted her.

Even though he hadn't consumed enough wine to get a buzz, his blood was hot and thrumming. Lines of text zipped across his monitor as his computer warmed up and ran through its virus checks, but all he saw was Julie, dressed in a soft, body-hugging blue sweater and a gently flared skirt. He saw her legs, propped up on the chair next to his, and the oval outlines of her knees—some women had the most alluring knees, and Julie was definitely one of them. Symphony Perfumes should have used her knees in their ads. A dab of perfume behind each knee, and Mac would be rendered incoherent with lust.

Julie's feet weren't so bad, either. Large, but then they'd have to be large to balance her tall frame. And they were slender. Her toenails, visible through her sheer nylons, had been painted a rosy shade.

He cursed again. Just thinking about her made his breath catch and his groin ache. And that was wrong, really wrong. Her sister was paying him to protect Julie, not to fantasize about "getting biblical" with her, he thought with a grin.

He and Frank had a stone-cold rule: never become involved with a client. Not that Julie was a client, but close enough. Mac couldn't touch her.

He'd already touched her once, though, yesterday morning in her office. He'd touched her face, and tonight he'd wanted to touch her toes. Hell, he'd wanted to touch every part of her from face to toes, not missing a single square inch.

"Stop it," he said aloud—as if he could order his libido to rein itself in.

Forcing himself to focus on the computer monitor in front of him, he found a message from Frank:

Nothing definitive on the money that disappeared from the Hotel Marchand. Did find some interesting background on the Marchands, though. Anne Marchand's mother is Celeste Robichaux. Old family with old money. Celeste's brother was implicated in a real estate scam years ago—tarnished the family's name a bit, but they recovered. Can't say if this has anything to do with the missing money, but I'm looking.

Also—interesting, possibly meaningless detail—Anne Marchand was traveling in Italy with her daughter Melanie around the time the money disappeared. Haven't been able to trace the money to Italy—it wasn't wired to Anne or her daughter there.

That's all I've got so far.

"Great. A mystery," Mac murmured, then clamped his mouth shut. He might be going nutty over Julie, but he wasn't so demented that he was going to keep talking out loud to himself.

The fact was, he and Frank were under no obligation to solve the mystery of the missing Marchand money. No one had hired them to find the million dollars that had inexplicably vanished. And even if they did find it, there was no guarantee it would restore the hotel to financial stability.

But if that missing money was the cause of the hotel's

fragile health, and Mac and Frank could locate it…well, that would make a lot of folks happy. Julie might throw herself at him in gratitude.

Yeah, sure. And the moon might fall out of the sky, too.

Julie would be grateful if he solved the money mystery, but she probably wouldn't forgive him for lying about who he was and what he was doing. She wouldn't forgive him for being her bodyguard. She wouldn't forgive him for knowing far more about her than she thought he knew.

But he'd tell Frank to keep investigating, because Julie or no Julie, he wanted to know where that money had gone.

FIVE E-MAILS from "4Julie." Julie laughed.

Whoever was trying to spook her was failing miserably. The first e-mail had shaken her profoundly, the second less so. The more she got, the more immune to them she felt. When five appeared in a single download the next morning, they almost seemed like a joke to her.

They'd lost their subtlety and their ability to shock. They no longer played delicately on the theme of Symphony Perfumes, with musical allusions. They were just stupid. "It's all your fault," one said. Another accused, "You think you're so hot?" The one that made Julie laugh out loud said, "Perfume girl, you stink."

When she'd been a kid, wounded by her schoolmates' taunts, her parents had always advised her to ignore the teasing and it would stop. This, Julie learned from experience, was an adult myth that lacked any relation to reality. Ignored teasing didn't stop. It just grew louder and more persistent.

But Julie wasn't a gawky, gangly, too-tall girl anymore. She was a confident woman and teasing couldn't get to her. Especially anonymous teasing via e-mail.

She left her office, feeling free and almost a little naughty about being away from her desk during business hours, even if she was taking care of business in other parts of the hotel.

No wonder Mac liked to prowl around the place. Going downstairs to check on the final menu and beverage orders for the Twelfth Night party wasn't going to fill her with Vitamin D, as a stroll down to Jackson Square might, but getting out of her chair and enjoying the scenery beyond her computer monitor was refreshing.

She took the grand stairway down to the lobby, even though that wasn't the most direct route to the dining room kitchen. She'd worked at the Hotel Marchand for nearly five years, yet the charm and elegance of the hotel's lobby impressed her almost as much as it had the first time she'd walked into the building, clutching her résumé and Charlotte's name, which had been provided to her by the employment agency she'd contacted when she'd traded the crisp cold of Montreal for the sultry heat of New Orleans. She'd been awed by the staircase that first day, and in truth she still felt like a bride when she descended those stairs.

The lobby was kept spotless by a silent battalion of housekeepers, and the honey-hued credenza waxed to a high gloss. Every last speck of lint was vacuumed from the rugs, the tables were free of dust, and decorative pillows nestled at just the right angle to the sofas and settees.

Some people might consider modeling a glamorous profession. Julie would take her current job over modeling any day. *This*—her gaze swept the lobby as she descended the last few steps—was glamour.

A few people stood at the counter checking in. She heard the voices of the two clerks on duty, soothing and competent as they processed the guests. A bellhop stood nearby, a matching set of suitcases stacked on his brass cart. The concierge desk was empty. No sign of Luc; maybe he was making the rounds of the hotel, just like Julie. She glimpsed the assistant concierge, Patrick, ushering a guest out into the courtyard.

She strode through the lobby, nodding a greeting to the check-in clerks. Near the exit to the hall, she felt a hand on her shoulder and turned to find herself face-to-face with Alvin Grote. As usual, his hair was pulled back into a ponytail, and the overhead lights glinted off the circular bald spot crowning his skull. He wore a black turtleneck and black slacks which gave him an almost sinister look from chin down. The ponytail was too cute to look sinister, however. And his expression conveyed middle-class, middle-aged pique rather than evil intent.

"Mr. Grote," Julie said pleasantly. "How are you?"

"I've been better," he grumbled. "I want to add another person to my reservation for the Twelfth Night party, and those inept fools at the front desk refused to help me."

Julie knew the clerks were neither inept nor foolish. She could just imagine how Grote had demanded their assistance. "I think our concierge, Luc Carter, can help you with this," she said in her most soothing voice. "Have you spoken to him?"

Grote glanced toward Luc's empty desk. "How can I talk to him? He isn't here."

"I'm sure he'll be back shortly. Or we can leave him a message and have him get back to you to confirm that your guest has been added to the list." She remembered Mac's obsession with identifying everyone slated to attend the party and added, "You'll have to provide your guest's name, of course."

Grote's expression softened slightly. "I met her yesterday. Maggie. She's a pistol. I want her hanging off my arm at that party."

Julie suppressed a grin as she imagined how this woman Maggie might react to an invitation from someone who described her that way. A pistol? Hanging off his arm? Maybe he ought to buy a gun and holster, if that was what he wanted.

"Why don't we leave a note for Luc?" she suggested, ushering Grote over to the concierge desk. She found a pad and penned the message for Luc, including Grote's room number. "What's Maggie's last name?" she asked him.

He hesitated, then muttered, "I'm not sure."

"Please find out," she said, once again imagining what Mac would say if some semi-anonymous arm candy named "Maggie" appeared on the guest list.

"Why isn't it enough that she'll be my guest? I'm paying for her, after all."

"We need the last name for security reasons," Julie explained. "I'm sure Luc will be able to help you out." With that, she smiled and moved on, aware that some guests would never be satisfied, no matter how hard the hotel staff tried to accommodate them.

The art gallery wasn't on her way to the restaurant, but she decided to detour there simply because strolling around the hotel was such a pleasant break from sitting at her desk. The door was open and she peeked inside. In the prime viewing location, Sylvie had hung an Andrew Wyeth painting from her grandmother's collection. Celeste had bought three Wyeths decades ago, just before he became famous. Now, of course, the paintings were practically priceless. To see one hanging on the wall of the hotel's gallery made Julie's heart beat a little faster.

The Wyeth painting undoubtedly helped to attract customers to the gallery. Several browsers wandered through the narrow room's two stories, studying the paintings, sculpture and jewelry by local artists with the same interest and respect they accorded the Wyeth.

Sylvie knew how to display art, and how to select it. She was an artist herself, having inherited her mother's eye for esthetics and visual harmony.

She was seated at a computer, but she glanced up at Julie's entrance. Her curly red hair was as striking as some of the artwork she displayed.

"The Wyeth looks magnificent," Julie called from the open doorway.

Sylvie grinned. "I can't believe I was able to borrow one of *Grand-mère's* precious paintings for the gallery. My daughter calls it the 'White painting.' She can't quite say 'Wyeth.'"

Julie laughed. "Too bad you can't sell that painting. You'd be set for life if you could."

"*Grand-mère* will never part with her Wyeths," Sylvie said, eyeing the soft landscape dominating the gallery's wall, "except for a temporary loan like this."

Julie nodded. "Are you planning to have the gallery open during the party?"

Sylvie shook her head vehemently. "All those people, all that revelry. All that booze," she added with a laugh. "The gallery would get a lot of traffic, but people wouldn't be in a shopping frame of mind." She glanced at the wall display one more time and sighed. "Is my mother around? She said she wanted to discuss the jewelry displays." She waved at the glass-enclosed showcases. "She claims she has some ideas."

Julie interpreted her tone and guessed, "You don't want her input?"

"She's got a great eye," Sylvie said. "I'd be crazy not to listen to her suggestions. I just wish she'd take it a little easier. She's knocking herself out on the party preparations. I can't help worrying."

Julie felt a swell of sympathy—for Anne Marchand as well as for her daughter. "I know you can't help it," she said, "but people don't like being worried about." She certainly didn't like Mac worrying about her.

Sylvie nodded. "Sometimes I think Mama wants to be running the hotel again. Charlotte's doing such a good job, though. Mama should take it easy and enjoy her retirement."

"I'm sure she'd appreciate that advice as much as you appreciate all the advice she ever gave you."

That got a laugh out of Sylvie. "All right. I'll let her rearrange the jewelry showcases if she wants. Maybe she doesn't really want to run the hotel anymore. It could be she's just stir-crazy. And she's living with *Grand-mère*. She probably wants to get out of the house as much as possible."

"Your grandmother can't be that bad," Julie argued gently.

"Anyway, I think your mother just wants to keep her hand in. She doesn't want all the responsibility of running the hotel full-time. She'd much rather let her daughters deal with the stress."

Sylvie tossed back her head and laughed again, causing her coppery curls to vibrate. "And we like dumping all the responsibility and stress on you, Julie."

Julie joined her laughter. She eyed the Wyeth one more time, sighed at its misty, moody beauty, and then said goodbye to Sylvie and left the gallery. As she crossed the lobby, she noticed Patrick at the concierge desk and Luc nowhere in sight. At least Alvin Grote wasn't pacing the floor and grumbling.

She entered Chez Remy. In the dining room, a few stragglers lingered over a late breakfast, but most of the tables were empty, and a busboy moved silently through the room, setting the polished wood tables with linen napkins and silverware and centering bud vases and ornate candlesticks on each table, preparing for the lunch crowd. The restaurant's ambiance was an intriguing mixture of formality and familiarity. Small tables were surrounded by mismatched but superbly constructed chairs which Anne and Remy had scavenged years ago at antique shows and estate sales. The tall windows and French doors opened onto the courtyard; the full-length drapes were tied back to afford views of the pool and the potted plants outside.

No wonder people lingered for hours over their breakfasts. Who would want to leave such a lovely dining room?

Julie couldn't stay, though, especially after having spent time in the gallery with Sylvie. She crossed to the kitchen, where she found Robert LeSoeur in a crisp white shirt and black trousers, presiding over rows of stainless-steel counters, an eight-burner industrial stove, an enormous griddle and banks of wall ovens. Young, handsome and endowed with the sort of arrogance a chef required to create exquisite cuisine out of chaos, Robert ruled his frenetic underlings like a not quite benevolent dictator.

Glimpsing Julie, he darted to his desk, which was tucked into a corner of the room away from the food preparation area, and lifted a folder. He must have known she'd be asking for the final menu and budget today, because he had all the information printed out and ready for her. "Thanks," she said. "Any potential disasters I need to know about?"

He smiled enigmatically. "In the kitchen, there are always potential disasters. You probably *don't* want to know about them."

"Then by all means, spare me," she said with a grin.

From the dining room she traveled to the bar, where Leo was counting bottles and marking an inventory list. A slight, silver-haired fellow sat alone at a table, nursing a brandy. Rather early for that particular refreshment, Julie thought, but she trusted Leo to keep the customer both satisfied and safe.

She headed straight for Leo, who was standing behind the bar. "Are we all set for the party?" she asked.

"As ready as we'll ever be," he assured her. "The champagne will be delivered the morning of the party. Wine deliveries should be arriving any minute. Folks who want the hard stuff will have to leave the function rooms and come here."

"Have we got strategies in place if anyone overindulges?"

"Always." Leo grinned. "Most folks don't need the excuse of a party to overindulge. We can handle them. We've got the police on our speed dial, just like the security office."

Julie realized she wasn't far from the security office herself. Work awaited her back at her desk, but… Why not pay a quick, friendly visit to Mac? He wandered past her office often enough, usually vanishing before she could see him and leaving nothing in his wake but his distinctive woodsy scent and a frisson of awareness in Julie. But he hadn't been by her office that morning. She hadn't seen him, hadn't smelled him or sensed him.

She owed him a thank-you for arranging their supper last night, even if it had been supplied by Melanie. Surely that was a reasonable excuse to stop by his office.

But he wasn't there. She glanced through the door and saw

the young security staffer, Carlos, behind the desk, viewing the images picked up by the hotel's security cameras with the intensity of someone watching a gripping dramatic film. Mac was probably making his rounds. Right now, he could be hovering outside her office door, wondering where she was.

That thought made her smile. She moved past the security office, figuring she'd take the back stairs up to the second floor, when she heard a murmur of voices, one male and one female. Following the sound, she spotted Luc Carter and a petite dark-haired maid emerging from the supply storage room, their heads bowed together as if they were swapping secrets.

Julie fell back a step, not wanting to embarrass them. From the corner of her eye, she saw Luc drop a light kiss to the chambermaid's cheek, then turn and saunter down the hall toward the stairs, right where she was standing. Even if she wanted to avoid him, she couldn't.

He saw her, faltered a step, then grinned sheepishly. "Hi."

She returned his smile. "I heard you had a sweetheart on the housekeeping staff."

He seemed mildly flustered. "We're just friends."

"Not that you're asking me for any advice," she said, "but be careful. Workplace romances can get messy." Which was a valid reason for her to have avoided the security office this morning. Not that she and Mac had a romance going, not that they ever would, but…yes, such relationships could get messy.

"Thanks for the warning, Miss Julie."

"You should get back to the lobby," she suggested. "I left a message for you there. A guest wants to change his reservation for the party. Alvin Grote."

Luc rolled his eyes. "Alvin Grote wants everything, and he wants it yesterday."

Julie couldn't argue that. "Unfortunately, it's our job to see that he gets it. And at the moment, it's your job."

"Lucky me." Luc and Julie exchanged a smile. "I'll take care of him."

"Thanks." She watched as Luc sauntered down the hall toward the lobby. Then she entered the back stairwell and climbed the stairs, her escape from the confines of her desk drawing to a close. Her long legs carried her efficiently toward her office, the slit in her slim-fitting skirt gapping with each step. A few paces from her open office door, she caught a whiff of his scent.

Mac had been here.

And he was still here, she discovered as she swung into her office. He was sitting at her desk, staring at her computer monitor and scowling.

"What are you doing?" she asked, too startled to take offense.

He spun around in the chair and aimed his furious gaze at her. "Why didn't you tell me?"

"Tell you what?"

"You've gotten a total of ten threatening e-mails. Five of them today." He rose to his feet, and she realized that he was struggling to keep his temper in check—and not quite succeeding. "Why the hell didn't you tell me?"

Her own anger belatedly kicked in. "Who gave you permission to read my e-mails?"

"Your door was open," he countered. "Your computer was on. I looked through the doorway and saw an e-mail on the monitor."

She was pretty sure she'd closed her e-mail program before she'd left her office, and she'd been gone long enough for her screen saver to have taken over.

Mac was lying. He'd entered her office while she'd been out, opened her e-mail program and read her mail. "My e-mail is none of your business," she snapped, marching across the office to confront him up close. "You have no right snooping through my messages."

"Of course I have a right. Of course it's my business. These are threatening e-mails. That's a matter for security."

"It's *my* e-mail—"

"Which you received on your work computer during business hours. Don't bullshit me, Julie. You promised you'd tell me if you received any more of these messages. You've gotten a bunch of them, and you didn't tell me."

"Because they're stupid," she retorted. "Because they don't mean a thing. Because I'm not going to let some jerk scare me for his own amusement. I can take care of myself."

Mac grabbed her by her shoulders and tightened his hands, as if he thought she'd run from him. But why would she? She was no more afraid of him than she was of the jerk sending the e-mails.

"Julie," he said in a low, intense tone. "You're not scared. Fine. *I'm* scared. Someone is targeting you for a reason. At the very least it's harassment."

His solemnity, his barely contained rage and the profound darkness of his eyes alarmed her in a way no e-mail ever could. "And what is it at the *not* very least?" she asked quietly, hating the anxious edge to her voice.

"At the *not* very least, someone wants to hurt you."

His hands were still on her shoulders, his face just inches from hers. His distinctive scent filled her nostrils. "Stop trying to frighten me," she said, her voice more hushed and tremulous than she would have liked.

"Who might have sent you those e-mails?" he asked. "Who wants to hurt you, Julie?"

She thought briefly of Glenn Perry, who'd wound up in prison on the strength of her testimony. But that had been so long ago. The world had changed in a million ways since then, and so had she. And so, no doubt, had Glenn.

And anyway, how could he have found out her e-mail address?

"No one," she whispered.

Clearly exasperated, Mac released her and paced in a circle around her office. Her shoulders felt chilled with his hands gone. The chill spread to her spine and down the length of her, causing her to shiver. She didn't like lying to Mac any more than he liked being lied to.

She wrapped her arms around herself and watched him storm from the windows to the file cabinets and back to her desk. He raked a hand through his hair, then faced her squarely. "Julie," he said. "Maybe you don't care that someone might have you in his sights. Maybe you don't care that you could be in danger. *I* care. So you're going to have to play this my way. We can trace those e-mails—at least find out where they're being sent from. I'm going to copy them, and I'm going to have an expert I know work on them, and we're going to figure out as much as we can about them. Do you understand?"

He didn't wait for her to answer, but instead lowered himself back into her chair and inserted a memory stick into a port on her computer. She watched apprehensively as he downloaded material from the machine, and hoped it was only her e-mails. Everything else on her computer was work-related—contracts, letters, spreadsheets and other files—and she had no reason to hide any of it from the head of the hotel's security department, but still…this felt like a violation. Mac was tapping into her computer and sucking her data out of it.

"I don't like this," she said, a halfhearted protest.

"I don't like you being threatened by a cyber-stalker." Mac clicked on an icon and removed his memory stick. Pocketing it, he stood.

"I'm not really in any danger," she said, attempting to convince herself as much as him.

"You don't know if you are or not," he said. "But if something happened to you…" His hands rested on her shoulders again, gently this time, not to hold her immobile but to emphasize the honesty in his words. "It would just about kill me."

She peered up at him. Not just his hands but his eyes, the grim line of his mouth, the faint roughness in his voice told her he meant it. He was that worried about her. He cared that much.

It seemed too easy to move from the emotion passing between them to something more. Too easy, too natural, too necessary. Too inevitable.

He bowed his head as she tilted hers, and his lips grazed hers. Just one fleeting, tender kiss, but it ignited a heat inside her, as dark and languorous as a summer delta night. If one tiny kiss from Mac could warm her so thoroughly, so deliciously, what could two kisses do?

She wasn't sure she could handle the answer to that question. Leaning back, she found him gazing steadily at her. "This is a bad idea," she said.

"Yeah." Then he bowed his head and kissed her again. His lips brushed hers, stroked, nipped. Devoured. One moment he was kissing her and the next he was taking her, conquering, claiming. His hands flexed against her shoulders, his teeth plucked at her lips, his tongue probed until she opened to him and he stole inside, sliding deep, filling her. Her body's temperature rose a hundred degrees. She felt as if she was melting, her soul liquefying so Mac could drink it in.

A faint groan escaped him, and she realized that he was every bit as staggered by this kiss as she was. The surge of desire flowed both ways. If he needed her at that moment, she needed him every bit as much. If he wanted her…she wanted this, his mouth on hers, his hands, his body pressing against her, tall and hard and scorchingly hot.

No man had ever told her that if something happened to her it would kill him. At that moment she was sure that ending this kiss would kill them both. Maybe it was a bad idea—but stopping, she was sure, was a far, far worse one.

His hands moved from her shoulders to the sides of her throat and up to her cheeks, holding her head steady. His fingertips seemed to sear her cheeks before they dug into her hair. His tongue teased hers, lured it, and she accepted its invitation, chasing it into his mouth. He tasted like coffee and mint and sex.

She reached for his waist, slid her hands under his jacket and sensed the heat of his skin through the smooth cotton of his shirt. His breath caught as she skimmed her palms across the taut contours of his chest, feeling ripples of response, the flexing of muscle, the fierce pounding of his heart.

She wanted to tear his shirt off, and her own. She wanted to taste not just his mouth but his neck, his torso, every part of him. She wanted to shut down her brain so it wouldn't keep nagging her to stop wanting Mac. This *was* a bad idea—and never had a bad idea felt so good.

"Julie?" Charlotte called through the open inner door. "Did you get the party menu from Robert?"

Julie and Mac sprang apart. Julie glanced toward the door and was relieved not to see Charlotte standing there. Lowering her eyes, she managed a shaky breath. Her mouth burned.

She felt Mac's gaze on her. Mustering her courage, she lifted her face and saw that he was staring at her, his eyes smoky, his nostrils narrowed as he struggled to regulate his breathing. He reached up and drew his hand the length of her hair, smoothing it back from her cheek.

She tried to guess what he was thinking. That her safety was a life-or-death thing to him? That this kiss had been a life-or-death thing? That they should pursue this bad idea or behave as if it had never occurred?

She cleared her throat. "I've got the menu, Charlotte," she called in an oddly hoarse voice, which she directed toward Charlotte's open office door even though she couldn't shift her eyes from Mac. "I'll bring it right in."

He caressed her cheek and the trembling curve of her lower lip with his fingertips. Then, abruptly, he turned, stalked toward the door to the hallway and walked out. His hand was in the pocket of his jacket where he'd stashed his memory stick.

Had he kissed her to distract her from the fact that he'd copied her e-mails without her permission? To make her forget, or at least not mind, that he'd breached her privacy?

To obliterate her anger over his bossy, self-important, know-it-all, smothering overprotectiveness?

Or had he kissed her for the same reason she'd kissed him—because at that moment, kissing him had seemed essential to her survival?

Whatever the reason, it shouldn't have happened, and she knew she'd regret it, not only because of the inherent dangers in workplace romances, which she'd been lecturing Luc about just minutes ago, but because this was Mac Jensen, a man who'd just stolen her e-mails. A man who could seize control of her life if she let him. A man she still wasn't sure she could trust.

CHAPTER EIGHT

"I'VE GOT TO SPLIT," Mac told Carlos. "I've got some business to take care of. I'll be back in an hour. Do you mind taking a late lunch?"

"Nah. My girlfriend makes me eat a big breakfast. She says she wants to fatten me up." He lifted the cup of coffee Mac had brought him from the kitchen. "This'll keep me going."

"My cell will be on, in case you need to reach me." With that, Mac bolted from the security office and out the service entrance.

The noontime weather was overcast and cool, half matching his mood. He was overcast but definitely not cool. Just thinking about the kiss he and Julie had shared—although the word *kiss* hardly seemed adequate to describe it—made him hot. His breath rasped, his scalp sweated and his groin… Damn. Talk about being on fire.

Julie was gorgeous, no question about that. When a man fantasized about a gorgeous woman, however, the fantasy generally entailed *him* doing things to *her.* She was the scenery, he was the actor.

But Julie wasn't just some beautiful scenery. She could kiss as if she was channeling the spirit of Venus and every other love goddess in mythology, with a touch of wild woman, a dash of hooker and a load of wide-eyed wonderment mixed in.

He could tell himself he'd kissed her because he'd had to change the subject from stealing her e-mails, or because those e-mails had genuinely scared the crap out of him, or because the minute he'd planted his hands on her shoulders, he'd known that all the pacing in the world wasn't going to keep him from pulling her into his arms. But here was the truth: he'd kissed her because he'd had to. And now that he'd done it, he wanted much, much more. One taste of the drug that was Julie Sullivan had addicted him and made him want to do that drug again and again, until his mind was gone.

He'd have to get a grip. He was a freaking professional, and he couldn't jeopardize his company or his own integrity by chasing after her.

Halfway to the parking lot, he had his cell phone out of his pocket. His thumb flicked the buttons to speed-dial the office. Sandy answered on the second ring. "Crescent City Security, can I help you?"

"I'm beyond help," he growled.

"Mac?" Sandy paused. "Are you all right?"

"I'll survive." *Maybe,* he added silently. To reassure Sandy, he said, "Yeah, sweetheart, I'm all right. Is Louise around?"

"She hasn't left for lunch yet, if that's what you're asking."

"Don't let her leave." He'd reached his car and unlocked it. "Tell her I'll treat her to lunch at the Commander's Palace when this job is done, but she's got to make do with a sandwich at her desk today. I'm bringing her a bunch of e-mails to decode."

"Now?"

"I'm in my car," he said as he slammed the door shut and jabbed the key into the ignition. "I'll be there ASAP. Louise is not to leave her desk until she finds out where these e-mails came from."

"If I keep her from leaving, will you treat me to lunch at the Commander's Palace, too?"

"If you keep her from leaving," he said, backing out of his space and maneuvering the wheel with one hand, "I'll treat you to Pizza Hut. Right now, darlin', Louise's skills are worth a hell of a lot more than yours."

"I'm insulted," Sandy said, then laughed. "I'll bar the door so the woman of your dreams can't escape. See you soon."

The woman of my dreams, he thought as he folded his phone shut. With her technical expertise, Louise ought to be that woman. But he knew the woman he'd be dreaming about tonight, and she was a tall Yankee with eyes the color of a bayou sunset and a mouth that could make him swear off sanity forever.

"THIS IS GREAT," Charlotte said, lowering the buffet menu Julie had carried upstairs from the restaurant. "I can't believe Robert came in under budget."

"It took some doing," Julie admitted. She'd had to veto several of his suggestions. No Alaskan king crab. Prawns would do. And no truffle miniquiches. Surely, Julie had insisted, he could prepare something equally interesting with portobello mushrooms.

"No one's going to leave the party hungry," Charlotte predicted. "That's the important part. Mama said the rooms are almost done. The flowers are arriving tomorrow morning, and she'll be placing them where they need to go." She sighed. "Would you mind terribly helping her with that? If she spends all day finishing the decorations, it might be too much for her."

Julie appreciated the opportunity to focus on flowers and Anne Marchand's health. It kept her from thinking about Mac. Thinking about him turned her brain to mud and the rest of her body to lava, molten and glowing.

"I have a feeling your mother is in better health than you realize," she said. "If you want me to help her with the flowers tomorrow, of course I will. But you and your sisters need to stop worrying about her. She's not about to keel over."

"How do you know that? Just last autumn—"

"I know, I know. She had a heart attack. But today she radiates health and energy. She's never looked better."

"You like her hair long?" Charlotte eyed Julie's long hair and grinned. "I suppose you would. I try not to worry about Mama, but I can't help it. You know how worried you were about your daddy just a week ago, when he was battling the flu."

Julie conceded with a nod. "My father's perfectly healthy now, and I think your mother is, too."

"From your mouth to God's ears." Charlotte smiled at Julie, tilting her head slightly as she appraised her. "You've got that look again."

"What look?" Julie discreetly touched her hand to her lips, as if to hide any evidence of what had occurred just minutes ago in her office.

"That Mac Jensen look."

Julie took a deep breath and reminded herself that he'd entered her office uninvited, breached the privacy of her computer and then kissed her senseless—probably to keep her from becoming angry about his downloading her e-mails. That only made her angrier. Anger was better than abject yearning, she decided.

"The man pisses me off," she said.

"I reckon that's part of his job," Charlotte said. "A good security director has to make people uncomfortable sometimes."

Not this kind of uncomfortable, Julie thought. "Maybe," she agreed without much enthusiasm.

"For the party tomorrow," Charlotte continued, "Mac and his staff get free rein. Make sure everybody knows this. We want no security problems. Whatever Mac says goes."

"I'll spread the word." Julie shuddered to think of Mac having free rein and her having to obey his every command. What if he ordered her to kiss him again? Would she have to?

Would she be able to stop herself?

"The party's going to be a great success, and we did it all without professional planners," Charlotte said resolutely. "I bet even that grouch in Room 307 won't find anything to complain about."

Assuming he was able to find out his tootsie's last name, Julie thought.

"Why don't you take a run downstairs and see how the event rooms are coming along?" Charlotte requested. "If my mother looks worn-out, make her take a break."

"If she looks like she needs one," Julie said, knowing full well that Anne would look like a world-class marathoner, barely breaking a sweat as she labored over the decorations.

Julie left Charlotte's office and veered toward the back stairway, wondering whether she should have locked her office first. Even if she had, Mac could open it with his master key. She had no way to keep him out.

Her legs felt a little wobbly as she descended the stairs, and she paused on the landing to collect herself. When she'd taken her last stroll around the hotel, she'd felt free and invigorated, as if circulating through the first floor was an exciting adventure. Now that she knew the devastating excitement of kissing Mac, she didn't want to run into him. She hoped he was as far from the event rooms as possible.

Her view from the doorway of the first room told her that a great deal had been done, and a great deal more needed to be done. Several men from the maintenance staff were perched on stepladders, hanging colorful panels of diaphanous cloth from the ceiling at Anne's direction. At least she wasn't climbing the ladders herself. But standing at the center of the room, shouting orders— "six inches to the left, please" and "could we try the sapphire blue cloth there instead?"— to the men scurrying around and repositioning the ladders, Anne made it very clear that she was the boss.

"It looks great," Julie said, sidling up to her.

"It looks terrible," Anne argued. "But by the time we're done, it'll look splendid. We've got about fifty miles of silver and gold beads to hang, along with the drapery panels. I'm hoping the effect will be an elegant variation on a carnival tent, fun but classy. Then we'll have candles floating in bowls of water on the tables—beautiful and also practical. If someone knocks over a candle, the water will douse it. And the flowers, of course."

"Of course."

"The band will be in the other room. Dancing there, food and drink here. This is going to be our best party yet."

Julie appreciated Anne's optimism. "Do you need my help with anything?"

"Charlotte asked you to babysit me again, didn't she." Anne's smile was tinged with irritation. "I'm perfectly fine. No, the green," she shouted to a man who'd been about to pin a yellow panel of cloth to the ceiling. "And fasten it about a foot closer to the window."

"Yes, ma'am," he responded.

"Anyway," Anne continued to Julie, "I'm happy to have your company, but I don't need you doting on me as if I were an invalid."

"I know. I've told Charlotte the same thing."

Anne shared a smile with her. "My daughters act as if I'm in danger of collapsing. I do hate being fussed over."

"So do I," Julie said, thinking of Mac's irritation over her failure to inform him about the e-mails. "At least in this case you know your daughters are fussing over you because they love you, not because they're playing power games."

"That's true. They love me—and I love them. It's amazing how people can love each other so much and still get on each other's nerves." She laughed. "If you really want to help, you can check with Nadine to see if the party linens have arrived. I ordered tablecloths to pick up the rainbow colors of these drapes. And multicolored cocktail napkins. They should be here by now."

"I'll do that," Julie said, sending out a silent prayer that Mac wouldn't be in the security office next door to the housekeeping department. Even if he was as busy doing his job as she was doing hers, even if there was not the sliver of a chance that he'd touch her again, she wasn't yet ready to face him.

MAC MIGHT BE OBSESSED with Julie Sullivan, but at four-fifteen that afternoon he was madly in love with the very short genius who performed feats of technological magic in the back room at Crescent City Security Services.

He sat at a table in a corner of the courtyard, ignoring the couple sipping colorful drinks by the edge of the pool as if they were vacationing on some tropical isle rather than in the French Quarter of New Orleans in January. The air wasn't quite tropics warm, and there was no sand or swaying palms or salty air, but they were making the most of the teardrop-shaped pool and the open sky above them.

As soon as Mac had gotten the message to call Louise he'd come out to the courtyard. Whatever she intended to tell him, he wanted to be alone to hear it, undistracted by the hotel surveillance cameras flashing their images on the monitor in the tiny security office. He'd sent Carlos off to have a cigarette, and once he'd satisfied his nicotine craving, Mac left him in charge of the desk and went to the courtyard to return Louise's call.

"This is weird, Mac," she told him. "I gather Sullivan received the last five e-mails all in the same download, but they weren't sent at the same time."

"They came from New York, though?"

"No. I was saving the bad news for last," Louise answered. "They came from airports. Most airports have WiFi now—wireless Internet service for anyone who has a laptop and an Internet card. The first was sent from LaGuardia, the second and third from Detroit, the fourth and fifth from Dallas. Judging by the times they were sent, I was able to narrow down the flights the sender might have taken. I've got schedules from Delta, American and United Air Lines, and, depending which airline our guy booked on, I can tell you what flights he was on. I couldn't get any of the airlines to release passenger manifests for those flights, though."

"So he's on the move." Mac frowned. Dallas was a hell of a lot closer to New Orleans than New York City was. "I thought that according to the terms of his parole he wasn't allowed to leave New York."

"You're assuming the person sending the e-mails is Glenn Perry," she pointed out.

One thing he liked about Louise—she didn't worry about trying to make her boss feel smart or superior. She just blurted out the flaws in his reasoning. "Who else would be harassing Julie?" he shot back, partly to soothe his ego and partly because Louise was so freaking smart she probably had an answer.

"An old boyfriend?"

"Her sister insists there's no one else. Julie didn't date much, and the few men she did date were sane. Marcie says Perry is the only person who's got a grudge against Julie."

"Then maybe he hired someone to send these messages for him."

That possibility had crossed Mac's mind, as well. It had troubled him, so he'd preferred to relegate it to deep storage. But now Louise had dredged it back up.

That Perry could have an ally roaming around the country, sending threatening e-mails on his behalf, definitely qualified as bad news. Those last five e-mails had differed from the earlier ones in tone. Why shouldn't Mac assume they were sent by someone else?

"So—we've got to get hold of those flight manifests and see if there's anyone on them who might have some connection to Perry."

"The airlines wouldn't release their passenger lists," Louise reminded him.

"They wouldn't release the lists to *you*, darlin'. That doesn't mean they won't release them to *me*." He pondered for a minute. Whoever had sent the e-mails could be using a false name. Or Perry could have asked more than one person to run his nasty errands for him. Maybe no one had flown anywhere. Maybe there were separate bastards in Detroit and Dallas sending the e-mails from the comfort of their own homes. "You're sure these were sent via airport WiFi?"

"As sure as I can be," Louise responded. "Which is never a hundred percent, Mac. You know that."

Mac ruminated some more. "We need to contact Perry's parole officer to make sure he's still in New York. If he's flying around the country, he could get pulled in for a parole violation."

"I'll ask Sandy to call his parole officer," Louise promised.

"Do you think Perry's got the money to buy folks tickets to fly around the country for him? What do they give ex-cons when they leave the joint? Twenty bucks?"

"I think it's a little more than that." Louise paused. "But Perry could have rich friends from his former life."

"Jet-setting friends. Buddies in the SkyMiles club, or whatever it's called."

"Or someone who works for the airline," she suggested. "Don't they get free tickets?"

Mac developed a cramp in the bridge of his nose from frowning so hard. He leaned back in his chair, stretched his legs and pinched the spot between his eyebrows where the ache had sprung. "As the head of a modeling agency, Perry must have traveled a bit. He could have accrued lots of miles…or he could have gotten friendly with a few flight attendants." Could be he'd gotten biblical with one or two, Mac thought with a reluctant smile.

"Maybe there's a way to find out what airline he used back in his jet-setting days," Louise suggested. "If he was loyal to one, we could assume that's where his frequent-flyer miles would be."

"Or his flight attendant girlfriend," Mac agreed. "Sweetheart, you're brilliant." Mac sighed. "Marry me. Throw over that doctor fellow and run away with me."

"Thanks. I think I'll stick with the doctor fellow," she said dryly. "I'll see if Frank has any ideas about how to get this information out of the airlines."

"Frank will have lots of ideas. Maybe I ought to marry him, instead."

"I don't know if Sandy would like that," Louise said.

If she and Frank hadn't negotiated a peace over their child-bearing decisions, Sandy might like it a lot. "Take this fool off my hands," she'd say. "I'm going down to the sperm bank to get myself knocked up."

Frank might be clueless about managing a successful marriage, but he knew how to pry information from difficult places. He could put the Garrick Insurance case aside for a day and poke around the airlines. Maybe he'd charm the flight manifests out of them.

"All right," he said. "Let's dump this on Frank."

"Consider it done," Louise said before disconnecting the call at her end.

Mac flipped shut his phone, rolled his head back until he was staring straight up into a sky that resembled a sheet of blue linen dotted with cottonball clouds, and processed what Louise had told him.

New York to Detroit to Dallas. Did the SOB even know Julie lived in New Orleans?

He had to go back to Julie's office. Maybe now she'd realize he was serious about her keeping him informed. Maybe she'd finally live up to her promise to tell him about all her sicko e-mails.

He doubted it. And he doubted that if he went back to her office, either of them would be able to think straight.

He'd go later, after she'd left for the day. He'd break in, as he'd broken in before, and monitor her in-box. She already knew he could—and would—do that. She knew she couldn't trust him.

He had nothing to lose by acting untrustworthy.

CHAPTER NINE

SHE SENSED HIM before she saw him. Once again he was lurking outside her door, watching her. It was more than just his scent that alerted her to his nearness. It was a charge in the air, a sudden heat, an awareness centered somewhere in the region of her solar plexus.

Thank God it was centered there and not lower.

Not quite ready to face him, she remained at her computer, finishing typing a response to an e-mail from Roxanne Levesque, who had written to remind her that if the hotel wanted to hire her for any services in the days leading up to Mardi Gras, it would have to act fast. Her calendar was nearly full.

Given what she charged, the hotel wouldn't be hiring her this year. Julie didn't mention that in her e-mail, of course. She simply thanked Roxanne and said the hotel would keep her in mind for future events.

She clicked the send icon and then, taking a slow, steady breath, rotated her chair to face the doorway.

Mac remained outside her office, the toes of his loafers less than an inch from the threshold and his hands gripping the door frame. Was he afraid of what might happen if he entered the room? *She* certainly was. Merely gazing at him from eight feet away reminded her of what kissing him had been like. If he crossed that invisible barrier—the line separating her office from the hallway, the line separating two professional colleagues—he might kiss her again. And since Charlotte was downstairs reviewing her final to-do lists for the party with her mother, Julie couldn't count on a helpful call from the office next door to stop another kiss before it blazed out of control.

"It's nearly six," Mac announced. "I'll bet you're starving."

"I'm always starving," she admitted.

"Lately, darlin', so am I."

His tone hinted that he wasn't discussing food. She refused to rise to his bait, though. Her cheeks felt warm, but she kept her breathing steady and held her hands quietly in her lap. "Have you been skipping lunch?" she asked, choosing the most innocent interpretation for his words.

He grinned. "I'm skipping more than I'd like. What do you say we get a bite?"

Dinner with him? Again? Now that their relationship had gone haywire? Since when did they even have a relationship, anyway?

Since before that morning, she knew. Maybe it had started the first time he'd eaten dinner with her. Or earlier that same day, when he'd tracked her down in the courtyard. Or even before then, when he'd first begun working at the hotel, back in November. She'd felt his nearness, his attention, right from the start. She'd been far too aware of him—and far too aware of his awareness of her.

"I think I should just go home," she said, as much to herself as to him.

He remained outside her office, his fingers flexing on the door's vertical moldings as if he literally had to hold himself back. "We've got to talk, Julie. We can do that here or over a plate of something edible. I vote for the second option."

She sighed. She'd skipped lunch herself today, and if Mac was going to insist on talking to her, she might as well eat. Food would give her the energy to ignore her attraction to him.

"All right," she said. "Let me just close up here." She swiveled back to her computer. As she hit the keys to close her e-mail software and shut down her computer, she could feel him staring at her back. His gaze was almost a tangible thing, a warm pressure between her shoulder blades.

Ten minutes later they were outside, ambling down a sidewalk swarming with people. As always, the French Quarter was bustling with locals and visitors, shoppers and browsers and rowdies primed for an evening of boozing and dancing. Julie didn't want to get separated from Mac in the crowd, but she didn't dare take his hand. She couldn't touch him. Too risky.

He made no effort to strike up a conversation as they worked their way down the street. A display of painted porcelain masks in one shop window caught Julie's eye, and Mac patiently stood by while she moved closer to the glass to admire the handiwork. Creighton had several gorgeous masks on display in his apartment. Julie wondered if they'd been created by the same artisan who'd done the ones in the shop. None of the masks had price tags visible, which meant Julie couldn't afford them.

Did Mac think she was a hopeless tourist? Did natives consider Mardi Gras masks a step below kitsch? Julie didn't care. Gazing at the delicately painted china kept her from thinking too much about the man lurking close behind her.

After a few minutes she reluctantly turned from the window and continued down the sidewalk with Mac. She could stall only so long. Sooner or later they'd have to talk. And eat. At least she was looking forward to eating.

The first restaurant they entered said they couldn't be seated without a reservation. The second told them they didn't need a reservation, but they'd have at least an hour's wait for a table. Back out in the cool, dark night, Julie kept pace with Mac—her legs were almost as long as his—and remembered the funky eatery he'd taken her to halfway down an alley a few nights ago. She wasn't sure exactly where that place was, or if it was within walking distance. In any case, Mac seemed to know enough about the restaurants in this part of the Quarter. He bypassed one without pausing, glanced through the arched entry of another and shook his head.

Whatever he thought they needed to talk about, he was clearly waiting to start the discussion until they were indoors, with food in front of them. His hands were in his pockets, leaving his elbows available if she chose to hook her hand around one, but she sensed no invitation from him. He hardly even looked at her. In her office doorway, he'd smiled, he'd teased her with double entendres, but here on the street he was all business, his chin jutting forward and his eyes steel hard as they scanned the teeming sidewalks.

At last they arrived at a restaurant he deemed worthy of his business. He gestured her through the door ahead of him, and she found herself surrounded by carved mahogany paneling and the aroma of herbs and butter. Even without reading a menu, she could guess this place was a lot pricier than the café in the alley where the waitresses fawned all over him.

"Isn't this a little ritzy?" Julie whispered as they approached the maître d's station.

"I'm wearing a suit and tie," he whispered back. "And you look…" At last he looked at her, and his eyes softened. "Fine," he finished the thought, although his expression said a lot more than *fine.*

The maître d' was able to seat them without a wait. Their table was covered in heavy linen, a bud vase holding a fresh pink rose in the center. "If we were going to dine at such a swanky place, we could just as easily have eaten at Chez Remy," she murmured. This was the sort of restaurant where speaking above a murmur wouldn't do. "I'm sure the food is no better here." *And the prices are no cheaper,* she added silently.

"We needed to get out of the hotel," he explained before opening his menu.

Julie opened hers, too, and sighed. Everything looked delicious and cost too much. She wished she earned more—

and she surely deserved more than Charlotte paid her. But the hotel couldn't afford raises at the moment, and Julie cared too much about the place and the Marchands to leave in search of a higher-paying job. During her modeling days, even after Glenn Perry had taken his commissions, she'd earned more per hour than she was earning ten years later, with a college education under her belt. But she wouldn't trade that life for the one she had now. Getting paid for what she thought and did was much more rewarding than getting paid for how she looked.

She supposed her budget could stretch to accommodate one of the appetizers. When a waiter in a pleated white shirt and bow tie came to take their order, she requested a salad from the appetizer list, mixed greens topped with crabmeat.

"You need more than that," Mac chided.

She couldn't very well tell him she wasn't hungry, after admitting back at her office that she was. "I think it'll be enough," she said instead.

Mac scrutinized her for a moment, then turned to the waiter and said, "She'll also have the Cajun shrimp. I'll have a bowl of gumbo and the grouper. And we'll share a half bottle of the Zinfandel." He pointed to an item on the wine list, then handed it and his menu to the waiter.

Julie seethed. Sure, she was hungry enough to scarf up everything Mac had ordered for her. But that wasn't the point. "I resent your making decisions for me," she said, her voice taut and her jaw clenched.

"You need to eat, darlin'. I'm paying, so don't worry about the prices."

"How can you afford this restaurant? And your fancy car, and your tailored suits…"

"I've got a little side business robbing banks," he joked, then whipped his napkin free of its elaborate folding and spread it across his lap.

"I'm serious, Mac. I know what the hotel pays you."

"I manage my money well." He smiled cryptically, then leaned back as the waiter arrived with their wine.

Julie ought to refuse on principle to drink any. But after Mac tasted and approved of the wine, the waiter filled a glass for her. The wine looked too tempting, the crystal stemware too pretty. Julie was tired, she was working so hard in the run-up to the party…and damn it, if she'd gone home she would have poured herself a glass of wine there, or accepted Creighton's offer of one of his heady alcoholic concoctions.

She took a sip and tried to convince herself that drinking the wine wasn't a mark of defeat. Lowering her glass, she scrutinized Mac across the table. If he could watch her, she could watch him.

Who was he? Too wealthy to be a hotel security guy—even the head of security. If he'd been telling the truth about his modest beginnings the last time they'd been in a restaurant together, then he hadn't inherited a fortune. She didn't believe he was a bank robber, but…

Success. That was a part of his charisma: he carried himself like a successful man. Not a man who'd won the lottery or married an heiress and taken her to the cleaners in a divorce, but rather someone who'd started with little and created something big. Someone who knew just how talented and capable he was. Someone used to admiration and respect.

He wasn't arrogant—well, not usually. But he exuded confidence. He knew he was hot stuff.

Yet he refused to explain himself. When she questioned him, he became evasive. How could she trust a man who was obviously keeping secrets from her?

"The e-mails you received came from different cities," he said.

So that was what he wanted to talk about. Not the security measures he was taking for the Twelfth Night party. Not the hotel's strained finances. Not the kiss.

To her, that kiss and her memory of it were like a thumbprint smudging her mind's window—she could look past it but couldn't stop seeing it.

She had no idea whether or not Mac had been as strongly affected as she'd been, but that kiss was not what this meal was about. Probably just as well, she decided. What could they say? That it shouldn't have happened? That it would never happen again?

Forget the kiss. They were going to talk about her damn e-mails. Mac had steered her into this restaurant, ordered for her, decreed that she would be his guest, and now dictated the topic for tonight's conversation. He was the boss, in control.

She didn't have to be happy about it, though. "So they came from different cities," she muttered. "What does that mean?"

"It could mean one of several things." He paused as the waiter delivered their appetizers, then ticked off the possibilities on his fingers. "More than one person could be sending them. It could be a coordinated attack on you. Or the person sending them is on the move, traveling from city to city."

"It's not an attack," she retorted, then lowered her voice. "It's minor harassment that turned into a joke."

"No one would fly around the country or solicit friends to do the same thing just for a joke, Julie. I don't know how to get you to recognize how serious this is, but—"

"If someone wanted to attack me, why would he fly around the country sending me e-mails? He could just as easily fly to New Orleans and punch me in the nose."

"Or worse," Mac said grimly.

"It just seems like an awful lot of effort for anyone to go to if they really wanted to get me."

"They may not know where you are. Your e-mail address is with a national ISP. They're stalking you with these e-mails while they try to figure out your physical location."

"Why are you so determined to scare me?" she asked.

Mac's eyes were profoundly dark and steady on her. She wished she could read them, wished she knew what he was really thinking and feeling. "I don't want to scare you, *chère.* But I think you're in danger, and you keep blowing it off like it's a game."

"I'm not blowing it off. I don't like getting these e-mails. But I'm not going to stop living my life because of them. And I'm definitely not going to run to some big strong guy and beg him to protect me."

"Am I supposed to be the big strong guy you're not going to run to?" Mac asked, the slightest hint of a smile on his mouth.

"I don't know what you're supposed to be," she said wearily. "But you're a pest and a nag."

"A pest and a nag." His smile widened as if she'd given him a compliment.

"I don't need protection, Mac." She struggled to keep her tone muted. "And I don't like being patronized."

Her bitter words didn't seem to trouble him. He tilted his head and studied her for a long moment before lifting his glass to his lips. After drinking a bit, he smiled tentatively. "Is that a general statement, or am I—" he groped for the right words "—stirring up something from your past?"

She opened her mouth and then closed it. She wasn't used to men being so perceptive—even men who'd studied psychology in college, as Mac told her he had. She ought to have come to terms with the fact that he simply wasn't like most men.

She didn't trust him…but maybe if he understood the source of her resentment, he'd back off a little. "The man I used to work for when I was a model was very protective of his girls, but all that protectiveness was actually his way of exerting control over them."

"You think I'm trying to control you?"

"Yes." The answer seemed so obvious she saw no need to elaborate. Instead she dug into her salad. Overpriced, perhaps, but delicious.

"Isn't it just possible that I'm trying to keep you out of harm's way?"

"Oh, I'm sure you've got lots of noble rationalizations," she said, softening the words with a hesitant smile. "Glenn did, too. He was our agent. He had to protect and control us because without him we wouldn't be able to work. And some of the girls in the agency were so vulnerable, they had no defenses against him."

"What did they have to defend against?" Mac stirred his gumbo, then consumed a spoonful. "As their agent, didn't he have their best interests at heart?"

"He had only one interest—his own. These young girls would come from all over the country, so eager to be high-fashion models. Maybe they'd won a local beauty pageant, or maybe, like me, someone they knew thought they had what it took and suggested they give the business a try. So they flocked to New York, sixteen and seventeen years old, some of them dropping out of high school. Of course they needed someone to protect them. And there was this big, strong, wonderful man, Glenn Perry, who promised to take care of them and turn them into models."

"If they were that young, they probably needed his guidance," Mac suggested.

"Guidance, sure. They didn't need his exploitation." She lowered her fork and sighed. Much as she hated to remember those awful days, they weren't exactly a secret. If Mac truly wanted to know, he could comb through the newspaper archives and find out what had happened ten years ago in New York. She might as well spare him the effort and tell him. "Some of the girls had trouble keeping their weight down. It's hard, let me tell you. But it's not as hard if you use amphetamines."

"Ah." Mac ate some more of his soup and nodded. "So this agent—Glenn, was it? He supplied them with drugs?"

"For their own good, of course," she said sarcastically. "So they could keep their weight down. Those drugs can be addictive. Cocaine helps you lose weight, too, so he made sure the girls had plenty of that."

"This guy was bad news, huh."

"He arranged for their housing. He arranged for their bookings. He managed their money—and he deducted the cost of their drugs along with their housing expenses and his commissions. He coached them. He molded them. He was kind of a Svengali—which I suppose isn't against the law. Giving them drugs *was* against the law." She shuddered. "He was sleeping with a couple of them, too."

"If they were over sixteen, that's not against the law," Mac pointed out.

"No, but it's not right. They were so dependent on him for everything. He was like some kind of god to them, and they worshipped him. Of course, once a few of them got addicted to drugs, they depended on him even more. He took care of them, all right," she concluded bitterly.

His bowl empty, Mac set down his spoon. He rotated his wineglass slowly, his thumb and forefinger maneuvering the stem, but his gaze remained unwavering on Julie. "So how did you avoid his evil clutches? You were working for him, too."

"I was living at home," she reminded Mac. "And finishing high school."

He smiled. "Plus, you were probably a hell of a lot smarter than the other girls. Tougher. Braver."

He listed these attributes calmly, as if simply stating the truth rather than deliberately buttering her up. She was more flattered than she should have been—especially since he was overstating her strengths. Ten years ago, when she'd taken Glenn on, she'd been less tough and brave than simply stubborn. She'd gone into modeling not for the glamour, not to fulfill a lifelong fantasy, but to prove a point with her tormenters. No dream rode on whether she won a contract with Symphony Perfumes. Seeing Glenn for what he was, and then calling him on it, hadn't taken all that much courage on her part.

Neither she nor Mac spoke while the waiter cleared away their dishes, then brought their entrees. Mac's bluntly expressed praise hung unchallenged in the air between them. Julie scrambled for another subject—Glenn Perry was definitely not someone she liked to talk about—but as soon as the waiter departed, Mac bore down on her. "So what did you do about the bastard? Did you sit quietly by and let him take advantage of all those foolish young girls?"

Though she couldn't guess why, she had the clear impression that Mac already knew the answer. She wasn't sure how he could know, but the way he phrased the question implied that he didn't for a minute believe she'd done nothing.

"I confronted Glenn," she said. "I told him the power games he was playing with the girls was wrong, and the drug stuff was really wrong. And I thought he was unethical and immoral and not fit to be working with teenage girls."

"And he…what? Told you to take a hike?"

She nodded and tasted her shrimp. It was spicier than she'd expected, and a film of sweat sprouted on her upper lip. It was also scrumptious. As long as she washed each bite down with a gulp of ice water, she'd be fine.

"Did you take a hike?" Mac asked.

He knew she hadn't. She could tell by the glint in his eyes and by his smile, which was a bit playful but also approving, warm with pride. "I reported him to the police. The drugs were criminal. And I also didn't trust his bookkeeping. I thought they might get him on larceny charges."

"You were how old? Eighteen? Nineteen?"

"Almost twenty when I reported him. Twenty-one when I testified against him in court. The wheels of justice turn slowly. But he was convicted and sent to prison."

"Is he still there?"

She sorted her thoughts. If she told Mac her sister Marcie had informed her of Glenn's recent release from prison, he'd probably link the e-mails to Glenn. She'd entertained the possibility herself, so she couldn't blame him if he reached that conclusion. But if, as he'd claimed, the e-mails hadn't come from New York City, Glenn couldn't have sent them. The terms of his parole prevented him from leaving the city.

"He was released in December," she told Mac.

"And you hate the way I worry about you because I remind you of him?" Mac was still smiling, but he sounded affronted. "You think that when I tell you to take those threatening e-mails seriously, I'm acting like some son of a bitch who supplied young models with drugs and coerced them into having sex? Is that what you think of me?"

"Of course not," she said quickly, then hesitated. It wasn't that she equated Mac's behavior with Glenn's. It was just… "I don't do well with overprotective men, that's all."

"What makes you think I'm *over*protective? Maybe I'm just the right amount protective."

She shrugged and took another drink of water. "I trusted Glenn until I saw how easily he deceived the girls who trusted him. I don't trust so easily anymore. And when someone tries to manage my life for me, I don't like it."

"Fair enough," he said, cutting a bite-size chunk of fish. "I'm not going to lay off, Julie. I'll protect you with my life if necessary, and I don't give a damn if that pisses you off. Having you angry with me isn't the worst thing in the world."

She settled back in her chair, trying again to make sense of him. That he would willfully ignore her feelings annoyed her, but hearing him swear that he'd protect her with his life was…*romantic*. No man, with the possible exception of her father when she was a child, had ever said such a thing to her. She hated it—but she loved it, too.

They ate in silence for a minute, Julie taking the time to absorb Mac's words and her own reaction to them. Somehow, his claim that he didn't care if she was pissed off made her a little less pissed off. If Mac was overprotective, it wasn't because he wanted to take advantage of her the way

Glenn had taken advantage of his protégés back in New York. That morning's kiss didn't count as taking advantage. Before she'd come to her senses, she had given as good as she got.

"How do you know the e-mails are coming from different cities?" she finally asked.

"I've got a friend who's a genius when it comes to technology. I asked her to trace them and she did the best she could. Apparently they were sent from WiFi connections at a few airports around the country."

Despite the importance of the information he was providing, Julie's mind snagged on that one pronoun: *her*. For some stupid reason, she experienced a pang of jealousy. Why shouldn't Mac have a brilliant female friend? Or a dozen brilliant female friends?

"I hope this friend of yours is discreet," she said. "I'd prefer not to have half the city aware that I'm getting nasty spam."

"Does Charlotte know?"

She shook her head. "Charlotte has enough on her plate. My job is to reduce her worries, not add to them." She used her napkin to dab her upper lip and inhaled deeply, her sinuses scorched from all the spicy shrimp she'd eaten. "Is this the same genius friend who got you thinking the hotel is for sale?"

"No, that's a different genius friend. I like to surround myself with geniuses," he explained with a laugh. "I keep hoping some of their smarts will rub off on me."

Mac was clearly well endowed with brain power. He had money, smarts, brilliant friends, and a face and body that could land him a job with any modeling agency in the country. So why was he working as a hotel security guard?

"You said you'd ask Charlotte about having an investigative firm try to track down that missing money," he reminded her, evidently done with the subject of her e-mails and her alleged bravery. "Have you talked to her?"

"Mac." She laughed and shook her head. "When would I have had time to discuss that with her? We're hosting a huge party tomorrow. We're still getting reservations—Luc has all the names. I assume he passed them along to you. We've got to deal with the final decorations, the food and beverages and, yes, the hotel security. Money that went missing four years ago is not our top priority at the moment."

Mac scowled. "Luc hasn't forwarded the new reservations to me."

His gaze collided with hers, and again she struggled to decipher his thoughts. "Luc's been busy, too."

"Everyone's busy. That's no excuse not to do your job."

"I'm sure if you ask, he'll give you the names. It probably just slipped his mind."

"I'll take care of it tonight."

"I'm sorry you have to work such long days," she said, meaning it. "Hotel jobs are like that sometimes—not exactly nine-to-five. Especially with a big event like the Twelfth Night party coming up."

"Security work is rarely nine-to-five, anyway," he said, setting down his silverware. The waiter approached, and Mac turned to him. "Can we see a dessert menu?"

"No," Julie cut him off. "Not for me, anyway."

He eyed her, then shrugged. "All right," he said to the waiter. "Just the check, please." The waiter cleared their dishes and vanished.

"Sometimes I think you're trying to fatten me up," she accused.

"It would take a lot of desserts to do that, Julie. You're as slim as a willow branch. Besides..." His smile took on a mischievous glint. "I like watching you eat. What are the chances you'll get the baby in the cake tomorrow night?"

She smiled. Before moving to New Orleans, she'd never heard of the Twelfth Night tradition of the King Cake, which tasted like a glorified cinnamon roll to Julie. The King Cake was frosted in green and gold icing and a tiny baby doll was hidden inside. Whoever received the wedge of cake with the baby in it was responsible for baking the following year's King Cake. Not that the hotel would force any of the guests to bake next year's cake, but they'd make a fuss over whoever received the piece with the baby in it.

"I won't get the baby because I won't be having any cake," she told him. "The food is for the paying guests, not me."

"If you go, you won't be working, will you? You'll be just another guest."

"I won't be working, but I won't be a guest." She looked at him pointedly. "You won't have to work tomorrow night, either. The night security staff will have things covered."

"I expect they will." He paused, then added, "But security is like police work. Even when you're off duty, you're still a cop. If I'm there, I'll be backing up my guys." He grinned again. "I'll be dressed to kill, though."

"I can't wait to see—" Julie let the words slip out, then pressed her lips shut. She shouldn't want to see Mac dressed to kill. He'd be far too handsome.

Once he'd settled the bill, they left the restaurant. If anything, the sidewalks were more clogged with pedestrians than before. A blues singer's gravelly voice, accompanied by a wailing guitar, spilled from the open doorway of a tavern, and Julie wished she could linger for a moment to listen to the plaintive song. But tomorrow promised to be a long day and a longer night—and Mac still had to return to the hotel to review the recent additions to the guest list before he could call it quits for the day. Lingering was out of the question.

"I'll walk you to your car," he offered, bypassing the hotel's welcoming front doors and broad, arched windows. Around the corner, he headed down the block to the parking lot where employees left their cars. The side street was darker and quieter, and he took Julie's hand so casually the contact seemed almost natural. His hand was much larger than hers, the skin smooth and warm. She didn't want to have to hold a man's hand to feel safe…but she *did* feel safe with Mac's fingers woven through hers.

He knew her car, having followed her home a few times, and when they reached the lot he led her directly to it. He released her hand so she could dig through her purse for her key, but once she'd unlocked the door he took her hand again and turned her to face him.

"Julie," he murmured, gazing down at her.

She wasn't accustomed to men being taller than her. Mac's height made her feel a little less safe now. So did the pressure of his hand around hers.

"About this morning," he said, then sighed. "You were right," he conceded. "You said it was a bad idea, and you were right."

Never had being told she was right hurt so much. He wasn't going to kiss her again. She should to be relieved, but all she felt was disappointment.

If he wasn't going to kiss her, he ought to release her hand. He especially ought to stop sliding his thumb back and forth over her inner wrist. He ought to let go and return to the hotel and do his job, and never look at her the way he was looking at her right now, the night's shadows etching his face, his gaze as soft as a caress.

After a long moment, he did let go. She all but dove into her car. The lot was small and crowded enough that she couldn't floor the gas and peel out, which was just as well. She didn't want to have to test her squeaky brakes with hard driving. More important, she didn't want Mac to know how frustrated she was, and how disappointed that what had happened that morning in her office for a few dazzling, dizzying minutes would never happen again.

As if roaring out of the parking lot would make any difference. Mac knew just how disappointed she was, just how much she would have welcomed another kiss from him, even though it was a bad idea.

Somehow, he seemed to know everything.

GOD, IT WAS HOT HERE. If she lived to be a hundred, she'd never get used to this kind of muggy weather just days into the new year. But muggy weather was what she needed right now. The heat had helped to turn her into Maggie.

Maggie, she thought with a sniff. She was Maggie now: the kind of girl who put on a skimpy little dress and high-heel sandals and stood across the street from a famous French Quarter hotel, angling for a way to get inside. As soon as she'd seen that bozo with the bald spot and the ponytail, everything had fallen into place.

I hope you're scared, Julie. I hope you're trembling in your size-nine shoes, because tomorrow night is showtime.

Julie should be scared. The other e-mails had been sent by now. They were meaner, blunter and, yeah, scarier.

A long time ago, before she'd become Maggie, she'd had a dream: she would be a model. She'd live a fabulous life in the heart of the fashion world. She'd earn tons of money and party every night, and men would fall in love with her. And she'd fall in love, too.

It had all come true, every part of her dream. Glenn had loved her. He'd sworn it. It didn't matter that he slept with a couple of his other girls. He told her they were nothing to him. She was everything. He'd gotten her good speed, good blow. He'd gotten her good jobs. He'd given her promises.

And then, thank-you-very-much-Julie, he'd gone to jail—and come out a changed man. No longer dazzling. No longer rich and fun and loving. When she'd tracked him down to the dreary little apartment he now called home, a world away from his cool thirtieth-floor condo overlooking the East River, he'd stared at her as if she were a total stranger, not the girl he'd once sworn that he loved.

"If there was ever anything between us," he'd said, his voice dull and lifeless, "it's dead, honey. Go away. Go home and get a life."

How could she make a life for herself when everything she'd wanted, everything she'd once had, was gone?

All because of Julie.

She lit a cigarette and stood smoking in the shadow of an awning. Across the street the Hotel Marchand stood like something out of a painting, a tourist poster of New Orleans. People inside there had lives. They probably had access to all the stimulants they could ever want, and liquor and money and fine clothes. They probably had lovers, too.

They had everything she didn't have, because Julie Sullivan had sent Glenn to prison.

Tomorrow night, she promised herself. Tomorrow night she'd go inside on the arm of that starry-eyed asshole with the ponytail. Tomorrow night she'd find Julie.

Tomorrow night she'd get a life: Julie's.

CHAPTER TEN

LUC WAS GONE for the day.

Mac should have expected as much. It was eight-thirty, and most of the hotel's day staff had left. Still, he'd hoped to get his hands on that guest list.

Patrick, the assistant concierge, didn't know what Luc had done with the list. "He probably locked it up somewhere safe," Patrick said, as if he expected Mac to be impressed that Luc had taken such precautions.

He wasn't. He didn't want the list locked up somewhere safe. He wanted it in his hands, now.

The housekeeping supply room was empty when Mac checked it on the slim chance that Luc might be there with his girlfriend. No tryst was taking place, but Mac took a few minutes to inspect the shelves. Everything seemed to be in pristine order, the way Nadine liked to keep her supplies. The towels were evenly folded and stacked. If anything had been tampered with, Mac couldn't spot it.

Hell. His impatience wasn't just over the list and the fact that, given everything else he'd have to do tomorrow, reviewing the new reservations might prove to be one task too many. Even if he'd found the list, even if Luc had hand delivered it to him right that instant, Mac would be in a foul mood.

He'd done the right thing by assuring Julie he wouldn't kiss her again, but… *Hell, hell, hell.* A fire was burning in his gut, in his soul, and the only thing that would quench it was Julie.

And it wasn't going to get quenched, not as long as he was being paid to protect her.

After shouting a quick greeting to Tyrell, Mac headed out the door. The night air did nothing to cool him off, and in fact his body temperature rose significantly when he entered the parking lot where he'd last seen Julie. He could still feel the imprint of her slender hand in his, the silky smoothness of her wrist. He could see her huge eyes, their unusual color not quite visible in the evening gloom, and the delicate shape of her lips, and the slim, graceful curves of her body, a body he longed to touch and taste and love.

He slumped into the driver's seat of his car, pulled out his BlackBerry and checked his e-mail. He found in his in-box a note from Julie's sister Marcie saying she was renewing her contract with him for another month, and a message from Frank promising "interesting stuff" and containing an attachment. Mac wasn't going to read it on the tiny screen of his BlackBerry.

He'd access the attachment when he got home. No stop at the office tonight, he thought, as he headed out of the lot. Tomorrow would be too long a day; tonight he deserved to refresh his memory of what his apartment looked like. It seemed as if he hadn't spent more than a few minutes a day there, other than to sleep, since he'd been forced to juggle two jobs.

His apartment was nothing special—roomy and airy, but decorating wasn't his forte. He still felt strange having four rooms to himself. Growing up, he'd had to share his bedroom with two brothers and a single bathroom with the entire family—five kids, his parents and his widowed grandmama. His brothers and sisters were doing well, one sister now a teacher and the other a nurse, one brother in the Air Force and the other making good wages on an oil rig that was once again up and running in the gulf. They all sent money home, and his parents could afford to expand their house, even add a second bathroom. But now that all the kids were grown and gone, they saw no need.

Once he reached his apartment, Mac wandered through the spacious rooms thinking that for all the square footage it really wasn't much of a home. The place needed some art on the walls, some knickknacks on the tables, touches of warmth. It needed a bigger-screen TV—if Mac was ever around to watch it—and maybe a pool table.

It needed a woman.

He was walloped by a mental image of Julie in this apartment, turning it into a home. The hell with a wide-screen TV and a pool table. If she lived here, he'd rather watch her than any show, and he'd rather play with her than play pool.

Cursing under his breath, he entered the kitchen, yanked open the cabinet where he kept his stash of booze and filled a glass with bourbon. He carried his drink to the small study, turned on his computer and sipped the smoky whiskey while the machine warmed up. Finally it had completed its virus checks and scans and he could open his e-mail.

He found Frank's message, clicked on the attachment and settled back in his chair.

We've been busy. Today's notes:

1. According to his parole officer, Perry is still in New York.

2. Remy Marchand's accident four years ago was really an accident. Lousy weather conditions that night, and the other driver was drunk. Some digging into the records indicates that Marchand wired the missing money to a bank in the Cayman Islands. No other name attached to the transaction.

3. Julie's picture appeared last summer in the *Times-Picayune*. The newspaper ran a story on the antebellum antiques the hotel has on display and how well they came through the hurricane. Julie's name appears, along with a bunch of Marchands, and

she's definitely recognizable in the picture. A person could identify her and locate her in New Orleans.

4. Sandy's wearing me out, but I'm having fun.

Mac suffered a totally unjustified pang of jealousy. He didn't want to be making a baby, but he wanted a woman to wear him out. Not just any woman—Julie.

Ignoring the fourth item on Frank's list, he reread the first three. Perry was in New York, so while he might have orchestrated Julie's e-mails, he wasn't sending them. Mac almost wished Perry *was* flying around the country, heading to New Orleans, just so Mac could meet the SOB and pulverize his face with a few well-placed punches. He tried to picture a teenage Julie, thin and insecure, yet strong enough to confront the man who'd made her a successful model, to report him, to testify against him. The woman had balls. Well, no, she didn't, but…thinking about how brave she was only made him desire her more.

Number two on the list was interesting but not immediately relevant to Julie's safety. When people wired money to the Caymans, they did so to hide the transaction. Maybe Remy was laundering hotel profits, or trying to shelter them from tax liabilities. Maybe he'd taken a high-risk loan from a shady operator who didn't want Uncle Sam to know about his operations. Mac would love to know who was on the receiving end of that money transfer, but obviously Frank hadn't figured that out yet.

Number three was the biggie, though. The bad news. Mac took a slug of bourbon and reread what Frank had written. Then he opened another window on his computer and called up the *Times-Picayune*'s archives. He typed in his password and did a search for Julie's name.

Damn it to hell. Anyone who'd seen a Symphony Perfumes ad would recognize Julie in that picture, even though she was nearly a decade older. If her cyberstalker had found this photo, he'd found Julie.

Mac sat back in his chair, took another long sip of bourbon and felt its heat spread down his throat and seep through his chest. Fortunately, the liquor clarified his thoughts instead of blurring them, and he sorted through them now. The pieces of this puzzle weren't fitting together.

Julie's sister had hired Mac because Julie's old boss was being released from prison. He'd been the one Marcie was worried about. But he was sitting pretty back in New York.

Yet someone was after Julie. Mac knew it. The e-mails were too personal to be random harassment. And the fact that the sender was moving around the country—from New York City westward, closing in on New Orleans—persuaded him that Julie was at risk. Perry might not be the one coming for her, but *someone* was. Could Perry be directing the situation from the comfort of his parole-imposed New York address?

Julie had said he was a Svengali. Mac wished he'd taken more literature courses, but he recalled that the character Svengali had hypnotized a young protégé and then controlled her career. Could Perry be controlling whoever was flying around the country, sending Julie e-mails via airport WiFi?

Dallas was too damn close to New Orleans.

He sucked in a deep breath. *Get through the party,* he ordered himself, *and then you'll find this creep and squash him like a June bug.* Whoever the guy was, Mac would find him. No question, no doubt. Anyone who threatened Julie Sullivan was going to wind up in Mac's crosshairs, and Mac would be smiling when he pulled the trigger.

"YOU LOOK FABULOUS!" Creighton gushed.

Julie wasn't so sure about that. She didn't *feel* fabulous. She'd gotten to work early that morning, aware of how much had to be done in the final hours before the party, and now she was wiped out rather than ready to cut loose. On top of her usual tasks, she'd helped Anne array the flowers around the event rooms. She'd overseen the maintenance staff's preparation of the courtyard; the party mob was bound to overflow through the French doors when the dance floor became too crowded or the band too loud. The pool had to be locked down to avoid having drunken revelers accidentally tumble into the water, and more floating candles had to be arranged on the tables scattered about the courtyard. In the middle of the afternoon, the band's manager threw a hissy-fit about the event room's acoustics, as if he'd expected an old hotel to resonate like Carnegie Hall. And in the kitchen Robert had freaked out over the delivery of what he considered inferior quality portobello mushrooms.

And then there was Mac.

His existence alone would have been more than enough distraction to Julie. Last night she'd conferred at length with her tropical fish, who'd offered no advice on the subject. What could they have told her, anyway? *The man isn't going to pursue anything with you. Get over it.*

It would be easier for a Tetra to say that than for her to get over Mac. As if there was anything to get over. He'd kissed her once. Big deal.

Very big deal. More than just a kiss had burned between them. Lying restless in her bed through the night, she'd been haunted not only by the memory of his mouth on hers but by his low, sexy drawl, his sly smile, his piercing gaze and that distinctive scent.

So she hadn't slept well last night, and she'd been in perpetual motion all day. The last thing she wanted to do was spend the evening mingling with the party guests and making sure everything from the champagne to the conversation flowed smoothly, while simultaneously avoiding Mac because he'd said he would be there, and if she saw him she'd plunge back into all those troubling memories of what a bad idea kissing him had been.

But Charlotte wanted her at the party, and she couldn't say no to Charlotte. So now she stood in Creighton's colorful living room, clad in a black sheath with a daring neckline and a skirt that fell in uneven petals just past her knees. She'd found the dress last October on a half-price rack at a boutique not far from the hotel—apparently size-six-tall dresses didn't sell well, and she was often able to find bargains. The price was so reasonable she'd snatched the dress up, figuring that sooner or later she'd find a reason to wear it.

Unfortunately, the shaggy hemline didn't work with low-heeled shoes, so she'd stuffed her tired feet into her black dress sandals with three-inch heels. The added height caused her to tower over Creighton, but if he had any ego problems, they didn't relate to his height. He eyed her up and down, giving her subtle makeup an approving nod and then beaming at her hair, which she'd pinned up haphazardly, preferring to have it off her neck while she was trapped in warm, crowded rooms.

"Absolutely spectacular," he murmured.

"You're the one who looks spectacular," Julie responded. Clad in a cream-colored jacket, a red silk vest, pinstriped black trousers and a black bolo tie fastened with a large garnet stone, he appeared brash and dramatic and very, very Creighton. "Stanley is going to fall madly in love with you."

"Been there, done that," Creighton said with a wave of his hand. "We're just friends, I swear." He circled Julie slowly, shaking his head in amazement. "That hem is fantastic. What it does to your legs should be declared illegal. Fortunately—" he'd completed his orbit and was once again facing her "—I'm immune. My only concern is that it's all a little black."

"Black is fashionable," Julie told him.

"For funerals, maybe. And in New York. I know that's what everyone wears there. Wait here." He held up a finger, then dashed off to his bedroom. When he returned, he was carrying a pink feather boa.

"Should I ask where you got that?" Julie inquired, wary yet amused.

"No, you shouldn't." He draped the feather rope around her neck and stepped back. *"Perfectamente."*

Ordinarily, Julie was not the pink-feather-boa type. But the flash of color and the sheer silliness of the accessory boosted her spirits.

Creighton clapped his hands, clearly exuberant about his success. "Now, are you sure you don't want to go to the party with Stanley and me?"

"You've got a two-seater sports car," Julie reminded him. "Where would I sit—in the nonexistent trunk?" She smiled and shook her head. "I'd rather have my own wheels, in case I decide to leave early."

"Oh, you mustn't leave early," Creighton clucked. "Promise me you'll stay at least until everyone has had a chance to ogle you."

"Everyone will ogle me the instant I walk in. They'll all think I'm a forward for the Hornets, dressed in drag."

"They'll all think you're the prettiest thing they've ever laid eyes on. I know about drag, honey, and you'd never pass." He glanced at his watch and adjusted his blazer. "I've got to go pick up Stanley. I'll see you at the hotel."

Julie preceded him out of his apartment, then continued across the hall into her own. She strode to her bedroom to check the effect of the pink boa in the mirror above her dresser and decided it worked surprisingly well, its texture mimicking the feathery shape of her hair. She freshened her lipstick, tucked the tube into her purse, then returned to the living room to shake some food flakes into the aquarium. "Behave yourselves, guys," she said to the silent, fluttering fish. "I don't care what Creighton says—I won't be out too late tonight." Busily consuming the flakes, they ignored her.

She'd learned how to walk gracefully in stiletto heels during her modeling career, and although she rarely wore such high heels now, her feet and ankles remembered how to balance her weight so she wouldn't teeter. By the time she reached the bottom of the stairs, she was confident and energized and actually looking forward to the party. Everything would go smoothly. Robert's portobello hors d'oeuvres would be delectable. The guests would have a blast. Mac would see her and decide that kissing her hadn't been such a bad idea, after all. And she'd drink just enough wine to agree with him.

This would be a splendid night, she thought, stepping out into the balmy evening and heading for her car.

THIS WOULD BE A GHASTLY NIGHT, Mac thought as he surveyed the crowds swarming through the hotel's lobby. Tyrell had assured him that the night security guys had everything under control, but Mac didn't believe it. Not because he doubted the abilities of his staff, but because he knew that in a mob scene like this one, nothing was ever completely under control.

He'd spent an exhausting day checking, double-checking and triple-checking every detail. Luc Carter had shrugged when Mac had demanded an updated reservation list. "I don't see why you need that," he'd balked. "These folks are paying to come. That's all that matters."

"It's not all that matters," Mac had argued, annoyed that anyone—let alone a charming slacker like Luc—should question his security decisions. "I need those lists."

"Well, they're here somewhere." Luc had rummaged through the papers on his desk and in his drawer. "Maybe I took them home with me last night…" Mac had been within seconds of throttling Luc when he'd finally produced the list.

Reviewing the names with Julie would have been easier than vetting them on his own, but he hadn't risked it. Seeing her would have tempted him too much, and as long as he was in her sister's employ, he had to act ethically. Integrity sucked, but Mac was unfortunately endowed with his share of it.

Unable to identify a few of the names, he'd asked Carlos to help him. "These are dates," Carlos had deduced. "They're all women. See this one, Maggie No-Last-Name? She's coming as the date of that head case in 307. You know who I mean? The guy with the ponytail who's always complaining."

"Alvin Grote," Mac muttered.

"Right. These other ladies, I'm guessing it's the same thing. Businessmen come down to the Big Easy and meet some of our fine women. It happens all the time. Ladies of the night, most of them. They don't pose any threat."

As he circulated through the crowded lobby that evening, Mac decided Carlos was right. None of the guests looked dangerous. Some were dressed formally, the women in gowns and the men in tuxedos, and some wore flamboyant costumes, but Mac detected no mysterious lumps or bulges in their apparel or their purses. He would have liked to set up a security checkpoint and run a wand up and down each arrival, but Charlotte would never have stood for that. She'd have told him the hotel was having a party, and its guests were not to be treated like prospective criminals.

Mac wasn't dressed as formally as the most elegant guests, partly because he didn't own a tux and partly because he wanted to stay loose and comfortable. He'd donned a slate-gray suit, a black shirt and a black silk tie. If he looked a little like a shadow, so much the better.

Music drifted down the hall from the event rooms. He detoured through the restaurant and the kitchen, taking the long route around the courtyard. "Everything okay here?" he asked one of the assistant chefs.

"Crazy but fine," the kid responded without looking up from a cutting board, on which he was chopping something green and mint scented. "If you need a cup of coffee, you'll have to get it yourself."

"No coffee. I just wanted to make sure everything was copasetic." Mac patted the walkie-talkie hooked on his belt. "You need anything, just buzz me."

He continued on through the bar, which was doing a bustling business despite the fact that a portable bar had been set up in one of the event rooms. Mac caught Leo's eye. The bartender tipped an imaginary hat at Mac, then busied himself fixing what looked from across the room like one of those sissified flavored martinis that were so popular these days.

From the bar, Mac entered the courtyard. The night was dry and mild, the sky speckled with stars, the wrought-iron fence surrounding the pool locked. Through the open French doors lining the hall to the event rooms he heard the happy chatter of hundreds of voices all yakking at once, as well as the rhythmic lilt of the band playing a vaguely familiar tune with a Dixieland flavor.

Mac wished he could relax and enjoy himself. This party contained all the right ingredients: lots of people, good music, booze, food and a classy old hotel in the heart of the French Quarter. But he remained edgy, hypervigilant.

He crossed the courtyard, entered the hallway and took another detour to make sure the gallery was locked up for the night. He hated having so many strangers wandering around the building with that damn Andrew Wyeth painting on display. God help them all if anything happened to that painting.

But the gallery was secure, the alarms set and the door locked and bolted.

Satisfied that the Wyeth was as safe as possible, he followed the flow of revelers toward the event rooms. Chatter and clouds of perfume surrounded him. He wondered if any of the guests was wearing a scent by Symphony Perfumes. He had no idea what the stuff actually smelled like.

The first event room was almost unrecognizable. He slipped inside the doorway and gaped at the gently draped fabrics, the strings of silver and gold Mardi Gras beads looped over light fixtures and dangling in glittering parabolas from the ceiling. Banks of flowers adorned windowsills and tables, and stubby white candles floated in the water-filled glass bowls on every horizontal surface. The tiny flames bobbed on the water and were reflected in the shiny beads above them. The effect was mesmerizing.

But Mac lost all awareness of the decorations the instant he spotted Julie. And the instant he did, he realized that she, not any concerns about safety, was the cause of his tension. She stood taller than the cluster of people with whom she was deep in conversation, and Mac acknowledged one of the many things he found most attractive about her: despite her height, she stood straight. Some tall women hunched over, shrank themselves, tried to downplay their statuesque dimensions. Not Julie. She had the posture of a drill sergeant. Not that any drill sergeant in the history of the United States Armed Forces could possibly look as ravishing as she did.

He hovered just inside the doorway, appraising her from a distance. Her hair was piled onto her head in a style that looked haphazard but probably wasn't. Wavy strands drizzled down to frame her face and tickle her long, slender neck. The sight of her exposed nape caused something to pull tight in Mac's groin. He wanted to nibble on that pale, vulnerable skin.

Hell, he wanted to devour her.

Moving his gaze downward, he let out a laugh. She had on a stylishly simple black dress—nice low neckline, though her breasts were too small to offer up anything resembling cleavage—but she'd draped a pink feather boa around her elegant shoulders. The boa was at once hilariously goofy and shockingly pretty.

Mac found himself besieged by visions of Julie wearing the pink boa and nothing else. He experienced another sharp pang of arousal and stifled a moan. Was every other man in the room fantasizing about her, or was he the only one suffering from hormone overload?

The men in the group surrounding her seemed to be functioning well enough, exchanging banter with her, laughing at something someone said. One couple was a bit older, the man's bald head so shiny it looked as if someone had waxed and polished it. The woman with him was dressed in an odd beaded dress that resembled something the flappers used to wear in the Roaring Twenties. Julie's effusive white-haired neighbor stood with her, his bright-red vest lending his face an unexpected ruddiness, and at his side stood a tall, thin, blond man with a wispy goatee and a glittering diamond stud adorning one ear. A younger couple clad in what appeared to be recycled wedding clothes—a prissy tux for him, a long white dress for her—and two unattached women completed the grouping. Julie stood with them like a lily surrounded by dandelions, cool and beautiful.

He should keep his distance—but he couldn't. Not with the back of her neck beckoning him. He recalled learning in college that the Japanese considered a woman's nape one of the most sexual parts of her anatomy. They sure had that one right.

Sighing with resignation, longing and despair at his own lack of willpower, he inched his way through the crowd. He spotted Charlotte Marchand at the bar, conferring with one of the bartenders, and Luc Carter circulating as if he were the party's actual host. He recognized quite a few of the hotel guests from his regular strolls or from the monitor in the security office.

But there was only one face he cared about tonight. As he drew nearer, he realized Julie was standing taller than usual. Nearer yet, he could see why—she had on the sexiest spike-heel sandals he'd ever seen. Had he admired her insteps before? Had he paid attention to how narrow her ankles were? He tortured himself with a revised fantasy vision of her in nothing but the boa and the shoes.

Julie's neighbor spotted Mac before Julie did, and beamed him a grin. "Oh, Julie, look who's here," he said excitedly, waving Mac over. "Looking devilishly handsome, too."

Compared to the neighbor in his blaring red vest, Mac thought he looked pretty drab. But he joined the group, smiling and nodding as they widened their circle to include him. When his eyes met Julie's, his smile felt a little forced. He didn't want to smile at her. He wanted to ravish her.

Her smile looked as artificial as his felt. "Mac," she said, holding his gaze for a fraction of a second too long before she turned back to the others. "This is Mac Jensen, the hotel's head of security." Then she introduced the others—some New Orleans old-timers, her neighbor Creighton and his friend Stanley.

"Head of security?" the woman in the flapper dress drawled, batting her eyes coquettishly. "Are we in danger?"

Mac opted not to tell her the Wyeth painting was at greater risk than she was. "I'm off duty right now," he said instead. "Just enjoying the party."

"Then go and enjoy it," Creighton insisted, motioning with his head toward the other event room, where the band was playing a tune that sounded familiar but had been so elaborately arranged Mac couldn't quite identify it. "You and Julie are off the clock now. Go take her for a spin around the floor."

"Creighton," Julie murmured, a halfhearted protest.

Mac should have protested, too. But the thought of wrapping his arms around her, feeling her body against his, dancing cheek to cheek—something they could actually do since her shoes brought her up to his height—was too tempting. With a polite nod to the others, he touched his hand to the small of her back and guided her through the crowd to the adjacent room.

"Is this a good idea?" she asked as he deftly steered her past the loiterers in the doorway and toward the center of the room.

"Dancing isn't kissing," he replied, turning her to face him and gathering her right hand in his left. "You're not going to break your ankle in those shoes, are you?"

"Not if you don't fling me around."

As soon as they began to move, he acknowledged that this

was as bad an idea as kissing her had been—and some bad ideas were wonderful. He was hardly a terrific dancer, but he had a feel for the music. And tonight he had a feel for his partner. She fit so perfectly in his arms. Her legs moved with his. Her eyes met his. She smelled like gardenias.

"Is everything all right?" she asked.

It took him a minute to realize she was asking about the hotel's security, not his current state of mind. Holding Julie was better than all right. Being so close to her he could count her eyelashes, knowing the shadowed hollow between her breasts was barely an inch from his shirt's front buttons, feeling the delicate ridge of her spine through her dress… *"all right"* barely scratched the surface.

She was awaiting an answer, though—and that answer couldn't be about the graceful contours of her back against his palm, or the alluring loops and curls of her hair. "The gallery looks secure, and no one here is sending off trouble-maker vibes," he said. "Tyrell knows what he's doing, and the staff is on its toes. So, yeah, everything's all right."

She eyed him speculatively. Maybe she knew the reply he'd given wasn't the first one that occurred to him. Maybe she'd been expecting that first one. "How about you?" he asked, testing her. "You okay?"

"I'm not used to wearing heels this high," she muttered. "I hope I survive."

"You look spectacular." The hell with discretion. A feather from her boa was tickling the back of his hand, and he slid it upward, under the boa to the neckline of her dress. To the nape of her neck.

She took a deep breath and let it out slowly. "Thank you," she said in a slightly shaky voice.

"The feathers are a nice touch." Maybe he shouldn't have used the word *touch.* Simply hearing the word emerge from his mouth gave him too many ideas. Bad ideas. Wonderful ideas.

He edged a fraction of an inch closer to her, and she drew

in another deep breath. "Mac." Her voice had gone from shaky to husky.

"Yeah."

"The way you're holding me…"

…wasn't the way he wanted to be holding her, but it would do for now. "My sisters tried to teach me how to dance when I was a kid. They told me I was hopeless, but I'm doing the best I can."

"You're a fine dancer," Julie assured him, amusement mixing with other, less easily defined emotions in her eyes.

He edged the slightest bit closer again, so close barely a whisper of air existed between their bodies. "And the problem is…?"

"The problem is, we sort of agreed…" Her words dissolved into a quiet sigh as he stroked a finger across her nape.

"Sort of," he conceded. Just standing this near her, moving in a simple rhythm with her, feeling her breath against his cheek and her hand resting on his shoulder caused heat to gather below his belt. He was like a high school kid, getting hard from nothing more than a slow dance with the girl of his dreams.

You're working for Julie's sister, he lectured himself. *You're supposed to be keeping Julie safe.* He desperately wanted her safe—from everyone but him. But no matter how soft her skin felt, how silky her hair, how sweetly she moved in his arms, she would remain safe even from him. That was how it had to be.

"Oh my God," she suddenly whispered, staring past him.

He glanced over his shoulder but didn't see anything remarkable. Just lots of other people swirling around the floor in their flashy apparel. "What?" he asked her.

"The woman with Alvin Grote. You know him?"

"The pain in the ass occupying Room 307."

She grinned. "He met a woman in town and decided to

bring her to the dance. She looks exactly like someone I used to know in New York City."

Mac's nervous system jolted to attention. He intently searched the crowd, even though he had no idea what he was looking for. "Someone from New York?"

"Relax, Mac. She was a friend of mine at the agency. A very sweet girl." She squinted slightly, surveying the crowd. "I don't know—I'm probably just imagining the resemblance."

"I want you to find her, Julie," Mac said. If she'd imagined the resemblance, so be it. But on the slim chance that a very sweet friend of hers from New York City—someone who'd known her during her time as the model for Symphony Perfumes—was here in New Orleans, in this room, Mac wasn't going to blow off the coincidence. In his business coincidences didn't exist.

"I can't even see her now," Julie said. She must have read his concerned expression, because she laughed. "You're thinking she sent those e-mails?"

"I wouldn't discount the idea."

"I would. Alvin Grote said he met her here in town the night before last. And I got that last batch of e-mails the next morning. How could Alvin Grote's date have been sending me e-mails from Dallas and who knows where else when she was in New Orleans, reeling Grote in?"

Mac conceded the point. The sweet friend couldn't have been sending e-mails from around the country while she was in New Orleans. Even so…he wasn't convinced that her presence at this party was a mere fluke. Flukes were right up there with coincidences in his view of things—worthy of skepticism and investigation.

"I'd still like to meet her," he said, trying not to sound too suspicious.

"If I ever spot her again, I'll—"

Abruptly the room went dark. The music clattered to a halt,

a woman shrieked, someone bumped into Julie and she stumbled against Mac. He tightened his hold on her—only to keep her from falling, he told himself, even as a jolt of erotic energy surged through him.

That was the only energy in the room—in the entire hotel, he realized as his eyes adjusted to the darkness that engulfed him and Julie and the Hotel Marchand's Twelfth Night party. His lungs filled with Julie's delicate perfume, and her hair brushed against his cheek, and her hands clung to his shoulders…and he couldn't do anything about it. They were caught in a blackout—and both he and Julie had to get to work.

CHAPTER ELEVEN

THE WORLD WAS BLACK—and it remained black even after Julie slowly, reluctantly leaned back from Mac and opened her eyes. All around her, people chattered anxiously. "Is it a storm?" someone asked, even though the evening weather had been tranquil. "Should we evacuate?" someone else—perhaps a veteran of Katrina—whispered loudly. The band's drummer must have bumped something, causing his cymbals to rattle and hiss.

"Stay calm, folks," Mac shouted, yet his voice seemed to be coming from miles away. "We've got a power outage. Nothing to panic about. The hotel will get the lights back on in no time."

"We will?" Julie whispered. Her hands remained on his shoulders, clutching the wool of his jacket. Her feet felt a little wobbly, and she doubted that had anything to do with her high heels—or, for that matter, with the blackout. It had to do with Mac, with the gentle way he clasped her waist and held her steady, with his erotic scent and the warmth of him so close.

His answer was to release her, reach under his jacket and pull out a walkie-talkie. He pressed a button and lifted it to his ear. "Tyrell? Mac. Have you checked? Right. You take the gallery. I'll take the generator." He hooked the walkie-talkie to his belt and muttered, "I thought I'd be off the clock tonight. No such luck."

How could he be so clearheaded? Everyone else on the crowded dance floor seemed confused, bemused, meandering and murmuring and bumping into one another. And they hadn't been dancing with Mac. Julie had, which only compounded her sense of disorientation.

"Last I saw Charlotte, she was in the other room. You'd better go help her." He pressed an object into her hand, then strode away, sure-footed despite the darkness.

She lifted her hand and squinted at the plastic cylinder he'd given her: a penlight. Pushing the button on one end sent a narrow beam of light out the other. Somehow, that skinny shaft of white jarred her brain, unscrambling it. "Please, everyone, watch your step and don't worry!" she shouted. Her voice didn't carry as well as Mac's, but what could she do? The band's microphones wouldn't work without electricity. Lung power was all she had. "It's just a power outage! If you'd like to go out into the courtyard, there might be more light there! Please be careful! No shoving!"

People surged toward the doors. She wished she was wearing comfortable shoes. A portly man hurrying past her snagged her boa and nearly yanked it from her neck, but she caught one end of it and managed not to lose it.

Her mind spun with all the possible catastrophes this situation threatened. The hundreds of guests attending the party could get injured in a stampede. They could lose their bearings and their balance. They could bang into walls and bruise themselves on doorjambs. There could be people upstairs, too, or trapped in elevators. Was the entire hotel without power, or just the first-floor rooms?

Mac was on his way to the generator. Armed with his trusty walkie-talkie, he'd round up some maintenance staffers and try to get power back to the public rooms, the hallways and elevators. Meanwhile, as he'd suggested, she should be helping Charlotte.

Fighting the tide of bodies heading in the direction of the courtyard, she struggled to reach the doorway into the other event room. The penlight Mac had stuffed into her hand offered too little illumination to guide her across the room, so she turned it off and clutched it tightly, not wanting to drop it. The other room was as chaotic as the one she'd left, although the candles bobbing in their crystal bowls of water indicated where tables were located. The tiny flickers of light reflected off the shiny surfaces of the Mardi Gras beads. Under other circumstances, Julie would be entranced by the effect.

Right now, though, she had to find Charlotte.

Through the drone of voices—some laughing, some edgy, some just this side of hysteria—she heard Charlotte doing her best to speak above the tumult. "No need for alarm," she was saying. "We'll get some more candles lit."

"Charlotte." Julie staggered to her side, as relieved as if she'd just reached the summit of Mt. Everest.

"Oh, Julie, thank God you're here. We've got to keep order."

"Mac's gone to get the generator running," Julie informed her. "Do we have more candles?"

Julie was able to make out Charlotte's nod. "I've sent word to Nadine that we need not just candles but flashlights and oil lamps. I can't believe that tonight of all nights the hotel should lose power. It's a disaster." Charlotte might have only soothing words to her guests, but tension vibrated in her tone as she whispered to Julie.

"It's not a disaster," Julie assured her. "The food won't spoil, and some of the band's instruments don't need amps. If we can get both rooms a little brighter, we can restart the party."

"Heaven help us if someone gets hurt. I can't imagine why this has happened. We pay our utilities bills faithfully—and those bills are staggering."

Julie chuckled and patted Charlotte's arm. "The electricity wasn't cut off because we haven't paid our bills. It's a technical glitch. Maybe a car struck a light pole down the block. Look." She tucked her hand through Charlotte's arm and steered her toward a window. Across the street, the buildings were all dark. So were the streetlamps. "It isn't just us. The whole neighborhood is out."

"If a driver was stupid enough to drive into a pole and knock out the power on Twelfth Night, he ought to spend time in jail," Charlotte grumbled, then managed a feeble laugh. "Help me keep these people in line, Julie. We don't want a riot on our hands."

Julie hardly thought people dressed in their finest and eager to party would resort to rioting. She handed Charlotte Mac's penlight and said, "You need this more than I do. I'll go out to the courtyard and organize things there."

The silver light from the nearly full moon wasn't enough to turn night into day, but compared to the darkness indoors, the courtyard was remarkably bright. Many of the revelers carried drinks in their hands, and some held small plates of food. A few waiters circulated, passing out fresh drinks, and the band had gathered near the pool. The guitarist and keyboardist wouldn't be able to play without their amps, but the trumpeter gamely burst into a solo of "When the Saints Go Marching In," which brought a burst of applause from the audience. The drummer tapped a rhythm with his sticks against the bars of the fence surrounding the pool, and the sax player threaded a harmony into the mix.

Julie smiled and made a mental note to add a fat gratuity to the band's fee.

She wandered about the perimeter of the courtyard, where the building cast shadows, to make sure no one was fretting or sulking or, God forbid, hurt. A few frisky guests started to dance, and more joined in. Julie checked her watch. How long would it take Mac and the maintenance crew to get the generator up and running? How long until Nadine and her assistants rounded up some candles and gas lamps?

However long, this party would survive. And people would be talking about it for years.

She spotted Creighton and Stanley—Creighton's white hair glowed vividly in the moonlight—and made her way over to them. Seeing her, Creighton slung an arm around her shoulders, careful not to crush the boa he'd lent her.

"I, for one, am devastated," he said cheerfully. "Without electricity, that talented mixologist over in the bar won't be able to prepare any drinks that require a blender." He lifted a tall, frothy glass of something watermelon colored and took a drink. "I guess I'll have to sip slowly and make this last."

"We've got a backup generator for emergencies," Julie told him. "I don't know if mixing drinks counts as an emergency."

"The hell with the blender," Stanley declared. "Who needs fancy drinks when we're having such a unique experience?"

Julie sent a silent prayer heavenward that everyone would view the party the way Creighton and Stanley did. And indeed, the people around her seemed generally happy, dancing and talking and making the best of a difficult situation.

Surveying the crowd, she spotted Alvin Grote and his companion. Again she was stunned by the eerie resemblance between Grote's date and Andrea Crowley, one of the girls she'd worked with at Glenn Perry's agency. This woman was older than the Andrea that Julie remembered, her face a bit worn, her hair spiky and bleached blond at the tips. Her makeup was harsher than anything Andrea had ever worn back when she and Julie worked for Glenn; his agency had had a reputation for youthful, innocent-looking models, and he'd coached his girls to use cosmetics that enhanced that sweet, milk-fed look. Of course, they *had* been youthful and innocent, at least when they'd started working for him. By the time he'd been convicted, they might not have been that much older, but they'd sure been a lot less innocent.

But why would Andrea have turned up at the hotel's Twelfth Night party, of all places and after all these years?

Julie eased her way around dancing couples, past a woman seated on a wicker chair, her shoe removed so she could massage her toes, past three men gesticulating with the skewers from their chicken satay hors d'oeuvres while they argued over the environmental impact of the rebuilt oil platforms in the gulf, and finally over to the pool, where Grote and Andrea's look-alike stood near the wrought-iron fence.

The woman caught Julie's eye and smiled slightly, but before either she or Julie could speak, Grote erupted. "Ms. Sullivan!" he bellowed, smiling as if he considered life utterly perfect and no complaint had ever sullied his lips. His ponytail trembled from his exuberance. Dressed in a dapper suit and smiling broadly, he looked almost handsome. "What an adventure!"

Julie said something she would never have imagined herself saying a day ago: "If everyone has your attitude, Mr. Grote, this party will be a triumph."

"I'd like you to meet my friend, Maggie Jones. Maggie, this is Julie Sullivan, who keeps this grand old hotel chugging along."

Maggie Jones? Julie accepted the name without blinking and extended her hand. The woman shifted her beaded clutch from her right hand to her left so she could shake hands with Julie. "I hardly do it by myself," Julie said. "We have a large, hardworking staff. And my boss, Charlotte Marchand, is really the one who makes it all happen."

"She owns the hotel, huh?" the woman called Maggie said. A decade had passed since Julie had spoken to Andrea Crowley, but this woman sounded an awful lot like her.

"Her family does. Her parents founded the hotel, and her mother still keeps her hand in it. Her sisters are involved in the business, too."

Maggie looked less than fascinated. Her gaze drifted to her beaming escort. "Alvie, would you be a dear and get me a martini?" she asked. "On ice."

Alvin Grote seemed surprised. "In the middle of a blackout?"

"They don't need electricity to make a martini," Maggie said.

"The ice cubes here aren't the cylindrical kind with the holes in the center," he warned. "The beverage doesn't flow through them."

"That's all right. I'll make do." She sent him an adoring smile, and he seemed to melt like a praline in warm water.

"I'll be right back," he promised, then spun and hustled through the crowd, clearly eager to satisfy Maggie's every whim.

Maggie turned back to Julie. Either this woman was Andrea or she had a punky twin sister. The moon shed enough light for Julie to recognize those pale, cool eyes, even though they were circled not just in inky eyeliner but in weary, wary shadow. "Maggie, is it?" she asked politely.

"For the time being," Maggie replied with a smile. "Shouldn't one of us say, small world? Or maybe long time no see."

"Both work." Julie relaxed. Now that she knew she was actually talking to Andrea, she wanted to give her old colleague a hug. But Andrea was sending don't-touch-me vibes, so Julie restrained herself. "Why did you change your name to Maggie?"

"Oh, I just..." She glanced in the direction Alvin Grote had vanished. "Let's face it, he picked me up on Bourbon Street. I wanted to come to this party, so I encouraged him, you know? But I didn't think he needed to know who I really was."

Julie supposed that made a kind of convoluted sense. "How have you been?" she asked.

"Hanging in there." She swept her gaze the length of Julie's body. "You've put on a few, haven't you."

Julie laughed. "And I've savored every single calorie. Are you still modeling? You look—" *terrible,* she thought but said, "—terrific."

Andrea snorted. "No, Julie. I'm not modeling. The agency I used to be with went under. Maybe you heard."

Julie detected a strong undertone of bitterness in Andrea's voice. "There are other agencies."

"Not for me, there aren't."

"So," Julie said brightly, not wishing to rehash the ugly days after Glenn had been arrested and all his models had found themselves bereft of any support. "What have you been up to?"

"We've got some catching up to do." Andrea slipped her hand around Julie's elbow. "But not here. It's too crowded."

"I can't leave the party," Julie protested, although she was tempted to find a quiet corner where she and Andrea could talk over old times. She'd always been fond of Andrea and as protective of her as Andrea would allow—which wasn't much. Although Julie couldn't prove it, she suspected that Glenn Perry had taken particular advantage of Andrea, who had arrived in New York City from a blink-and-you've-missed-it Midwestern town, armed with big dreams but not much savvy. Though Glenn hadn't gotten her a great deal of modeling work, he'd definitely kept her tightly under his control. At his urging, Andrea had dropped a lot of weight, and when Julie had pressed her, she'd admitted that he was supplying her with amphetamines. Julie had suspected she might be one of the girls sleeping with Glenn, too, but Andrea had been evasive about that.

Once Glenn had been arrested and Andrea had returned home to wherever she'd come from—Wisconsin or Indiana, Julie couldn't remember—Julie had felt confident Andrea would put her life back together. She'd always seemed hard-headed and stubborn, traits Julie could identify with, given her own stubborn streak.

While she knew she ought to remain in the courtyard, doing her part to keep the party going, she was curious to hear about Andrea's life and find out what had brought her to New Orleans. And really, the party seemed to be faring quite well without any assistance from her. So when Andrea gave her arm a little tug and said, "Come on, just for a few minutes," Julie shrugged and strolled with her toward the lobby doors.

Through the glass she could see that the lobby was dark except for a few candles burning inside glass chimneys. Thank goodness the hotel had a supply of glass-enclosed candles. Open flames in a hotel crammed with antiques and high-energy revelers would have been hazardous.

She'd thought they could stand at the edge of the courtyard to talk—after all, Alvin Grote would be returning soon with Andrea's martini—but Andrea swung open a door and led Julie into the dark, eerily quiet lobby. One clerk stood behind the check-in credenza in the amber glow of a hurricane lamp. He looked generally helpless with his computer out of commission, but except for him the lobby was empty. Andrea steered Julie away from the desk, toward one of the candles, and then released her arm. "I want to show you something," she murmured, lifting her purse and popping open the clasp. She reached in and pulled out a silver pistol no bigger than her hand.

"Andrea! What—?"

"Shh," Andrea silenced her. "We're going for a walk."

Julie stared at the gun. Why the hell was Andrea carrying that—that *thing?* Julie had seen guns in movies and on TV, but the closest she'd ever come to an actual firearm was when she'd talked to police officers. People she knew didn't own them. Or if they did, they kept them carefully locked up, not stashed in their elegant evening purses.

She forced her brain to stay focused. Andrea Crowley had a gun and she was taking Julie for a walk. Julie was being abducted. The hotel was without electricity, the party was gearing up again, and a woman Julie had once worked with and had considered a colleague and a friend was brushing the tip of her tiny, deadly gun against Julie's back, exactly where Mac had brushed the tips of his fingers just minutes ago, when they'd been dancing and the hotel had been filled with light.

Okay. Julie took a deep breath. *Okay.* She was being kidnapped. She had to stay alert. She had to save her life. "Put that away," she whispered. "I'll go wherever you want, but put that thing away."

Andrea smiled. Her teeth were still model white and even. "No, Julie. You don't get to tell me what to do. I'm the one with the gun. Let's go." She used the weapon to nudge Julie toward the door to the street.

Julie moved stiffly, under no obligation to act as if everything was normal. Her fingers fidgeted so intensely with her boa, a feather came loose in her hand. An idea sprang to her mind. She discreetly dropped the feather. It landed on the carpet just inside the door.

The street outside the hotel was a scene of festive bedlam. Thousands of people milled around on the sidewalks and in the streets, where cars, trapped in gridlock without traffic lights or police officers to guide them, blared their horns. Their headlights slashed the night, but they were aimed straight ahead, not toward the dark, crowded sidewalks and shrouded buildings.

The French Quarter always teemed with people, but tonight the throngs stared at one another rather than the historic buildings. The neon signs of fortune-tellers weren't flashing, and the display windows of jewelry stores and souvenir shops remained dark. Upstairs, people gathered on the balconies overlooking the street, singing, shouting, drinking and viewing the blackout as an excuse to party—as if folks in New Orleans ever needed an excuse.

Julie wondered if she could lose Andrea in the crowd. She felt the pistol's barrel jab her spine and decided not to risk it. If she broke free, Andrea might fire and hurt someone else. The better choice was to argue some sense into Andrea, to learn what she was up to and talk her out of it.

Meanwhile, she plucked another couple of feathers from the boa and let them fall. They landed where the front facade of the hotel met the sidewalk. Julie prayed they wouldn't blow away or get trampled. Surely if someone found a trail of pink feathers, they'd think to follow it, wouldn't they?

Mac would. That understanding was so forceful, so irrefutable, she nearly smiled. Mac would follow the feathers and find her.

After he was done getting the hotel's generator up and running, she reminded herself. And double-checking the gallery to make sure the Wyeth painting was safe. And returning to the party and discovering Julie was gone. By which time God knew how far Andrea would have dragged her. Would she run out of feathers before he found her?

"Why are you doing this?" she asked, trying to keep her tone even. She refused to let Andrea know she was frantic, her heart thumping against her ribs at twice its normal tempo. As long as she remained outwardly poised, she had a prayer of keeping Andrea calm, as well.

Andrea's voice barely carried over the din of horns honking, engines rumbling and people shouting and, in a few inebriated cases, singing off-key. "You ruined everything," Andrea told her. "You destroyed my life."

"Me?" Julie laughed, even though nothing about this situation was funny. She was keenly, painfully aware of that gun poking the center of her back. She tugged a wad of feathers from the boa and let them fall to the sidewalk.

"Where's your car?" Andrea asked.

Julie gave her a sharp look. "You must be joking. We can't drive anywhere tonight. The neighborhood is blacked out. Look at the traffic!"

"I don't care. Where's your car?"

Sighing, Julie turned left at the corner. The side street was marginally less crowded. She plucked another bunch of feathers from the boa and dropped them. "Andrea, I always liked you. I worried about you in New York. It infuriated me that Glenn took such advantage of you. How did I destroy your life?"

"He didn't take advantage of me," Andrea snapped. "I loved him."

Julie wanted to give Andrea a good shake, but she didn't think that would be a wise idea, given that Andrea had a gun. Instead she helped the boa shed a few more feathers. "How could you love him? He was twenty years older than you, and he was pumping you full of drugs."

"I liked those drugs," Andrea muttered. "You think getting off the drugs was easy? I went nuts, thanks to you. You were so self-righteous, Julie. You knew what was right for everyone. You took Glenn out of action because you knew better than the rest of us. So we all lost Glenn. We lost our chance to model. We lost our chance to make it. And Glenn—I lost Glenn."

"He was an asshole," Julie retorted, forgetting for a moment that she was supposed to be trying to keep Andrea calm. "He used you, he exploited you—"

"He *loved* me," she insisted. "And I waited for him. I waited. He got out of jail and I flew back to New York to be with him, and..." Her voice faltered slightly, and a quick glimpse informed Julie that Andrea's eyes had teared up. "Prison changed him. He didn't love me anymore. God knows what happened to him while he was there, but he didn't want me. And it's all your fault."

"All right—so this romance didn't work out," Julie said, once again placating. She tried not to choke on the word *romance.* A forty-something businessman having sex with his teenage models hardly qualified as a romance. "I'm sorry, Andrea. I really am. I was only trying to keep you and the other girls from getting hurt."

Andrea said nothing. They reached the corner near the lot where Julie had parked. She couldn't imagine where they'd drive. The intersection was jammed with more vehicles, some abandoned, others with their engines still running and the drivers shouting at each other through their open windows. A helpful volunteer wearing a Cat-in-the-Hat striped stovepipe hat stood at the center of the intersection, alternately swigging from a bottle of gin and attempting to direct traffic.

"Glenn was the only good thing that ever happened to me," Andrea said, shoving Julie across the street. "He cared about me. He gave me what I needed and he told me he loved me."

"Did you send me the e-mails?" Julie asked suddenly. For

some reason, as they inched their way through the crowd and across the street, her brain started clicking.

"Did you like those?" Andrea giggled, sounding for a moment like the sweet young girl she'd once been. "Did they scare the hell out of you?"

"No." It didn't add up. Andrea couldn't have been the source of the e-mails. Alvin Grote had met her two days ago, and Julie had gotten all those messages from around the country yesterday. How could Andrea have sent e-mails from Dallas and Detroit when she'd been in New Orleans?

"You're lying—you were scared," Andrea insisted.

"All right. I was scared." They'd reached the parking lot, and Julie dropped another handful of pink feathers. She was desperate to slow Andrea down, to keep from getting into her car. Once they were in the car, her trail of feathers would end. "How did you send e-mails from around the country when you were in New Orleans?"

"I was in New York for a while," Andrea said. "I sent those. I had a friend who's a flight attendant send the others from around the country. Pretty clever, huh?"

Actually, Julie recalled that the e-mails that had come in a bunch yesterday had been much less subtle than those sent from New York. She should have guessed they'd been written by a different person. "That's an awful lot of trouble to go through, just to spook me."

"Not as much trouble as pulling this trigger," Andrea pointed out. "Which car is yours?"

"That one." Julie pointed to the decrepit old car. "I don't have my keys with me."

Andrea whacked the gun against her back, bruising her. "Damn it! Where are the keys?"

Julie blinked back the tears that sprang to her eyes from the pain of the blow. "They're locked in my office," she said.

"You're lying!" Andrea began pawing her, searching the layered fabric of her dress's skirt for a pocket. Julie bit her lip. She'd locked her purse in her office, but her office key was on the same ring as her car key—and that ring was nestled in the discreet pocket in the side seam of the dress.

Unfortunately, Andrea found it. "You effin' liar," she muttered, then whacked Julie's back again, banging the butt of the gun against her ribs and causing Julie to wince. "Get in the car."

Julie clung tenuously to hope. She dropped another few feathers and nudged them under her car with her foot, then let Andrea push her behind the wheel. She started the engine before Andrea climbed into the passenger seat, entertaining the thought that she could drive away before Andrea got in, but her hands were shaking and she couldn't shift into reverse and back out of the space quickly enough. Andrea stumbled in as the car lurched backward, then she smacked Julie's arm and rammed the gun's muzzle into her side.

"Drive," she ordered.

CHAPTER TWELVE

"WHAT DO YOU MEAN, the generator won't start?" Mac growled at Eddie, one of the two maintenance men who'd met him in the furnace room, where the emergency generator shared space with the furnaces, central air conditioning units and hot water tanks.

"It's been tampered with," Eddie told him. "I'm guessing someone added something to the fuel tank."

"Added something? Like what?"

"Sugar, maybe," Eddie guessed. "No way this baby's gonna work till we get the fuel tank emptied and cleaned out."

Mac closed his eyes and erupted in a veritable tide of curses. Eddie *had* to get the generator started. The safety of the hotel's guests depended on it.

Who the hell would have sabotaged the generator? And why?

"How long will it take you to fix it?" Mac asked, trying to keep his tone free of exasperation. None of this was Eddie's fault.

"I don't know. Could take awhile. We've got to drain the tank, clean it out, clean the fuel lines…" While Eddie dipped a metal stick into the tank, pulled it out and stared at the glistening fluid coating it, the other man turned on a battery-powered lantern. The lantern's fluorescent bulbs flickered on and cast a bluish glow.

"Son of a bitch," Mac muttered. "Did you see anyone down here? Any of the guests? Anyone who might have poured sugar into the tank?"

Eddie shook his head. "Nah. Nobody."

"'Cept the concierge," the fellow holding the lantern said.

"Right, him. What's his name, Luc? He was heading up the hall as we were coming down. Said he was collecting flashlights."

"He was carrying 'bout a half dozen," the other maintenance man added helpfully.

Luc Carter, Mac thought, his brain whirling. Why was it that the golden-boy concierge always happened to be leaving the scene right before some mess was discovered? Broken glass imbedded in towels, a ruined generator… Something was definitely up with him.

Or else he was just doing his job, collecting flashlights. And the incident with the glass splinters in the towels—it was always possible he'd been fooling around with a chambermaid and his presence near the supply room that night had been pure coincidence.

Mac didn't believe in pure coincidence.

"This is gonna take awhile," Eddie repeated as his colleague lugged over a red gasoline jug and a funnel. "No need for you to stick around, Mac. Go tell Miss Charlotte she's gonna have to make those candles last."

"Thanks," Mac said, filtering the rage out of his voice. He was furious, but not at Eddie. He gave the burly guy a slap on the back, then stormed down the hall, ignoring the fact that he couldn't see where he was going. He *knew* where he was going. As a security consultant, he'd often worked in dark spaces. He didn't even have to count steps to know when he was approaching the security office. He was used to relying on all his senses, not just his sight.

Tyrell won points for remembering to lock the security office when he'd left to check the gallery. Mac had no difficulty unlocking the door by feel. Inside, the monitor was dead, no projections flashing on it from the idle cameras, no hum of electricity, only a faint whiff of coffee lingering in the air. Mac squinted at the desk until he discerned where

Tyrell had left his cup. Mac didn't want to knock it over accidentally.

He yanked his walkie-talkie from his belt and summoned Tyrell. "There's a problem with the generator," he said.

Through the crackling static, he heard Tyrell's response—a clear reference to body waste. "What kind of problem?"

"The kind of problem that means we're going to be without emergency backup for a while. Where are you?"

"Can't see three inches in front of me. I could be anywhere and not know it." Tyrell laughed. "I'm on the second floor, checking the offices. Stu and Chris are upstairs, making the rounds of the rooms, knocking on doors to see if anyone needs help. We've already checked the elevators. They're all unoccupied."

"We caught a break there," Mac said, relieved that no one would have to be shimmying up and down the elevator shafts, performing rescues. "Listen, Tyrell, if you see Luc Carter, I need to talk to him."

"Sure thing."

Mac turned off his radio and hooked it back onto his belt. He left the security office and headed for the lobby. Flickering golden candlelight beckoned. The spacious hotel entry was occupied by a few people, some ensconced on the plush sofas and sipping wine, one couple sitting on the stairs and discreetly pawing each other—they were just silhouettes to Mac, but it sure looked as if the man's hand was sandwiched between the woman's knees—and a clerk posted behind the check-in desk, a cold beer by his elbow. As soon as he saw Mac, he reached for the beer, as if to hide it.

"Don't bother," Mac said. "I don't think you're going to be working the computers tonight. May as well enjoy yourself."

The clerk gave him a sheepish smile. "Thanks."

"But sip it slowly, buddy. One's your limit tonight. We need you clearheaded."

"Right." The clerk nodded earnestly.

Mac peered through one of the French doors into the courtyard, where the party seemed to be in full swing. "I take it nobody's fallen into the cake yet?"

"If they have, word hasn't reached me," the clerk told him. "And the pool's locked up, so no one's fallen into that."

Mac nodded and crossed that worry off his list. "Have you seen Luc Carter?"

"He was here a few minutes ago," the clerk said. "He gave me this." The clerk held up a flashlight. "I'm keeping it off to save the battery."

"Smart. Where did Luc go after he was here?"

The clerk shrugged. "He could be anywhere. You might just trip over him if you don't watch your step."

Mac reflexively glanced down. He didn't see anyone lying on the floor, but if someone was, he'd be easy to miss. "I'll watch my step," he promised. "You watch the steps of everyone in the lobby. If everything stays as calm here as it is now, we should survive this mess in good shape." With a smile, he ventured into the courtyard.

Julie should have been easy enough to spot. In those sexy shoes, she towered over most of the guests, and there was enough moonlight for Mac to get a pretty good look at the crowd. She definitely wasn't in the courtyard.

He shrugged off his disappointment. She was undoubtedly as busy as he was, making sure the guests were safe and enjoying themselves. And really, he shouldn't be thinking about her at all, except as a fellow Hotel Marchand employee with a truckload of responsibility tonight.

Still, blackout notwithstanding, Mac would sure like to take her out onto the dance floor again. For those few precious minutes when he'd had her in his arms, he'd forgotten who he was, what he was supposed to be doing and who was paying him to do it. She'd just been a woman and he'd been a man, wanting her.

He eased his way through the crowd, no longer looking for

her because he knew he wouldn't find her there. Instead he searched for Luc Carter. No luck spotting him, either.

At the opposite end of the courtyard he reentered the building and made his way to the event rooms. The one where the band had been set up was nearly empty, but people managed to circulate in the other room, where the floating candles offered modest illumination and a feast of food remained on the buffet tables. Mac noticed Charlotte surveying one of the tables with a tiny penlight. He wandered over.

"How are you doing?" he asked.

She spun around too quickly, obviously strung tight. Seeing Mac, she seemed to unwind slightly. "I'm checking to make sure the food isn't spoiling. People aren't eating much—I guess because they can't see where the food is." She laughed faintly.

"We ought to get the waiters to refill their trays and take the food out to the courtyard," Mac suggested, then frowned as he recognized the penlight in her hand. "Where'd you get that?"

"Julie gave it to me. Why? Do you need a light? Nadine got some battery-powered lanterns, and Luc was passing flashlights around. I'm afraid to have any more candles burning."

"The candles in the water are safe," Mac assured her. "And I'm okay, lightwise. You hang on to that." He folded her fingers around the penlight, then asked, "Do you know where Julie is?"

"She's out in the courtyard. Having fun, I suspect. That seems to be the place to be. Why don't you go join her?"

Mac refrained from telling Charlotte that Julie wasn't in the courtyard having fun. An undefined worry gnawed at him, but he saw no reason to infect Charlotte with his own concerns. "I'm sure I'll find her," he said, plucking a fat strawberry from one of the platters and popping it into his mouth before he abandoned Charlotte.

The strawberry was sweet and juicy, but it lodged in his throat. Where was Julie?

He returned to the courtyard and scanned the crowd,

hoping to spot Creighton. As Julie's friend, he might have an idea of where she'd gone. But before he could find her flamboyant neighbor, someone collided with him. He turned and found himself face-to-face with a slightly paunchy man whose sparse hair was pulled into a pretentious ponytail.

"Why don't you watch where you're going?" the man fumed, even though he'd been the one to bump into Mac.

Mac realized who he was: Alvin Grote, the whiner from 307. "Hey, buddy, we're all having a little trouble seeing," he said in a placating tone. Keeping tempers from flaring was vitally important. "Anything I can help you with?"

"No, damn it," Grote retorted.

"There's plenty of food inside," Mac told him. "And the bartender's doing his best, if you want a drink."

"I don't want a drink. I already have a drink. Two drinks," Grote said, lifting his hands. He was holding a martini in each one. "What the hell am I supposed to do with two drinks?"

"I can think of a few options," Mac said, trying to tease a smile out of the guy, who seemed close to snapping. "You could drink one and then, when you were done with that, you could drink the other."

"One of them is for my date," Grote informed him coldly. "But she's disappeared. I don't know where she's gone. This hotel—how could it have lost power? Do you know how much I'm spending to stay here? And they don't even have a generator for emergencies like this? I'm tempted to file a report with the Better Business Bureau. Or the tourist board. Or someone. The governor's office, maybe."

"You do that," Mac told him, his mind racing. Hadn't his date been the woman Julie had recognized from New York City?

Oh, Jesus. Without a parting word, without a care about whether Alvin Grote went ballistic, Mac hurried through the crowd, past the dancers and back into the lobby.

Where was Julie? Where was that woman from New York? Damn!

"Are you looking for someone?" the clerk called from his station.

"Yeah." Mac sprinted over, sure-footed despite the darkness. "Julie Sullivan. Have you seen her?"

"She was in here a few minutes ago."

"Was she alone?"

"No, she was with another woman. I could hardly see. I didn't recognize her as a guest here, but—"

"Where did they go?" Mac demanded.

"Um..." The clerk thought for a few seconds—long enough for Mac to want grab his shoulders and shake an answer out of him. "They talked for a couple of minutes and then they left."

"Left the lobby?"

"Left the building."

Mac swore, then shoved away from the desk and sprinted toward the front door. The world beyond that door was as dark as the world on this side of it. He shouldn't have been able to see anything—especially on the ground. But as he shoved open the door, it created a breeze which kicked up a feather that had been caught on the threshold.

Not just a feather. Mac bent over and snatched the feather up. In the light of the moon filtering through a drifting gray cloud, he was able to see that the feather was pink.

IT TOOK FIVE MINUTES to drive half a block.

All Julie could think about was getting out of the damn car. As long as she was in it, she was an easy target for Andrea's horrid little pistol. But if she could get out of the car, she might escape within the crowds of people packing the streets and sidewalks. Surely Andrea wouldn't fire her gun with so many innocent bystanders around, would she?

Who the hell knew? The woman was clearly deranged. She'd decided that Julie was somehow at fault for ending her modeling career—such as it was—and ruining what she'd perceived to be a great love affair with Glenn Perry, a bastard who'd bedded any sweet young thing foolish enough to believe his crap.

Because Julie had spoken the truth about the guy ten years ago, Andrea wanted to kill her. The irony burned inside her. She'd been concerned that Glenn himself would want revenge. But Glenn wasn't in New Orleans right now, pointing a gun at her.

The car rolled forward another few inches in the grid-locked traffic, and Julie braked. The resulting squeal sounded like a startled pig.

"What was that?" Andrea asked, glancing toward the dash-board.

Julie glanced toward the dashboard as well. Her brakes had been squeaking for months…but Andrea didn't know that. "There's something wrong with the car," she said. "I think it's dying."

"You're kidding."

"I'm not," Julie swore. She hit the gas and brake pedals at the same time. Her car lurched, and the brakes issued another plaintive noise. "I don't know what's wrong with it."

"What the hell is going on? This town has no electricity, your car is dying—does anything in this whole effin' city work?"

I hope your gun doesn't work, Julie thought, trying to swallow her nausea. But she said nothing, just jammed her feet on both pedals again, causing the car to jerk and squeak. "This car is going nowhere," she said. *Please,* she prayed fer-vently, *believe me, Andrea. Please believe me.*

"Well, what are you going to do? You can't just leave the car in the middle of the road."

She believed. Julie suppressed a grateful sigh. "Let me try to roll it to the curb." She played her feet on both pedals with the finesse of a street-corner tap dancer. With a chorus of squeaks and stutters, the car rolled to the side of the street. Julie twisted the key to turn the engine off.

Andrea's wrist was surprisingly steady as she held the gun on Julie. With her free hand, she reached behind her and opened her door. "Get out of the car," she said, "and don't do anything funny."

Julie couldn't think of a single funny thing to do under the circumstances. She shoved open her door, swung her legs out and searched the crowd for any gaps she could slip into. She didn't consider fleeing for her life funny, but Andrea might.

She opened her mouth to shout for help, but before she could utter a word, a crowd of inebriated young men swaggered past her, singing "Roxanne" loudly and poorly. She tried to cry out for help, but tension sealed her throat, and when she reached to grab the arm of one of them, he swung right past her, jostling her against the car. By the time she regained her balance on her teetering heels, Andrea was beside her, the pistol's barrel jabbing her side.

"Let's go," she said.

Julie blinked away the tears that blurred her vision and took a step in the direction of the hotel. Andrea yanked her back. "Where's the water? There's a river here somewhere, right? Let's go to the river."

Great. She was going to shoot Julie and dump her body into the Mississippi. "The river is this way," she lied, heading toward Jackson Square.

Fortunately, Andrea didn't know New Orleans well enough to realize that Julie was leading her in the wrong direction. Unfortunately, the mobs filling the streets didn't allow Julie a chance to escape. Instead, all the happy, tipsy humanity sharing the sidewalk with Andrea and her forced them together. No one noticed how close Andrea was standing to Julie—or the gun she was poking into Julie's ribs.

Julie plucked a few more feathers from her boa and released them. As if Mac would ever find them. As if the fluffy feathers would even reach the sidewalk. As if detouring to Jackson Square was going to buy her enough time to get away from this maniac who believed Julie had destroyed her life by testifying against a drug-dealing, cradle-robbing scumbag like Glenn Perry.

She stumbled over a curb, nearly spraining her ankle. Her knees were trembling too much; she couldn't handle three-inch heels right now. She wiggled one foot and then the other out of her sexy sandals.

A fresh burst of tears quivered on her eyelashes, and she blinked hard. She couldn't afford the energy it would take to cry, or the self-pity, and she sure as hell couldn't wait for Mac to rescue her. She broke off another large feather, sent it adrift and let a surge of people carry her across the street. She didn't lose Andrea in that intersection. Maybe the next one. Or once they reached the park... Sooner or later, an opportunity to break free would arise and Julie would grab it. Without the sandals, she'd be able to run faster.

The pavement chilled her soles through the thin nylon. No matter; the stockings would be torn to shreds by the time she reached the park. Someone stepped on her toe and she winced but trudged onward, searching the crowds for an opening, a friendly face, a police officer.

Where *were* all the cops, anyway?

Block after block lacked power, yet the people swarming around her had enough energy to light up the entire city, if only their high spirits could be transformed into electricity. People were carousing as if it were Mardi Gras, not Twelfth Night. Someone somewhere was playing a saxophone. Even a power outage could be turned into a party in New Orleans.

But Julie was in no mood to party. Could she duck down that alley? No—Andrea would follow her and shoot her dead. Alleys were not a good option.

She saw the park up ahead. A little more open space, at least, some dead winter grass to cushion her feet and moonlight to light her surroundings...and maybe, please God, an opportunity to escape that she wasn't finding on the street.

She was taller than Andrea. She'd been stronger than her ten years ago in New York City; she was probably still stronger today. If the crowds in the park were a little less dense, she might have enough room to turn on Andrea, knock her down, get the gun away…

Or die trying.

Oh, God, she didn't want to die. She loved her life. She loved her sister, her parents, her job, her friends. She loved the people she worked with—Charlotte and her sisters and…

No, she didn't love Mac. She'd loved dancing with him, and she'd loved kissing him, and she loved talking to him and looking at him, but damn it, where was he when she needed him? Some security expert. He was probably busy reviewing her e-mails in search of a threat to her life. Or he would be, if there were any electricity. And meanwhile, here she was entering Jackson Square with a gun jammed into her side.

Not surprisingly, the park was filled with people, and moonlight sifted through the thin clouds, replacing some of the light the decorative streetlamps would have provided if they'd been working. "Where the hell are we?" Andrea asked, nudging Julie with the gun.

"Jackson Square," Julie told her.

"Where's the river?"

"We haven't reached it yet." Julie worked her way through the crowds, searching for something, anything that might resemble a chance to escape. That group of teenagers chugging beer didn't look promising. The woman doing a suggestive dance atop a park bench? No help there.

Save yourself. Julie limped toward the statue of Andrew Jackson at the center of the park, her bruised toe throbbing. She thought the crowd looked a little thinner by the statue. She'd have room to move there. Room to fight back.

"Julie, I'm warning you—if you're screwing around with me…"

A sudden rush of rage overtook Julie. "If I'm screwing

around with you, what? You're going to shoot me?" She spun around and slammed her arm into the side of Andrea's head.

The gun sounded like a bomb exploding inside Julie's skull as it fired.

THE BEAM OF MAC'S FLASHLIGHT picked up another pink feather on the sidewalk just beyond the hotel entry's awning. Julie's boa hadn't looked so flimsy that it would be leaking feathers. She must have pulled them out. She was leaving him a trail.

He continued down the street, his gaze fixed to the ground as he searched for more feathers. With so many people tramping along the sidewalk, and only a little moonlight and the occasional glimmer from inside a building with a working generator to light his way, finding pink feathers would be next to impossible.

For Julie's sake, he had to accomplish the impossible.

He couldn't believe his stupidity. He'd been so sure her old boss would come after her. That was what her sister had feared, and her fear had made sense. Perry was the guy Julie had sent to prison.

But just as the parole officer had kept assuring them, Perry was being a good boy back in New York, and meanwhile one of Julie's fellow models had sneaked into the Twelfth Night party on the arm of that idiot Alvin Grote and dragged Julie away. Mac didn't have time to beat himself up for having failed to imagine this scenario. But once Julie was safe, he'd do a nice, long number on himself.

For now he'd concentrate on feathers. The beam of his flashlight picked up another tuft of pink just around the corner. Trying to move fast in a crowd oozing along at the speed of mud was a challenge—but Mac's goal for the moment was to accomplish the impossible.

And, impossibly enough, he saw a small, trampled wad of pink feathers.

The trail led him to the parking lot where hotel staff left their cars, and his heart squeezed tight. Julie's car was gone.

He spat out a curse. If that skinny blond psychopath had forced Julie to drive off somewhere, Mac would never find them.

Do the impossible, he ordered himself. He darted to his own car, grabbed the licensed pistol he kept stashed under the floor mat behind the clutch pedal and tucked it into the waistband of his slacks, then ran back to the parking lot's entry and searched the street. Which way would they have driven?

How could they have driven? The cars in the road were moving more slowly than the pedestrians swarming past them, taunting the drivers by waltzing back and forth across the street and impeding their already snail-like progress.

The kidnapper would probably have wanted to leave the city with Julie, or at least get her out of the French Quarter. Ignoring the hooting, singing and shouting around him, he took a chance and headed north.

Two blocks up, he found Julie's car abandoned beside a hydrant and unlocked, with the key still in the ignition. He searched the interior—no blood but no clues, either. He grabbed the keys, locked the car and searched the area for a feather.

"Come on, come on," he muttered under his breath. The woman was smart enough to leave him a trail. She was smart enough to figure out a way to get out of her car. She'd better be smart enough to have left him another signal. He'd been too stupid to see the danger she'd stepped into, so she had to be smart enough for both of them.

A break in the crowd revealed a mangled pink feather lodged in a crack in the pavement.

Away from the river, toward Jackson Square. Mac picked up his pace, pushing past people, several times grabbing someone and asking, "Did you see a gorgeous woman with a pink feather boa walking this way?" Two pedestrians shook their heads. Up ahead he heard the soulful wail of a saxophone, and he elbowed his way through the crowds until he spotted the player. Reuben.

Mac charged toward Reuben and nearly knocked the guy's sax out of his hand. "Hey, Mac! I lost my stage—no juice at the club," he said. "Thought I'd entertain the crowds out here, pick up some spare change. What d'ya think? Are folks more generous during a blackout?"

Mac didn't have time for banter. "I'm looking for a tall, gorgeous woman in a pink boa," he said. "Have you seen her?"

"That lady you were with the other day? Man, she's a looker. Yeah, I saw her headin' toward Jackson Square."

"Thanks. I'll catch you later." Mac forged back into the crowd.

Jackson Square loomed a few blocks ahead, a dark opening in the midst of dark buildings. His eyes fixed on the park, he tripped over something in his path. Glancing down, he saw a spike-heeled black sandal.

Julie's shoes. Reuben had been right. Mac grabbed the sandal at his feet, then located its mate a few steps away and grabbed it, as well. Smart, smart woman. She knew she could move faster in bare feet than in those sexy stilts. He stuffed them into his jacket pockets, the heels sticking out, and continued toward the square.

A festive atmosphere enveloped the park. People pranced around with glow sticks and toy light sabers, chanting and rapping and laughing too loudly. The predominant aroma was booze with undertones of marijuana.

He collared a giggling teenage boy. "Have you seen a tall, gorgeous woman here?" he asked.

"I've seen a million of 'em," the boy said unhelpfully.

"Really tall," Mac persevered. "Taller than you. She had a pink feather boa."

The kid shrugged and Mac shoved him away. He accosted another, slightly older fellow who was equally uninformative. Then he tried a woman.

"Oh, yeah—two of them. A blonde and a brunette. Coulda stepped out of the pages of a fashion magazine."

"Where?" Mac demanded. "Where did you see them?"

"Over by the statue, I think. If you strike out with them, honey, you come back and find me. I don't have any plans, and it's gonna be a long night."

"Thanks." He was grateful enough to spare her a smile and a pat on the arm before he raced toward the statue.

Before he reached it, he heard the gunshot.

CHAPTER THIRTEEN

JULIE'S HAND AND WRIST ached from slugging Andrea. Her knee was scraped raw from the pavement. But wherever that bullet had gone, it hadn't hit her.

She shook her head to clear her vision. All around her she heard voices screaming —"A gun, she's got a gun! Catch her!"—and the pounding of footsteps as people ran. The world was so damn dark, and everything had happened at blinding speed. But she didn't see any bodies on the ground, oozing blood. Andrea's gun must have missed the bystanders.

Despite her dizziness, Julie pushed herself to her feet and looked around. Andrea's spiky platinum-tipped hair was visible in the stampede of people. A few were racing away, but more were running toward Andrea, getting between her and Julie. Julie wanted to shout at them to try to stop Andrea, but her voice wouldn't work, and Andrea vanished as the crowd closed in on her.

Powerful hands clamped onto Julie's shoulders from behind, and she let out a shriek and tried to jerk away. "Shh, Julie. It's me."

Mac.

She wanted to collapse in his arms, burst into tears, let him take over. But she gathered her wits and refused to blubber. She wasn't the sort of woman who depended on men to take over.

He turned her toward him and scrutinized her face, his expression a blend of fear and relief and unadorned rage. "You're okay?"

"I'm fine," Julie said. Not a complete lie, she decided. Physically she was fine. Emotionally she was battered. But the mere sight of Mac's dark, worried eyes, his delectable mouth, the harsh line of his jaw and the warmth of his hands on her… *Fine* would do for now.

He touched his lips to hers, and she felt a lot more fine. Then he pulled back. "Where did she go?"

"I don't know, maybe that way." Julie pointed in the direction where she'd last seen Andrea's bobbing head.

"Don't move," Mac ordered before releasing her and forging into the crowd.

Like hell she wouldn't move. For one thing, she was as enraged as Mac, as determined to stop Andrea. For another, Julie had to be with Mac right now. The moment he'd removed his hands from her, she'd stopped feeling fine. She wanted his nearness. And although she wished she didn't need it, she did.

Besides, her sandals were sticking out of his jacket pockets, and she wanted them back.

She followed in his wake. People seemed to know enough to clear a path for him. Maybe it was his fierce expression, maybe his determined strides, maybe the aura he emanated. Whatever it was, the crowds instinctively backed away and let him through.

Ignoring her stinging knee and throbbing toe, Julie trailed close behind.

He finally caught up to Andrea near the gate leading out to Royal Street. She was racing to escape the park, her purse dangling from her wrist on a strap. Where was her gun? Could she fire it again? Could she fire it at Mac? If she did, if he got hurt… Julie was not a violent person, but she could easily kill Andrea with her bare hands if Andrea hurt Mac.

He launched himself at Andrea, gracefully avoiding the crowds that had stopped to gawk at the confrontation, and brought her down with a clean tackle. She let out a scream, and someone yelled, "Get the police!"

"Yeah, do that," Mac shouted over his shoulder as he

pinned Andrea to the ground. She writhed under him, and he slammed her hand against the pavement. The gun went flying from her fingers.

Julie pounced on it before anyone else could pick it up.

Mac shifted his weight on Andrea until he could force her hands behind her back. "Give me your boa," he called to Julie.

The poor boa was nearly bald, a featherless strip of knitted pink cording. Surely, given the circumstances, Creighton would forgive her for destroying the thing. She promised herself she'd buy him a new one.

Mac took the scrawny boa from her and used it to tie Andrea's hands behind her back. "All right," he said, his voice tight but calm as he eased off her. "Did anyone call the police?"

"They're all directing traffic on Canal Street," someone shouted.

"Great," Mac muttered, pushing himself to his feet and then helping Andrea up. She glowered at him, her bony shoulders straining against her improvised shackles. The two words she uttered were far from ladylike.

"I believe the correct term is 'getting biblical,'" he said, shooting Julie a faint smile. "You've got her gun?"

Julie lifted it up for him to see. She'd never held a gun before. This one was heavier than she'd expected, a dense sculpture of lethal metal. Holding it filled her with a weird mix of potency and dread.

One hand clamped firmly around Andrea's skinny arm, Mac extended the other and Julie placed the gun in it. It looked so small against his large palm.

He shifted his jacket to slide the gun into his trouser pocket. Julie glimpsed another, larger gun tucked into his waistband. Where had that come from? The hotel security staff didn't carry guns.

She'd ask Mac later. Once her mind settled down, once her bloodstream was no longer polluted with adrenaline, once her pulse stopped hammering in her temples. There would be plenty of time for questions later.

Together the threesome made their slow way out of the park and back toward the parking lot. Julie felt her respiration slow. Her chest stopped hurting with every breath. Her throat muscles gradually remembered how to swallow.

She'd nearly died. Andrea Crowley had tried to kidnap her with the purpose of killing her. Why? Because Julie had helped to put a bad guy in jail? A shiver racked her body, causing her legs to wobble beneath her. She was glad Mac and Andrea were ahead of her. She didn't want them to see her falling apart.

They reached the parking lot and he headed directly to his car. After unlocking it, he shoved Andrea into the backseat and strapped her in. "My arms hurt," she whined.

"I'm real sorry about that," he drawled sarcastically before slamming the back door.

"You have no right to tie me up like this," Andrea squawked as Julie opened the passenger-side door. "You aren't the police. I could have you charged with kidnapping. And assault."

"Be my guest," Mac drawled as he settled in behind the wheel.

Julie sank into the leather cushion of the front passenger seat. All her strength drained from her. She felt limp, exhausted.

"What happened to your leg?" Mac asked.

She glanced at him, astonished by the tenderness in his voice. Lowering her gaze, she noticed the blood oozing from her knee. "I guess I scraped it," she said.

He reached into the console between their seats and pulled out a tissue. She expected him to hand it to her, but instead he leaned across the gearshift and gently pressed the tissue to her wound. "We'll get you patched up as soon as I've handed our friend over to the police. Any other injuries?"

She flexed her hand, which no longer hurt. Her toe was still sore, but she decided not to tell him about that. He seemed so unnecessarily worried. "Really, Mac, I'm fine," she said, wishing her voice sounded a little stronger.

"You are amazing," he whispered, then straightened up and started the engine. "I found your car," he said as he maneuvered out of the lot. "You left your key in the ignition. I took it and locked up."

"I think I parked illegally."

"I've got friends on the force," he said. "A parking ticket is an easy thing to fix. How did you get out of the car, once she got you in it?"

Julie permitted herself a smile. "I think I told you my brakes squeak. I convinced her the squeak was an engine malfunction and the car was dying."

He laughed. "Brilliant."

"It wasn't brilliant," she argued. "It was sheer desperation. I didn't know what I was doing, I—" She broke off, aware of how close she was to crying.

"You told me your car was dying," Andrea grumbled in the backseat. "You bitch, you lied about your car!"

Mac snorted and shook his head, then let go of the gearshift and squeezed Julie's hand. He said nothing, for which she was thankful.

The drive to the police station took an eternity. If cops were directing traffic on Canal Street, Julie didn't see them. The traffic resembled downtown rush hour to the tenth degree. Only headlights illuminated the streets; the lack of working traffic signals at the intersections made driving through them perilous. The city spread around Mac's car like a vast ocean of black with massive schools of people swimming through it.

But eventually they arrived at the city's main police headquarters. Mac seemed to know his way around the building, which either hadn't lost power or had several generators keeping the lights aglow and the computers humming.

The night sergeant who stood behind the main desk greeted

Mac by name. "Hey, Mac—looks like you've got more than you can handle tonight," he joked, eyeing Julie and Andrea with a bit more interest than Julie appreciated.

"We've got a bad situation here, Joe," Mac said. "You'd better call the D.A.'s office. And we'll need a doctor."

"I'm fine, Mac. Really," Julie insisted. "All I need is a sink and a Band-Aid."

The sergeant signaled a female officer from the sparsely populated squad room. "Come with me, honey," the woman said, leading Julie away from Mac.

Separated from him, she once again acknowledged how soothing his presence was and how much she would have preferred to stay with him. She tried to listen politely while the officer ushered her down the hall and rambled on about how most of the squad was out dealing with the city-wide power outage, helping people stuck in elevators and assisting with medical emergencies. "I'll tell you this—a lot of new babies are gonna be arriving nine months from now," the woman said with a snort. "What a night. Never a dull moment in New Orleans. You look like you've had a time of it."

Julie pushed open the door to the women's washroom and thanked the officer for having brought her there.

"I'll find you a first-aid kit," she said. "You get yourself cleaned up."

Alone in the bathroom, Julie peeled off her shredded stockings and threw them in the trash can. Then she lifted her leg across one of the sink basins and washed her knee, which looked worse than it was. She examined her toe and found the nail blue but unbroken.

She dabbed her knee with a wet paper towel to wipe off the excess blood, then tossed the towel into the trash can with her stockings. Glimpsing her reflection in the mirror above the sink, she cringed. She looked like hell, her hair half up and half down, her dress wrinkled, her cheeks tearstained. Where had those tears come from?

Wherever they'd come from, she discovered she had plenty more. She slumped against the wall and let the sobs overtake her.

Julie wasn't a weeper. The last time she'd cried was when her beloved Bella had died. When her classmates had teased her, they'd only toughened her. When she'd found out about Glenn Perry's criminal behavior, she'd reported him. When her life as a model had ended, she'd created a new life for herself.

Girls like Andrea Crowley cried. Not Julie.

She supposed crying was allowed for someone who had come as close to being killed as she had. Tears were forgivable for a crime victim. But this meltdown wasn't just over what Andrea had done to her tonight. It came from deep inside her, a wrenching understanding that her life had somehow changed.

She'd always been her own person. When she'd decided to report Glenn to the police, Marcie had cautioned her against it. "Just quit his agency," her sensible older sister had said.

"But he's taking advantage of young girls," Julie had argued. "Someone has to stop him."

"That someone doesn't have to be you," Marcie had argued. "If you report him, you're going to bring a whole lot of grief down on yourself."

Marcie had been right—but Julie had been right, too. Reporting him had saved naive young girls from being exploited. She had never expected that Andrea would resent being saved.

She'd done the right thing then—by herself. She'd gone off to college in Canada by herself, and she'd moved to New Orleans by herself. She was used to her autonomy, used to depending on herself alone to get through each day.

But tonight... Tonight she'd needed Mac. She'd prayed for him to find her, and he had. That was what had changed: for once in her life, she'd wanted someone to help her, to stand by her and protect her, to be her partner. To save her.

Not just someone. Mac Jensen.

She washed her face, blew her nose, pulled the remaining pins from her hair and finger combed it. The female officer entered the bathroom with a first-aid kit, and Julie smeared her knee with antiseptic ointment and taped on a bandage. "Thanks," she said.

"Would you like a cup of coffee?" the woman asked as she escorted Julie back down the hall to the squad room.

"No, thanks." If Julie tried to drink anything right now, she'd probably choke. Or burst into tears again.

"Boy, I remember when Katrina hit a year and a half ago. We were without power for weeks. A good cup of coffee was so rare, it was like the nectar of the gods." The officer sighed at the memory. "You don't realize how dependent you are on something until you have to go without it."

How true. Julie hadn't realized how dependent she'd been on Mac tonight until she'd been taken away from him.

The officer led Julie to a small interview room, where a policeman in street clothes sat at a table. Julie's sandals lay on the table next to his folded hands. Her shoes were scuffed and battered, trampled by the armies of people traipsing around the French Quarter in the dark. Mac stood, holding his cell phone. "How are you?" he asked as the policeman rose to his feet.

"I'm fine." She'd lost count of how many times she'd spoken those words. Mac probably kept asking her how she was because he didn't believe she was fine. He was waiting to hear the truth from her.

Her knee was fine, though. That much wasn't a lie.

"Listen, Julie—there's a problem at the hotel. I've got to go back there."

"What problem?"

He smiled half-heartedly. "Tyrell just called. Nothing for you to worry about. I'll go over, check out the situation and then come back. Okay?"

"I'm fine," Julie said automatically. Her eyes met Mac's, and his smile grew. No doubt he'd also lost count of how many times she'd recited those two false words, but he'd accept them for now.

"This is Detective Rick Pelletier. He'll take good care of you until I get back," Mac promised.

"Okay."

Mac held out a chair for her, and she sat. He brushed his hand against her shoulder, then turned and left the room.

Detective Pelletier resumed his seat as well, opened a notepad and smiled at Julie. "I think he's more shaken up than you are," he said.

Julie smiled back. "I'm pretty shaken up, too."

"Why don't you tell me everything?"

Julie sat back in her chair, rubbed her stinging knee and sighed. Then she proceeded to describe her strange night to Detective Pelletier.

MAC STRUGGLED through the crazy traffic, trying to get back to the police station as quickly as possible. The dark, the erratic drivers, the giddy pedestrians—everything about this godawful night was getting to him. He hadn't wanted to be dealing with a crisis at the hotel. His real job was to be Julie's bodyguard. He'd nearly failed at that. Self-recrimination ate at his gut like battery acid.

But a body had been found in one of the guest rooms back at the hotel. "I don't know if it's foul play," Tyrell had reported, "but you'd better get over here."

Lucky he'd been at the police station. He'd arranged for Joe, the night desk sergeant, to radio for a patrol car to meet him over at the hotel. A body, regardless of the circumstances surrounding the death, was police business.

The party at the hotel had still been raging when Mac had arrived. Fortunately, Tyrell had kept the discovery of the body quiet, and the guests in the courtyard were having a grand old time, dancing to the unamplified band's music and stuffing their faces with food the restaurant was cooking on its gas-powered grills.

Mac didn't belong there. He belonged with Julie.

It was well past 2:00 a.m. by the time he got back to the police station. He wondered if Julie would still be there. Ricky Pelletier might have driven her home by now.

It would serve Mac right if she'd already left. Why should she wait for him? He was useless, the world's worst bodyguard. He ought to return Marcie's money. He'd been busy chasing down e-mails and targeting Glenn Perry, and meanwhile a skinny psycho woman had nearly stolen Julie away from him.

He parked, locked up the car and entered the station. Joe waved him over to the front desk, then motioned toward a bench where Julie was sleeping. "We offered to take her home, but she insisted on waiting for you," Joe told him. "She said she was sure you were coming back."

Mac's heart constricted. She looked so vulnerable asleep, lying on her side with her knees bent—one of them bandaged—and hair spilling over her shoulders. Her lips were parted and her thick, dark eyelashes shaped delicate crescents against her cheeks. Maybe she was vulnerable now, but trekking through a blacked-out French Quarter with a gun digging into her back, she had been strong and courageous.

She'd saved her own life. Mac felt guilty for not having been able to protect her, but his admiration for her—her brains and her guts and her stubborn will—soared.

And she'd waited for him.

He tiptoed over to the bench, hunkered down and touched her arm. Her eyes immediately fluttered open, and she smiled.

"Are you okay?" he asked. "Give me a better answer than 'I'm fine.'"

"Take me home," she said.

That answer would do.

She sat up, pushed her hair back from her face, gathered her sandals and yawned. Mac took her hand and eased her to her feet, then slid his arm around her and led her down the corridor to the door and out to his car. She moved slowly, whether from fatigue or her banged-up knee, he couldn't say. "What was going on at the hotel?" she asked.

No need to alarm her. "There was a problem in one of the guest rooms," he said vaguely as he helped her onto the passenger seat. Tomorrow—or the next day, whenever she felt up to returning to work—she could learn about the mysterious body found in the first-floor room of Matt Anderson, one of the hotel's guests. "Did Ricky Pelletier take good care of you?"

She nodded. "I hope Andrea pleads to some charge. I don't want to have to testify in court. I've done that once, and it didn't work out so well."

"It's history now," Mac assured her, hoping he was correct. Damn it, if he wasn't, if she was still at risk, he'd protect her for the rest of her life. He'd failed her once; he vowed never to fail her again.

Some stretches of the city were still without power, but now, in the space between very late night and very early morning, the streets were relatively quiet, only a few cars and die-hard rowdies out and about. Julie let her head sink against the leather headrest and sighed. Mac suffered a sharp pang deep in his soul. It went beyond anger at having misread the threat to her, beyond guilt that he hadn't protected her. It was a feeling that if he hadn't found her, if that lunatic had actually used her gun on Julie, he would not have been able to go on.

"Why her?" he asked, trying to drag his thoughts away from the scary place they'd wandered. "She was…what? A fellow model, right?"

Julie nodded, her eyes focused straight ahead into the black night on the other side of the windshield. "She was one of the younger girls at the agency. She came from some small Midwest town, and she had big ideas about fame and fortune. She hadn't even finished high school. Someone told her she had what it took to be a model, so she came to New York."

"She had guts. It takes guts to stalk a woman and kidnap her."

Julie shrugged. "Back then, Andrea was kind of timid and

insecure. But Glenn Perry took her under his wing. He promised to take care of her. And man, did he ever. She was one of the girls he got hooked on amphetamines to keep her weight down. And then he started sleeping with her. She was convinced he loved her."

Mac made a face. "Somehow, this starry-eyed romantic picture isn't fitting with the gun-toting bitch I dragged into the police station."

"She changed," Julie said, her bland tone emphasizing what an understatement that was. "Apparently, she carried a torch for Glenn the whole time he was in jail. When he got paroled, she went to New York to be with him. He showed her the door. He wanted nothing to do with her."

"And she blamed you," Mac guessed.

Julie nodded wearily. "It *was* my fault. If I hadn't gone to the police, Glenn would have still been running his modeling agency."

"And that woman would have still been washed up, drug addicted and dumped," Mac said. "All you did was save her a few years of wear and tear and heartbreak."

"Maybe I was wrong," Julie said quietly. "I was so self-righteous, Mac. I thought Glenn was ruining people's lives, so I called him on it. Maybe I should have just kept my head down and my mouth shut."

"And let the guy continue breaking the law and screwing girls young enough to be his daughters? No, Julie. You weren't wrong."

"I'm always so sure of myself," she muttered. "I was sure of myself when I turned Glenn in. I was sure I was saving these girls and making the world a better place and all that." She paused, cast a soft, melancholy gaze his way, then said, "I was so sure that a woman should fend for herself, that she should never trust a man who claims he's going to take care of her. Because too often, he takes care of himself at her expense. So she's got to watch out for herself, be dependent only on herself."

"That's not the worst way to get through life," Mac said.

"But when Andrea was dragging me at gunpoint around the French Quarter…" Julie sighed again. "I wanted you to save me. I kept leaving feathers for you to follow, because I wanted you to save me."

"I wanted to save you, Julie." His voice broke slightly, and he swallowed. "It kills me that I wasn't able to."

She looked at him again, startled. "You *did* save me."

"Not until after she took a shot at you." He swallowed again, reliving that ghastly moment when he'd heard the pop of a gun firing. How could Julie think he'd saved her? By the time he'd made the scene, Andrea was already on the run.

Julie believed he'd saved her because she wanted to. He could argue or let her believe what she wanted. Right now the last thing he wanted was to argue with her.

Julie's neighborhood in the Garden District was as dark as the French Quarter had been. Mac pulled up the driveway and parked in the paved area near the door. He shut off the engine and turned to her.

"What happened to the city?" she asked. "Where did all the electricity go?"

"I'm sure they'll figure it out sooner or later. Probably a breakdown in a regional center."

"Do you think we'll be without power a long time?"

He brushed a strand of hair back from her cheek and smiled. "You'll never be without power, Julie. You're the most powerful woman I've ever known."

"A regular Wonder Woman," she said dryly. She glanced toward the shadowed front porch of the seedy old mansion. "How will I get inside? I don't have my keys."

Mac reached into his jacket pocket and produced the key ring he'd pulled from her car. "Yes, you do," he said, then shoved his door open, got out and circled the car to help her out.

Her sandals in one hand, she swung her legs to the brick front walk. Standing, she winced.

Mac didn't bother to ask how she was. She'd only say she was fine, and clearly she wasn't. He lifted her into his arms, surprised at how light she was, given her statuesque height.

"Mac, put me down," she complained even as she clung to his neck. "I'm not a cripple."

"Not crippled, just a little wounded." He carried her up to the porch, lowered her gently to her feet and unlocked the front door for her, groping only briefly before he found the keyhole.

"Mac," she murmured. Her hands had slid from around his neck to his chest when he'd released her, and his lungs filled with her sweet gardenia scent. Her hair brushed against his chin, soft as mink. And she was so close to him, so damn close, and her hands rested on him, and her eyes were so large and pleading.

He'd almost lost her tonight. But he hadn't. She was here.

His brain shut down and his heart took over. Bowing, he took her mouth with his.

CHAPTER FOURTEEN

HER KNEE HURT. Her toe hurt. But neither of them hurt the way her body did, a sweet, womanly ache that only Mac could ease. His hand was closed around hers as she climbed the stairs to her apartment, her free hand on the railing and Mac's tracing the wall so they could feel their way safely up to the second floor.

The upstairs hall was so dark she couldn't see Mac. She could feel him, sense his warmth, smell his alluring aura. He pressed her keys into her hand, and she fumbled for a few seconds until she finally got her apartment door unlocked. The entry was as dark as the hall outside and unnervingly silent.

"The aquarium pump," she said, naming the noise that was missing. Her poor fish! Would their water get too cold with the heating filter pump out of commission?

"Have you got a flashlight?" Mac asked, halting her before she could charge through the darkness to the tank.

He was right. She wouldn't even see her fish without a light.

"Wait here," she said. In the dark she'd have enough difficulty walking to the kitchen, where she kept a flashlight as well as candles, and she knew the apartment. Mac had never been inside it before.

Fortunately, she reached the tiny kitchen without stubbing any toes or tripping on anything. The flashlight was on the shelf in her broom closet, and once she had its light to guide her, she gathered a few candles to fit the candlesticks she owned. After wedging two tapers into holders and locating a box of safety matches, she returned to the living room, carefully aiming the flashlight at Mac's chest so she wouldn't blind him.

The circle of white light struck his loosened tie and unfastened collar. Julie eyed the skin at the base of his throat and shivered—not from the lack of heat. *Mac is in my apartment,* she thought, lifting her gaze to his face. Enough of the flashlight's beam bled upward to define the edges of his chin and nose, the contours of his cheeks and brows. Another shiver gripped her—and she definitely wasn't cold.

So much hadn't made sense tonight: the unexpected appearance of Andrea Crowley using the name Maggie Jones, the blackout, the abduction. The hours at the police station. The fear, the stubborn determination to survive, the sheer joy of being found by Mac in the midst of the bedlam in Jackson Square. The only thing that made any sense at all was having Mac here with her now.

"Let's check your fish," he said.

The flashlight guided them across the living room to the silent tank. She set the candles on her coffee table and dipped her pinkie into the water. It was still warm. Her fish glided back and forth from glass wall to glass wall until the flashlight attracted their attention. They flurried over to the tank wall, their unblinking eyes fixed on Mac. *This is what a man looks like, guys,* Julie wanted to say. Other than Creighton, these fish rarely saw men in her apartment.

"I think the water's warm enough for now," she said. "I should wrap the tank with some towels to insulate it, just in case this blackout lasts a long time."

The flashlight got her safely to her linen closet and back. Mac helped her swaddle the base of the tank with thick towels. She didn't know if that layer of terry cloth would make any difference, but she hated the thought of her fish suffering in this dark, noiseless world.

Mac must have sensed her worry. "They'll be okay," he said, bringing his arms around her.

She rested her head against his shoulder, grateful that he'd taken her concern seriously rather than scoffing that she was making a ridiculous fuss over a half-dozen fish worth only a few dollars. They were her pets, her companions, and he respected that.

She felt his lips brush the crown of her head and lifted her face to him. His mouth covered hers, gentle and restrained, but she sensed the hunger in him. He didn't have to be restrained with her. She was a little wounded, as he'd said, but she felt whole, solid, strong, and she wanted to be kissed with everything Mac had to give. She wanted him to light her dark world with his kiss.

She parted her lips, and he took what she offered, his self-control melting away. His tongue swept deep into her mouth, claiming, devouring. *Yes,* she thought, *yes, I want this. I'm alive and I want Mac.*

His hands moved on her back. One slid up into her hair, and he drew back a little, then tilted his head and kissed her again, capturing her lower lip with his teeth before tangling his tongue with hers. For a moment, enveloped in his arms and the soft darkness, she imagined making love with Mac right here, standing in her living room.

Mac had other ideas. He pulled his mouth from hers, kissed her cheek, grazed the edge of her earlobe, then whispered, "Where's your bed, darlin'?"

She loved hearing him call her *darlin'*—not only because it sounded so damn sexy in his gravelly drawl but because it meant he was finally accepting that she was fine. He'd been so somber in the car, so grim and anxious. Now, at last, he seemed able to accept that she was safe, that he'd saved her and she didn't resent him for it.

Far from resenting him, she desired him. Because he'd saved her. Because he'd come for her. Because he was Mac.

She took a step back and turned to light the candles. Mac

lifted one, and she took the other. Together they walked down the short hall to her bedroom.

She set her candle on the night table next to her bed, and he placed his on the dresser. The two flickering flames gave them just enough light to find each other, to see what they had to see.

Mac pulled her into his arms again. He scooped her hair into his hands, smiling as if the mere feel of it sifting through his fingers turned him on. He dropped a light, teasing kiss on her lips and whispered, "I've got to do something," before turning her around. Lifting her hair away from her neck, he kissed her nape. She heard him sigh, then kiss that sensitive skin again. She sighed, too.

"When I saw your hair pinned up this evening," he whispered, "all I could think of was kissing you there." He kissed her again and again, hot, eager kisses that stoked the ache inside her.

She breathed his name. He responded by inching down the zipper of her dress, and when he grazed her bare shoulder with his mouth, she gasped.

"Julie." He touched his lips to the place where her bra strap would have been if she'd been wearing a bra. "I don't have anything with me."

Of course he didn't. He hadn't expected to be seducing her tonight. She hadn't expected to be seducing him. Maybe she'd hoped—without ever admitting it to herself—that he'd be entranced by her appearance. Maybe when she'd chosen this dress, which she couldn't wear with a bra because of the daringly low-cut front, and when she'd pinned her hair up, she'd been secretly imagining that her appearance would knock Mac sideways. When he'd danced with her at the party—it seemed like a century ago, rather than just a few hours—she'd believed he found her tempting. But she hadn't expected him to act on that temptation.

Neither, apparently, had he.

"I think we're okay." She slipped out of his arms and

moved to her night table. In the drawer, along with her phone book, notepaper, pens and assorted other clutter, she located a three-pack of condoms, the sort of item single women tended to keep in their drawers, just in case.

Mac took the package from her, kissed it, grinned and kissed her. He opened the package and dropped it onto the night table. Then he shrugged off his jacket and tossed it into a dark corner across the room from the candles.

His elegant suit—didn't he want to take better care of it? Evidently not. He pulled his loosened tie over his head as if he were escaping a lasso and sent it sailing into the same dark corner.

Julie reached for the buttons of his shirt before he could open them. No longer having to undress himself, he concentrated on her, easing her dress over her shoulders and down her arms. The bodice went slack at her waist. A sigh escaped him as he gazed at her naked torso.

He backed up to the bed, sat and drew her close, sandwiching her with his thighs. Then he buried his lips in the hollow between her breasts. Julie leaned into him, her legs shaky beneath her. She pushed his shirt down his arms and off, exposing the most gloriously male shoulders she'd ever seen. She ran her hands over their warm surface of muscle and bone, flexed her fingers, dug her fingertips into the firm flesh and provoked a gasp from him.

He pulled back, and she saw no trace of his smile. His eyes were glazed, his breathing unnaturally deep as he peered up at her. "Oh, Julie," he said, half a groan, half a plea.

He peeled the sleeves of her dress from her arms, and it slid over her hips and onto the floor. He tugged her panties down, letting them join her dress. Then he pulled her into his lap and kissed her.

She loved the way his naked chest felt against her breasts, and she was suddenly desperate to strip the rest of him, to feel his entire body against hers, to make him as vulnerable to her as she was to him. He must have read her mind, because he shifted, allowing her to tumble onto the bed, and then yanked open his belt and stripped off his trousers and briefs with ruthless efficiency.

Whatever power problems afflicted New Orleans, Julie's bedroom was ablaze with energy. Mac's skin was hot; his body seemed to glow as the amber light from the flickering candles glazed the rippling muscles of his torso, the taut surface of his abdomen, the sparse hair texturing his chest and the darker hair at his groin, framing his erection. Julie touched him the way the candlelight did, imparting heat and light with every stroke.

Mac let her explore his body as he explored hers, his caresses nearly as gentle as hers. His hands were large and warm against her skin. His mouth ignited her, making her burn everywhere it touched. His tongue sent fire along her nerve endings.

As eager as she was for him, he held back, taking his time to nip first one breast and then the other, tenderly massaging her belly, planting healing kisses in a circle around the bandaged scrape on her knee. An eternity passed before he finally settled his fingers between her legs, stroking her where the fire burned most fervently, where all the energy in the universe seemed to gather, waiting just for him, for this.

She filled her hands with him. He was so hard, and with each caress he grew harder, until he thrust against her palm and then groaned and eased her hand from him. After kissing her fingertips, he reached for the condom. He tore open the packet and handed its contents to her.

His eyes never left her. She had to look down to perform the intimate act of sheathing him, but she felt him still watching her. When he was ready, she glanced upward, and their gazes merged.

From the very first time their paths had crossed, Mac had been watching her. And she realized she'd been watching him, too. Less purposefully, perhaps, but just as intensely.

She opened to him, guided him to her, and he thrust deep.

This was a joining like no other. For the first time in her life she knew what it meant to depend on a man, to give herself completely to a man, to trust that a man would give her what she needed. She trusted Mac and let go, and to her amazement she felt infused with power. Depending on him seemed like a remarkable act of independence.

His surges were slow and controlled and so deep she was certain he was reaching parts of her that had never been touched before. She lifted her legs around his waist, clutched his hips, urged him deeper. She met his gaze until she had to close her eyes. What she was feeling was too personal, too exquisite. She couldn't look at him while her entire being, heart and soul, lay exposed to his perceptive gaze.

Still moving inside her, he propped himself up. "Julie," he murmured. "Look at me, *chère*."

She opened her eyes and saw the need illuminating his, the want, the love. Her body convulsed, deep spasms racking her, so fierce they hurt. She heard herself moan, then heard Mac moan, as well, his body pumping hard and fast, all control gone. He went rigid in her arms, stopped breathing—but never stopped watching her, his eyes mating with hers as thoroughly as his body did.

He let out a ragged breath, then dropped a weary kiss onto her mouth. She felt his weight on her, his sweat mixing with hers, his body still locked tight inside her as she pulsed around him. She wanted him there forever, joined to her, a part of her.

But eventually he went slack and pulled away. "Ah, Julie," he murmured, sounding almost wistful. He rolled onto his back and stared at the ceiling. The candlelight didn't reach that high, and a stretch of black loomed above them like a starless, moonless sky.

Something was wrong. Julie knew it just as surely as she'd known that making love with Mac had been right, opening herself to him had been inevitable, trusting him had been essential. Now that the love and trust were there, he was withdrawing from her.

"What is it?" she asked.

He eyed her with surprise, smiled, looped an arm around her and drew her against him, cushioning her head with his shoulder and sliding one leg between her thighs. "What is what?" he asked.

"You seem..." She struggled for the right word. "Apprehensive."

"No."

Resting against his shoulder, she could see only the line of his jaw. He no longer met her gaze. Maybe *apprehensive* described her more accurately than him. "Don't lie to me, Mac."

He stroked his hand up and down her arm. A long, tense minute passed, and he said, "I've been lying to you all along, *chère.*"

That statement, at least, was the truth. She knew it from his resigned tone, from his hesitancy. He was speaking honestly now—and what he had to say was that he'd lied to her.

She pushed away from him, even though that meant losing the warmth of his arm around her and his body next to hers. Sitting, she felt a chill that had nothing to do with the fact that the heat hadn't come on in her apartment all night. As long as Mac avoided her gaze, ice would settle inside her where just moments ago she'd been on fire.

I've been lying to you all along. "What have you lied about?" she asked, even though she feared his answer. Maybe, despite his personnel records, he was married. Maybe he had a criminal record. Maybe he was leaving town tomorrow and she'd never see him again. Maybe he had an incurable disease.

Whatever he'd been lying about, she knew it was bad.

He glanced her way and smiled. "Come here, darlin'," he said, extending his hand. "We don't have to discuss this now."

They sure as hell *did* have to discuss it now. She deflected his touch, then sighed as he circled his fingers around her wrist and brought her hand to rest on his chest. "You'd better tell me," she warned. "Whatever it is, it can't be as bad as what I'm imagining."

He steered his gaze back to the ceiling. "I'm not a hotel security guard," he said.

Given all the worst case-scenarios that had zoomed through her mind, his confession struck her as hilarious. "Of course you are," she said, suppressing a laugh. He'd filled the job of hotel security guard every day for more than six weeks. He'd run the security office, managed the security staff, uncovered mishaps like the glass in the towels and addressed the needs of guests. Even if he chose not to call himself a hotel security guard, that was what he was.

"No." He let out a long breath. "I'm a security consultant. A private investigator."

"You worked at that place, I know. Before the hotel hired you, you worked at…what was it? Crescent City something?"

"Crescent City Security Services. I don't just work there, Julie. I founded the business with a friend. I own it."

This still didn't seem like a tragedy. Why Mac seemed so grim puzzled her. "So…you wanted to supplement your income by working at the hotel?" she guessed.

"No." Once again, he turned to gaze at her. The candle on her night table was reflected in his eyes, twin yellow flames flickering in the darkest parts of his irises. "I was hired to watch you. I took the job at the hotel so I could do that."

"You were hired to watch me." The words came out in a shocked whisper. Even his hand covering hers couldn't impart warmth to her. Oh, God, she'd been right all along. He'd been watching her. *Because someone had hired him to.* "And that's why you're in my bed right now? Because someone hired you to watch me?"

"No!" He pushed away from the mattress, but he must have noticed her recoiling from him because he lowered himself back to the pillow. "I'm here in your bed because I'm crazy about you."

"Oh. Right." Sarcasm vibrated through her voice. "Is that why you watch me? Because you're crazy about me?"

"I watched you because I was paid to."

"Who paid you?"

"Don't ask me that, Julie. I've already said too much."

Anger bubbled up inside her, surprising her with its ferocity. She wasn't a violent person, even after what she'd been through earlier that night. But she wanted to hit Mac, hit him hard. It took all her willpower to keep from swinging at him. "I've asked," she retorted. "You'd better tell me."

His smile became placating. "I can't. The client doesn't want to be known, and I've got to respect the client's wishes."

"I suppose that's more important than respecting me," she said sharply.

"It's completely different." He propped himself up on his elbows, then sat fully, his eyes now level with hers. "I respect you with all my heart, Julie. I respect you in ways I can't even put into words. But I've got a contract with a client, and I have to respect that, too." He cupped his hand under her chin and caressed her cheek with his thumb. "Would it have been better for me to keep lying to you? I respect you too much to do that."

She couldn't digest his sweet words. They returned on her like something rancid. "Who hired you?" she demanded. "Glenn Perry?" Was her old boss after her? Now that she'd escaped Andrea Crowley's insane revenge, would she face Glenn's? Was Mac, the man who had just made love to her so sublimely, setting her up for Glenn? Damn it, would Mac do that to her? The mere possibility made her want to scream.

"It's not Glenn. The person who hired me wanted me to protect you from Glenn. My client thought he'd be coming after you, darlin'. He's not doing that, though, and at this point I'm convinced he won't. He's busy being a law-abiding citizen back in New York City, rebuilding his life and checking in regularly with his parole officer. You're safe from him."

But she wasn't safe from Mac. "Then who is it? Who hired you? Who wants me watched?"

He shook his head. "Someone who wanted me to protect you from harm, that's all. And I didn't do a very good job," he muttered, staring past her at the candle on her dresser. "You could have gotten killed tonight."

"Maybe you'd better phone your client and let him know," she said bitterly. "Gotta keep your priorities straight, Mac. The client always comes first."

"The client has nothing to do with what happened here," Mac argued, gesturing toward the bed. "Even before, when I was following your trail of pink feathers, I wasn't thinking about the client. Just you. Saving you, keeping you in my life."

"I don't want you in my life," she said. The words sounded false—but then, Mac had lied to her. Now it was her turn to lie. She wanted Mac, desperately. But not when he was receiving money to watch her. Not when he was answering to someone else. Not when, even after calling himself a liar, he refused to tell her the whole truth.

"Julie—"

"Get out. Get the hell out of here." She wrapped her arms around her legs, rested her chin on her knees and closed her eyes. He wanted her to look at him? Forget that. She never wanted to see him again.

And she sure as hell didn't want him to see the tears leaking through her lashes. She prayed the room was dark enough that he wouldn't notice.

She heard him sigh, then felt the mattress heave under her as he shifted to the edge and stood. At least he respected her enough to leave her.

She listened to the sounds of him getting dressed—the rustle and whisper of fabric, the rasp of a zipper as he closed his fly. Her hero, she thought resentfully. Earlier that evening, when she'd felt Andrea's gun jabbing her, she'd wanted Mac to be her hero. And he had been. He'd come, he'd found her, he'd captured Andrea. He'd taken her home. He'd made love to her.

But she'd wanted him to make love to her because his heart was as filled with her as hers was with him, not because someone was paying him.

So much began to make sense: his expensive suits, his expensive car, his friendship with police officers and street musicians. His gun. Even with her eyes closed, she was aware of his easy grace and confidence as he wandered through the dark bedroom, gathering his clothes. In a bedroom he'd never been inside before, and with the whispering light of two small candles, Mac moved as if he owned the ground he walked on, as if he'd memorized every nub in the rug, every seam in the floorboards underneath it.

He wasn't the Hotel Marchand's security chief. He wasn't a knight in shining armor who'd saved her life because he loved her. He was a slick, suave private eye, getting paid by the hour to watch her.

And she'd thought being kidnapped at gunpoint had been horrible.

Hero for hire. Goddamn liar. How much longer until he walked out her door and she could open her eyes again?

CHAPTER FIFTEEN

HE THOUGHT ABOUT DRIVING to his office, but if it had been affected by the blackout, he would never be able to get inside. The building's security system was powered by electricity, and only the building's management possessed keys that could override the system. So he drove home instead.

The empty streets matched the emptiness in his heart. He was too tired to sleep, too wired to think. His skin was imprinted with Julie. If he closed his eyes, he could imagine her hair swirling through his fingers, her breasts firm and sweet in his hands, her body hot and wet and throbbing around him.

If he closed his eyes, he'd drive into a light pole. That actually didn't seem like such a bad idea, but he kept his vision on the road ahead, cruised through empty intersections and found a parking space near the entry to his building.

The power was on here, for what that was worth. He went inside, climbed the stairs, unlocked his door and stormed directly to the kitchen, to the cabinet where he stored his bourbon. He took a swig straight from the bottle.

What a bastard he was. He'd betrayed just about everyone who mattered. When Julie's sister had hired him, she'd made him promise not to let Julie know he was guarding her, and he'd betrayed Marcie by breaking that promise. He'd betrayed Frank by failing to honor a client's trust, which was really bad for their business, and by making love to Julie, which was incredibly unprofessional. He'd betrayed Charlotte Marchand and the hotel's staff by pretending to be something he wasn't.

And Julie. God, he'd betrayed her.

He crossed to the living room window and stared at the dark, sleeping world beyond the pane. No carousers paraded up and down the sidewalks here. No lights illuminated the windows. No headlights stabbed the night. He gazed out and saw nothing at all.

He couldn't see the bottle from which he was drinking, either, but he was able to gauge from its weight and the sound of liquid sloshing inside it that it was at least half-full. Enough bourbon to knock him out cold, but not enough to wash away the guilt and pain that roiled his gut and tarnished his soul.

At least Julie was safe. He was convinced Glenn Perry posed no threat. And Andrea, in police custody, would never cause Julie any harm. The only person who could hurt her now was him, and he'd done a damn good job of that.

He didn't suppose she'd feel better knowing he was hurting far worse than she was.

The bourbon slid down his throat, warm and potent. A few gulps and Julie's scent, a mix of gardenias and female arousal, faded from his memory. A few more gulps and he could almost ignore the need humming through his body. There wasn't enough bourbon in the bottle to enable him to forget the dread that had stormed through him when he'd heard the pop of Andrea's gun, or the staggering relief that had replaced the dread when he'd found Julie alive. There wasn't enough bourbon in the entire world to enable him to forget what making love to her had felt like.

He'd have to get by with what he had—in bourbon and in life. In bourbon, half a bottle. In life, a resplendent array of screw-ups. Maybe he could repair some of the damage. Not tonight, not when he was too busy hating himself to think straight. But eventually.

He dozed off before he could drain the bottle. Seated in an easy chair near the window, he dreamed about Julie, the way her hands had floated over the length of his back, the way her hair had snagged in the stubble of his overnight beard, the magnificent length of her legs, the taste of her tongue. He dreamed about the loss of light and the heedless crowds clogging the streets of the French Quarter. He dreamed he was stranded on a corner, searching desperately for a pink feather, utterly convinced that his existence depended on finding it.

When he woke up, the sky outside the window was a milky white, and his refrigerator's motor was churning. His head pounded as if someone was wielding a sledgehammer inside his skull, and the muscles in his neck seemed to have turned to concrete. The aches in his joints when he stood gave him some idea of what his father must feel like when his arthritis flared up.

He staggered to the bathroom, peeling off his clothing as he went, and took a long, hot shower. Then he brushed his teeth several times to scrub the sour residue of bourbon from his mouth. He swallowed a couple ibuprofen for his headache, pulled on a pair of sweats and trudged to the kitchen to brew some coffee. He added chicory. He needed the strong stuff.

Six-thirty in New Orleans would be seven-thirty in New York—not too early to begin reclamation work on the disaster he'd wrought last night.

He carried his mug of coffee to his desk, turned on his computer and listened to it click and hiss as it warmed up. Why minutes spent waiting for a computer to warm up took longer than ordinary minutes he couldn't say, but eventually the familiar blue of his Windows screen filled the monitor. He called up his phone book, found Marcie Sullivan's home number and dialed.

She answered on the third ring. "Hello?"

"Marcie Sullivan?"

"Who is this?"

He sipped his coffee and cleared his throat. "This is Mac Jensen in New Orleans."

"Oh." A brief pause. "Oh, God. I heard about your power outage. The French Quarter was out."

"I've got power," he told her. "I'm hoping the rest of the city does by now."

"Is Julie okay?"

"She's fine," he told her. "She ran into a little trouble, but it's been taken care of and she's fine." He proceeded to tell Marcie about Andrea Crowley, whose name meant nothing to Marcie. He explained that Andrea had waited for Glenn Perry all the years he was in jail and blamed Julie for having ruined his life and Andrea's.

"Andrea Crowley is under arrest," he reported. "And every indication says Perry had nothing to do with her attempt at revenge and wants nothing to do with Julie. I know Perry's the one you were worried about. Turns out we were wrong to focus on him, but right to worry."

Marcie demanded several more times that Mac swear her sister was safe and sound. He could manage that without too much difficulty. But when Marcie started gushing about how wonderful he was, he couldn't bear it. He was in no mood to let anyone say anything positive about him.

"Listen, Marcie," he said, cutting her off. "I'm not wonderful. I told Julie I'd been hired to watch her."

"Oh, no," Marcie said, anxiety edging her words. "You told her? You swore to me you wouldn't."

"I know."

"She'll hate me. She'll be so mad—"

"I didn't tell her *you* hired me," he clarified. "Just that *someone* hired me to be a kind of bodyguard for her."

Marcie digested this news. "She isn't an idiot. She'll figure out it was me."

"Maybe."

"Why did you tell her?" Marcie railed. "She hates when people try to take care of her. That's why I made you promise not to let her know. How could you—"

He wasn't about to tell Marcie what had happened. If Julie wanted to share the details of her sex life with her sister, that was her business. "I'm sorry. I'll refund your money."

"You don't have to do that," Marcie said without much enthusiasm.

"We had a deal, Marcie. I made a promise and I broke it. That puts me in breach of contract. I'll have a check cut and sent to you." Before she could argue, he disconnected the call.

Wasn't confession supposed to be good for the soul? Mac had done the right thing in confessing to Marcie, and his conscience would emerge even more purified once he'd returned the money she'd paid him. But he still felt like hell, and the quantity of bourbon he'd consumed mere hours ago wasn't the reason.

His next call was to Frank. Unlike Marcie Sullivan, Frank lived in the same time zone as Mac, and the call awakened him. "What are you, nuts?" Frank growled. "I spent half the night trying to get Sandy pregnant. I deserve some sleep."

"It's not that early," Mac argued. Just as Marcie didn't need to hear about Julie's sex life, Mac didn't need to hear about Frank's. "I screwed up, Frank. I told Julie Sullivan."

"You told her what?" Frank asked, sounding less irritable than concerned.

"Everything. Everything except who hired Crescent City."

Frank cursed. "Why?"

"That's personal," Mac said.

Frank was a good enough friend not to press him. He was also a good enough friend to speak honestly. "You blew it, buddy."

"Tell me."

"What happens now?"

"I informed the client I'd reimburse her for the fees she'd paid. That'll come out of my pocket, Frank, not out of the firm."

"Don't turn into a martyr on me, Mac," Frank shot back. "It'll come out of the firm. At least you're bringing in a salary from the Hotel Marchand. Crescent City can absorb the hit."

"Can it absorb the hit to its integrity?" Mac asked.

"Sure," Frank said, though he didn't sound as positive as Mac would have liked. More of that damn honesty, he reckoned.

"All right, look. The shit hit the fan last night. Someone from New York—not Glenn Perry but some model who'd been in love with him—tried to kidnap Julie and took a shot at her. Julie's okay, the model's in custody and, as they say, my work here is done. I've still got a ton of stuff to take care of at the hotel. While you and Sandy were making babies last night, I was dealing with more crap than you can imagine. So I've got to go and tie up loose ends, and then maybe help the hotel hire a replacement for me as their head of security. It's the least I can do."

"Don't quit the hotel yet," Frank said. "I'm still trying to track down that missing money. Did you know Anne Marchand had a baby brother?"

"Is he in the hotel business, too?"

"Nope. He's in the black-sheep business. He wasn't a Marchand, anyway. He was a Robichaux. Disappeared from New Orleans years ago. Makes you wonder, doesn't it?"

Mysteries like the disappearances of family black sheep were why Mac and Frank had set up Crescent City Security in the first place. Mac had majored in psychology for a reason; he liked trying to figure out why people did the things they did. On any other occasion, he'd be sharing Frank's curiosity about Anne Marchand's brother.

But today he was in too much pain. His head hurt, his gut hurt, and his heart... *Hurt* didn't begin to describe what his heart was experiencing.

"It's not like the hotel's hired us to track down the money," Mac reminded him. "We were just pursuing this on our own."

"Right. And it's interesting, don't you think?"

"I've just cost us a bunch of money with Marcie Sullivan," Mac argued. "I don't know that we ought to be taking on another case for free. We can talk about it later, okay?" He said goodbye and disconnected the call. His coffee had gone cold but he drank it anyway for medicinal purposes, then stalked to his bedroom to change into suitable clothes for work.

The city looked relatively normal as he drove across town to the French Quarter. Some cars were illegally parked and ticketed—Mac would have to clear up any parking tickets stuck under Julie's windshield wiper—and more trash than usual sullied the sidewalks, but the storefronts remained intact and no signs of vandalism marred the buildings gliding past his car. Pedestrians ambled slowly, many of them looking hung over, but they probably would have looked that way without the blackout. Twelfth Night was a time for heavy-duty partying in New Orleans.

He drove to the street where he'd seen Julie's car last night. It was no longer parked by the hydrant. He hoped she'd moved it herself. If she hadn't, he'd have to assume the car was towed or stolen. The police had had more important things to do than tow illegally parked cars last night. A stolen car was always a possibility, though.

A few ripe curses tripped over Mac's tongue as he continued to the parking lot. Those curses died on his lips when he saw Julie's car next to a hulking SUV. Mac parked his own car and then jogged across the lot to check hers out. He noticed no obvious damage. No ticket lying on the passenger seat, either.

All of which meant Julie might be in a marginally better frame of mind than if her car had been stolen. But she still wouldn't want to see Mac.

He tugged the door handle to make sure her car was locked, then headed down the street toward the hotel. As he walked, he gave himself a firm mental lecture. He reminded himself that he was a professional, that his firm's reputation rested on his shoulders. How he acted at the hotel would reflect on Crescent City Security, on Frank, on Mac himself. That he'd made love to Julie was irrelevant. That she'd kicked him out of her apartment and her life…that was between him and her. No one at the hotel had to know.

"Some night, huh," Carlos greeted him as he entered the cramped office near the service entrance. "How'd you make out?"

Mac tried not to cringe at Carlos's unfortunate choice of words. "My building never lost power," he said. "How about you?"

"My girlfriend and I ate a lot of ice cream," Carlos said with a grin. "We found other ways to pass the time, too."

Cripes. Had New Orleans been one big orgy last night?

"Then I arrive at work this morning and find out things were insane here," Carlos continued. "I read Tyrell's report. I hope you don't mind."

"Not at all," Mac said, accepting the folder Carlos handed him. Tyrell had done a comprehensive job reporting the discovery of the body last night in Matt Anderson's room. The folder included not just Tyrell's report but also a police report and a coroner's preliminary report, as well as a statement from Eddie in maintenance concerning the damage to the generator. He didn't mention Luc Carter in his description, and Mac mulled over whether to add that bit of information. He couldn't prove Luc had had anything to do with the sabotage, but Mac would be having a little discussion with the kid soon.

Of course, he wouldn't be having any kind of discussion with Luc if he lost his job as the hotel's head of security. Julie might have informed Charlotte about his true identity, and Charlotte might have already asked Julie to type up a resignation letter for Mac to sign.

If so, he assured himself, Tyrell could handle Luc Carter. In fact, Tyrell could probably run the Security Department successfully, if he was willing to adjust his inner clock and work days instead of nights. Mac reckoned he'd be willing, since switching to working days would mean a huge promotion for him. With an ace like Carlos backing him up, Tyrell would make an excellent head of security. Mac would be sure to recommend him.

As if Charlotte would be open to any suggestions he might have.

Get it over with, he ordered himself, tucking the folder under his arm. "I'm heading upstairs to review this with Miss Charlotte," he told Carlos.

Carlos's gaze was fixed on the monitor above the desk. "Go ahead. I've got everything covered down here."

Mac avoided the lobby route, unsure of whether he had the authority to interrogate Luc Carter—assuming Luc was at the concierge desk. Instead, he took the back steps to the second floor and strode down the hall to the administrative offices. He paused at the open door to Julie's office. His gaze took in her desk, the computer he'd hacked into, the spot near her door where he'd kissed her the first time, where he'd acknowledged that keeping his hands off her was the most difficult challenge he'd ever have to face. As things turned out, it was a challenge he'd failed at.

The chair behind her desk was empty now. Julie wasn't in the office. A blend of disappointment and relief washed through him. Sooner or later he'd have to confront her, even if that involved dropping to his knees and begging her forgiveness. He ought to take care of business before he humbled himself before her. Surely Charlotte Marchand would want to spend a few minutes humbling him first.

The door to the adjacent office was also open, and when he glanced in, he saw Charlotte seated at her desk. She looked attractive, but a bit fatigued, her hair mussed and her eyes circled with shadows. He hoped he hadn't added to her exhaustion, but he suspected he had.

He tapped lightly on the door frame. Charlotte glanced up and smiled, such a warm, natural smile that he had to wonder whether she knew the truth about him. "Mac. Thank goodness you're here," she said, beckoning him inside.

He hadn't bothered to put on a tie, but his open shirt collar still seemed to press on his windpipe. Charlotte's office looked pretty, as always, and sunlight streamed through the tall windows overlooking the courtyard. She was dressed neatly, and her eyes seemed to brighten as he entered the room. She stood, sidestepped the desk and startled him by intercepting him in the middle of the office. She wrapped her arms around him and gave him a warm hug. "I'll never be able to thank you enough," she murmured, "but I am so grateful."

For what? Bewildered, he gingerly patted her back, then leaned away from her embrace. "Excuse me?"

"You saved our Julie. Of all the things that happened last night, the scariest was Julie's abduction. If you hadn't saved her…" Charlotte pressed her hand to her chest, as if holding her heart in place. "But you *did* save her. I owe you—all of us here owe you so much, Mac. Julie is like a baby sister to me. Not that I need any more baby sisters," she added with a laugh.

"I'm not sure who your source is," he said, "but I didn't save Julie. She saved herself."

"That's not the story she's telling. Now, Mac, stop being so modest and accept the fact that you're a genuine hero." She gestured toward one of the chairs facing her desk and resumed her own seat on the other side. "I was surprised she came to work today, after all she went through last night. She certainly deserved to take the day off. The week, if she chose. But she insisted she wanted to be here."

"She's an amazing woman," Mac said.

"Yes, she is." Charlotte grinned. "And thanks to you, she's alive and well."

"She's not in her office right now," Mac noted. "Do you know where she is?" *Avoiding me? Searching for me? Searching for me while armed with a carving knife from the restaurant kitchen?*

"Well, there was a scene with Alvin Grote," Charlotte explained. "When he realized the woman he'd brought to the party as his date had tried to kill Julie, he underwent a bit of a meltdown. He insisted that Julie have a cup of coffee with him so he could clear his name. Not that he has to clear much of anything. He gave a statement to the police, and I don't think he's in any way guilty."

"He's guilty of being an asshole," Mac said.

Charlotte chuckled. "Indeed. When he pleaded with Julie to have coffee with him, he simply had to mention that the coffee at Remy's is much too strong and the cups aren't big enough. He finally subsided when Julie reminded him that refills were free and he could use as much cream as he wanted to dilute the flavor."

Mac should have stopped in the kitchen to grab a cup of coffee. Maybe he would have seen her and Grote in the dining room. If he had, maybe he would have stormed across the room, hauled Grote out of his chair by his ponytail and beaten him to a pulp for having brought Andrea Crowley to the party. Of course, Mac was at fault for having failed to run a security check on her—or he would be, if her full name had ever appeared on the guest list.

He lifted the folder from his lap. "Did Tyrell get you a copy of his report?"

"He did." Charlotte patted a folder on her desk.

"He did a phenomenal job last night," Mac said. "The next time you're handing out raises, he deserves one."

"If I could afford it, he'd be getting a raise today," Charlotte agreed.

That had been her opening to drop the gratitude and let it rip. Unlike Tyrell, Mac didn't deserve a raise. Quite the contrary, he deserved the ax. Yet Charlotte continued to gaze at him, smiling benignly.

He sighed and pushed the words out himself. "I can arrange for my resignation as soon as you want it," he said.

She didn't look as startled as she might have, which implied that she knew the truth about him. "You mean, because you lied about your background when you applied for this job?"

"My background and my reason for wanting the job," he said.

"Mac." She tapped her fingers together as she regarded him. "Number one, your background made you more qualified than you had to be. I hardly think a person should be fired for being better than advertised."

"But my reasons—"

"Were somewhat deceptive, yes. Julie told me a little about what you revealed to her last night. I understand that in your line of business—private investigations and security—you can't always be forthright. Your work entails secrecy, am I right?"

He nodded reluctantly. "Sometimes, yeah, I've got to be secretive. But when I have to lie to people like you and Julie, I regret it."

"Regret is your own problem, Mac, not mine. Because you are who you are, rather than who I thought you were, Julie is safe today, and a dangerous woman is behind bars. I hardly think that constitutes grounds for letting you go."

"I don't know what Julie told you," he repeated, "but I didn't save her. She saved herself."

Charlotte's smile grew gentle. "What Julie told me was that you saved her. And for that alone, you will be welcome here as long as you wish to stay. If you need to go back to your other job, I hope you'll stay until I can find a replacement for you. That's not asking too much, is it?"

Not asking too much? The woman should have lopped off his head by now. If Julie had told her the whole story about last night, she'd probably want to lop off his balls as well.

He raked a hand through his hair and considered her request. "I'm sure there are folks who'd be better at this job than I am," he said. "I'll help you find one. Tyrell would be at the top of my list," he added, lifting his folder again. "I know he's young and I know he prefers working nights. But he's more than qualified for the job. He was a champ last night."

"So were you," Charlotte said. "Mac, it's none of my business but..." She drew in a deep breath. "Whatever is going on between you and Julie, please fix it."

"If I could—if I *can*," he corrected himself, "I will." He rose and started toward the door. Pausing, he turned back to Charlotte. "I'm keeping an eye on Luc Carter," he said. "He was seen in the area just before Eddie discovered that the generator had been tampered with."

Her smile faded. "I like Luc," she conceded. "Do you really think he had something to do with that mess?"

"I don't know. Apparently he was carrying a bunch of flashlights. It might have been nothing more than bad timing that put him in the vicinity of the generator just before Eddie realized it had been vandalized. But as I said, I think I should keep an eye on him."

"I trust your judgment, Mac."

He felt unworthy of that trust, but if she wanted to give it, he'd better strive to deserve it. With a nod he left her office.

Feeling a little less like an impostor, he descended the main steps to the lobby. No one would have guessed that the hotel had hosted a slam-bang party last night, or that the only illumination for the party had come from candles, flashlights and the moon. Nadine and her crew had tidied the lobby up—not even the scent of melted candle wax lingered in the air, which smelled of lemon furniture polish and fresh flowers. Leftovers from the party, Mac guessed as his gaze took in the bouquets in vases arrayed on tabletops and counters. Whatever drinks and snacks had been consumed in the lobby last night had been cleared away. Fresh tracks indicated that the carpets had been vacuumed that morning.

The concierge desk was vacant, which was probably just as well. Mac had promised Charlotte he'd deal with Luc, and he would. First, though, he had to deal with the woman haunting him, the woman who last night had tossed him out of her life for lying and this morning had spread flattering lies about him at the hotel.

He ran into Alvin Grote in the hallway outside Chez Remy. The man looked sheepish and grim, and he carefully avoided Mac's gaze. Mac could just imagine why. If his eyes were guns, he'd be shooting them straight into Grote's pudgy face. That man, that whining, cranky man, had brought Andrea Crowley into the hotel last night, nearly costing Julie her life. Mac would never forgive him.

He whipped past Grote and swung into the restaurant. Julie wasn't there.

Cursing, he cornered one of the waitresses. It took incredible restraint not to grab the poor girl by her collar. "Is Julie Sullivan around?"

"She just left," the waitress said.

"Where did she go?"

The girl shrugged.

Deciding he'd never forgive the waitress, either, Mac raced out of the room. He was used to moving stealthily around the hotel, spying on Julie while trying not to alert her to his scrutiny, but right now he'd be happy to grab a megaphone and bellow her name through the halls. The guests might not appreciate that, though. Given how few people occupied the restaurant and lobby, he assumed most of the guests were still sleeping off last night's excesses.

He returned to the lobby, wishing Julie had left him a trail of pink feathers. No such luck today. Maybe she didn't want to be found.

The last time she didn't want to be found, he'd located her in a corner of the courtyard, fretting over the first threatening e-mail she'd received. He shoved open one of the French doors into the courtyard.

A few maintenance men were at work there, tidying up the

last vestiges of the party. Crumpled napkins lay scattered across the ground, and a small pile of soggy debris sat at the edge of the pool, where one worker wielded a long-handled net to fish garbage from the turquoise depths. Chairs and tables had been pushed askew to clear space for dancing, and another worker was busy returning furniture and planters to their proper places.

Julie sat at the corner table, just where Mac had found her that first day. As always she was dressed attractively. Today's outfit was simple—a black tunic and matching black slacks that hid the scrape on her knee. The ensemble made her look absurdly tall and long-legged. And beautiful. Heartbreakingly beautiful.

She saw him as soon as he stepped into the courtyard. Her gaze followed him as he wove among the misplaced tables and chairs to the corner where she sat. She didn't order him to stop, didn't accuse him of terrible things. Her expression was, while not welcoming, not quite forbidding, either. If he had to choose one word to describe it, it would be sad.

He didn't stop moving until he was standing right before her. He dragged over the closest chair and planted it in front of her, then sat. And said the first words that came to him: "I love you."

She sat straighter and blinked in surprise. Her eyes were sleepy but still a mesmerizing violet, the color of a morning sky before the sun broke over the horizon. Her hair hung loose and her cheeks were hollow, her lips temptingly soft.

Maybe he should have eased into this conversation more subtly. "How are your fish?" he asked. "Did they survive the night?"

"Yes," she said quietly. "Better than I did, probably."

"Better than I did, too." The hell with her fish. The hell with easing into the conversation. He'd lied to Julie before, but he wasn't going to lie to her ever again. "I'm a son of a bitch. I know you're angry with me. You have every right to be. But damn it, Julie, I love you. I always thought you were smart and interesting and great company, but last night..." He swallowed, trying to slow down the words, to hold back the emotion rolling over him like the storm waves of a hurricane. "Last night I realized that if you'd been killed, my life wouldn't have been worth living. It would have been empty, pointless. I need you, Julie. I need you to make my life worth living."

Her eyes remained on him, gorgeous but unreadable.

"So okay, I'm a son of a bitch. You can hate me now. But I'll fight for you. I'll do what I have to, to convince you—"

"Mac," she said, so quietly he almost didn't hear her. "You aren't a son of a bitch."

"Just a liar."

"Yes." A smile teased the corners of her mouth. "You'll have to work on that lying habit."

"I only lie in my work," he told her. "I have to sometimes, and I won't apologize for that. But I don't lie in my private life. And I won't lie to you." He gathered her hand. It felt cool and slender, sandwiched between his palms. He remembered the way her hands had felt on his body last night, and a jolt of arousal gripped him.

"And anyway, I'm not the only liar around here," he went on, in part to distract himself from the tug of desire in his groin. "You told Charlotte I saved your life last night. That's a lie."

She looked startled. "It's the truth, Mac. The only thing that kept me going was the knowledge that you'd come for me. I had to stay alive until you came. And I was right. You did come."

"Because you left me a trail of feathers and shoes."

"Because I needed you," she argued. Her fingers flexed against his hand and her eyes seemed to glisten. "You were right when you said I was in danger. You were right to want to protect me, and I was too stubborn and sure of myself, thinking I was perfectly safe and I didn't need anyone looking out for me. Last night—" her voice broke, and she took a minute to regroup "—last night, at least half my anger came from the understanding that I need to depend on other people sometimes. On you," she added, her gaze so poignant he felt his own throat choke up a little. "I don't want to depend on anyone, but I can't help myself, Mac. I need you."

He hadn't realized he'd been holding his breath until it escaped him in a happy rush. "Then you forgive me?"

"Only if you forgive me for being such a dope."

"You're the bravest, strongest, smartest, most beautiful dope I've ever known," Mac said, rising and pulling Julie to her feet. "And I love you."

"I love you, too," she whispered, then tilted her face and pressed her lips to his.

They kissed, a soul-deep kiss that brimmed with her courage, her strength, her wisdom and beauty—and even her stubbornness. Everything Mac loved about Julie was in that kiss. And Mac realized, to his great relief, that he'd be able to forgive himself. He'd be able to do anything, as long as he had Julie's love.

HOTEL MARCHAND

Four Sisters.
A family legacy.
And someone is out to destroy it.

A new Harlequin continuity series
continues with
THE SETUP
by Marie Ferrarella

A bohemian artist is everything Jefferson Lambert
never *knew he wanted in a woman.*

The minute he meets his date for the night,
Jefferson Lambert knows someone tampered
with his matchmaking profile.
How else would a conservative lawyer end up
with a gorgeous, spirited woman
like Sylvie Marchand?

Here's a preview!

"I'LL CALL YOU LATER," Jefferson promised. About to hurry down the corridor, Sylvie looked at him quizzically. "To let you know if I hear anything," he added, gently reminding her of his offer to keep his eyes and ears open about the missing painting. That he wanted to call her because of last night was something he needed to quietly explore himself before he admitted it to her. He doubted if she'd be receptive anyway. Women like Sylvie had to beat men off with a stick.

"Right."

At this very moment, Sylvie felt as if there were a thousand random thoughts swimming around in her head at the same time. As soon as she tried to focus on one, something else came flying at her.

She needed to get hold of herself, to think clearly about one thing at a time.

She took exactly two steps before she swung around and doubled back. Jefferson stared at her as she grabbed him by the lapels, raised herself up to her toes, and kissed him on the mouth quickly and hard.

The next moment, she was off and running again.

Jefferson ran his index finger along his lips. The woman did leave an impression. For a moment, he thought of hurrying after her and walking with her as far as the elevator, but then decided that maybe Sylvie could use a little time alone to pull herself together.

So could he.

Last night was like a page out of someone else's book, not his. It was more like something that Blake would have experienced.

Blake. He realized that he'd lost track of the man. If he knew Blake, his friend had probably made the most of the situation.

Well, hadn't he done the same himself?

And then Jefferson reconsidered. Last night hadn't been about making the most of an unexpected opportunity, it had been about discovering himself. About discovering life. He hadn't felt this alive, this vibrant, this—okay, happy—in years.

And confused. Definitely confused. But when it came to Sylvie Marchand, he had a strong feeling that being confused kind of went with the territory.